SIMPLY A MATTER OF TIME

KATHRYN K. MURPHY

Caraway Press

For my family

CHAPTER 1

"You need to get out of there." Timothy Chappell's thick English accent, which he kept on principle despite being in the United States for almost four hundred years, would've brought a smile to Ethan's lips were it not for what he had just suggested.

Ethan sighed. "How long do I have?"

"How much notice do you need to give without drawing attention?"

"Probably two weeks."

"That'll do. You'll need to change names and change cities as well. I imagine you're still able to pass for a young man leaving university, so you'll need to assume that role again."

Ethan's hand tightened on the phone. He blew out a breath while looking around the sumptuous corner office on one of the highest floors in Manhattan.

"What about the accounts? Yours and the others? I won't be able to manage as much without drawing suspicion."

"I'd already considered that. We're under so much scrutiny, we can't afford any unnecessary attention."

"No one has questioned me. I hardly think—"

"We cannot have people getting too close. As it is, your brother had to marry that girl—"

"Caitlyn," Ethan said with a smile. He had only met his new sister-in-law a few times, but from what he had seen, he approved of Austin's choice.

"Yes, well, that's hardly what we need right now."

"With all due respect, she saved a bunch of us. I think I could contribute more if I remain as I am. I've lived this long without drawing any attention."

"We can't take the risk. I need you to move." The old man's voice always held a firm tone with everyone. Ethan enjoyed more familiarity than most as he managed the entire island's wealth, including the substantial holdings of the man with whom he was speaking.

The old man took a breath on his end of the line, a rare moment of pause.

"I'm sorry, Ethan. We're in extraordinary circumstances. All of us have to make changes."

Ethan couldn't imagine what changes Timothy needed to make but accepted the apology without comment.

"I still feel that given the current trends in the market, remaining in a position where I can have more insight and access to greater funds would be of benefit."

"I see your point, but you must leave and start over. We can't afford any more leaks. We're not talking money, Ethan. We're talking lives. You do realize what almost happened, don't you?"

Ethan's mouth thinned, and he gritted his teeth, biting back the response he had ready.

"I'm aware," he said dryly.

"The police have questions about Austin. I've arranged for a name change, and I'm hoping all this attention will die down in a couple of months. Something about his face all over that dreaded man's house."

"You can't make him assume a new name."

"He'll need to take one soon. I don't want to attract attention, but I would rather have this wrapped up."

"How does Austin feel about this?" Ethan asked, knowing the answer. Though his brother had lived at home since serving in the navy, he didn't like to be confined. Having to fake his own death would mean not being able to leave the island for months until everyone forgot about him, and he adopted his new identity.

"I haven't brought the matter to his attention." Timothy's voice told Ethan everything he needed to know. Apparently, the old man was looking forward to it about as much as Austin would be once he found out.

"Austin still looks young."

"The photographs were military—his military service through the modern-day. We have to rid ourselves of the chance for additional interviews. The more they talk to us, the less likely it is we can keep this a secret."

Ethan couldn't fault Timothy's logic. "Has there been additional questioning?"

"Not for about a week, but the questions have started to get more specific. They want to know about Austin."

Ethan made a noise in his throat.

"As he is your brother, this will extend to you."

"New name?"

"Yes."

Ethan tapped his fingers on the large, sleek desk in front of him. It represented so many years of hard work, hard work that he had prided himself on. Work was all he had, that and how he provided for the people who had raised him. With a life expectancy of at least four hundred, he couldn't possibly stay in the same job forever, but he had never left, and though he knew the day would come, the idea didn't sit right with him. He tried to catch up with what Timothy had been saying.

"...Your new apartment will be in Boston and—"

"Boston?" Ethan frowned, eyeing the New York skyline through his floor-to-ceiling windows.

"Yes, I think it's best if you're closer to home. After that, you'll need to leave in another three months to go elsewhere. I don't want anyone catching on to us any more than they already might have. Mark Schmidt figured it out, so we must act fast."

Back in December, Mark Schmidt had bombed the old meetinghouse where the renewals had taken place every season. Renewals on Brightrock were what made the people on the small island off the coast of Massachusetts different. A sip every now and then of the water from the secret spring and they almost stopped aging in its path. One year turned into seven, stretching their lifetime into hundreds of years. Before Mark had shot himself, he had screamed their carefully guarded secret was out. He was gone, but now the police had been asking questions for months as they uncovered more and more evidence about the island, and everyone on Brightrock wondered how a down-on-his-luck drunk had figured out what they had successfully protected for almost four hundred years.

"It's July, I thought they would've gotten tired of us by now."

Timothy sighed on the other end of the line. "I had hoped so too, but it seems every time the terror alert goes up, we're back on their list of priorities. Also, the police don't have a motive yet. Given what happened in Boston a few years ago, they're very thorough with their terror investigations. Not that they'll figure out that horrible man's motive, but until they're satisfied here we are. Besides it's not just them. We've been keeping a low profile for years, but since December even the Department of Health has realized they haven't been out for a while and want to come out for a full audit. All of us are on alert."

"What about Lizzy?" Ethan wished he could've taken the words back the moment they left his mouth. His cousin preferred to fly under the radar.

"Yes, I need to speak with her tonight. I haven't spoken with the other founders on the council about her situation. As Austin's cousin, she could be questioned. It would be best."

"She just started her doctoral program. As it is, didn't she have to come back early for a so-called family emergency last year?"

"Yes, and I've taken that into consideration."

"She's wanted to do that program for a long time."

"To use your sentiment, I am aware of that, but security measures must remain our top priority. There will be time for her to go to school, perhaps in another decade or so."

Ethan couldn't help himself. "A decade?"

"Of course. Lizzy has plenty of time. I'm going to propose to the council that we order her to return as soon as possible."

Ethan bit back the argument he had at the ready in Lizzy's defense. The town council consisted of the original settlers who founded Brightrock, having found the spring that extended their lives. Keeping both the secret and the islanders safe had always been a top priority for all of its members. Timothy Chappell sat as the most conservative voice, steering against all modernity. He held two doctorates, each from a different century, and no doubt saw no issue with Lizzy following a similar timeline.

"I see. Well, is there anything else you would like to discuss tonight? We have that conference call with the other members later in the week."

The old man took Ethan's cue and launched into a series of concerns and questions about various accounts and funds. While Ethan answered each one with ease, he looked out at the fading sun over the skyline while a sense he was being trapped closed around his chest.

CHAPTER 2

As the sun dropped behind the skyscrapers outside his window a week later, Ethan slid open another desk drawer and emptied the few contents he cared about into a box when the door to the other side of the office opened. He turned around, expecting to see another well-wisher saying meaningless words of congratulations, and instead saw the same night cleaning lady who had been with him during the attack on Brightrock. She had been the only other person in the office that fateful night he had stood rooted to the spot, unable to do anything but watch cell-phone video on the news networks showing the most sacred building on Brightrock engulfed in orange flames, while all of his friends and family ran away covering their mouths to ward off the smoke. He had called their numbers over and over getting nothing except their voicemails until, after an agonizing wait, Austin picked up and filled him in about the attack.

Ethan returned her quiet smile and eyed the clock, wondering if he had stayed late without meaning to again. The clock said only five thirty.

"I'll be out soon," he said to the lady whose name he did not know and now never would. After leaving so many jobs and cutting ties with everyone, he had found her quiet companionship comforting on nights when she walked in to tidy up while he still worked. She nodded, waved, and left, leaving the door open.

"Mr. Brooks?" A woman stepped around the corner in an ill-fitting, cheap suit. She placed an overstuffed black tote bag on the floor by the door. Her heavy black boots didn't match her outfit but fit her purposeful stride across the room.

Ethan would have frowned at her intrusion, but something about the hardness of her body and her hair tied back in an austere knot compelled him to sit and listen to what this stranger had to say.

"You just caught me," he said. He set down the tape and came around the front of the desk to take her outstretched hand, which was strong despite the fineness of the bones under the skin.

In a smooth motion, she reached behind her and held up a badge.

"I can see that. I'm Lieutenant Nora St. Clair, and I have a few questions for you." Her golden eyes were flat, her voice direct, both of which marked her as a veteran. The toned lines of her body looked relaxed, but judging by the way she carried herself—tense like a large cat—seeing her in action would be a performance in deadly beauty.

"To what do I owe the pleasure?" He leaned back onto his desk, drinking in the sight of her. She stood in his office like a Celtic warrior, all quiet tension, and for the first time in forever, something stirred within him.

"I understand you're from Brightrock. I have some questions about your brother Austin."

A warning sounded deep inside him, but after so many

decades spent living a half-life off the island, Ethan slid his usual mask into place.

"Well, I'm not sure how much I'll be able to help. Can I offer you a drink? Coffee?"

"Sure, thanks."

He felt her eyes on him as he walked to the kitchenette on the side of the room. Despite his imminent departure, everything remained in the cabinets for the next occupant. Business, like his life, moved on whether people left or stayed— his absence would make no difference. He had fixed coffee countless times on this machine, preferring not to have a secretary like all of the other fund managers. Ethan needed to keep his distance from everyone lest they caught on to the cyclical returns to Brightrock or any reference to how much experience he had in the city.

"Cream? Sugar?" he asked, turning around.

"Just straight, thanks," she said, accepting the cup from him and sitting on the couch when he gestured toward the small sitting area he seldom used.

Ethan took a sip, feigning being relaxed while watching her, waiting for her to speak first. His secret and all of Brightrock depended on discretion, and he had mastered the art of volunteering nothing and making it seem like a lot.

"I'm sorry for your loss," she said, watching him like a cat over the rim of her white cup.

A quick study, Ethan gave a slow nod, not wanting to confirm or deny. "What would you like to know?"

Those golden eyes tracked his movements, not hiding her ongoing assessment of him, which only made him more careful.

"I'm investigating the attack on Brightrock."

Ethan frowned. "I thought that investigation concluded a while ago."

"Following up on loose ends."

"I'm not sure I follow." Ethan knew they were dancing together with words, and both of them wanted to lead. The challenge entertained him.

Nora leaned back on the brown leather sofa, watching him, assessing. Her golden eyes narrowed the slightest bit, her jaw setting as she reached her conclusion. Ethan admired how much care and thought she put into her words.

"Mark Schmidt had a lot of information—papers, photographs—all scattered around his house."

"Austin." Ethan didn't need her to confirm, but her curt nod, with a professional and appropriate amount of sympathy, did it anyway.

"Why him?" Nora's intelligent eyes watched him, sizing him up, warming his skin, making him want to sit all night, talk, and watch her.

Ethan folded his leg over a knee, feigning relaxation though getting a thrill out of the risk every word held. He shrugged.

"That's what I want to know. When the case was transferred to my department, I hadn't realized Austin passed until I called to interview him about the attack." Her face, unmoving, told him everything he needed to know without saying a thing. Sitting politely across from him, another person would have mistaken her features for polite, professional interest, but those golden eyes gave her away. She had no proof, but she knew Austin wasn't dead.

Ethan looked down into his coffee, counting in his head, orchestrating a look of grief for his happy, healthy, pain-in-the-ass brother, probably sitting in his tiny shack back on Brightrock with his new wife on a hideous couch in front of a fire.

"I'm not sure I can help you," he said, meeting her gaze. "I have lived away for some time."

"But you visit."

Ethan paused. Of course, she would have researched him, and though he tried to be discreet, not everything had been wiped or ordered under a different name. She had found where he worked and judging by the wrinkles in her suit and the large bag she brought with her, had left with little notice. In the silence, he let his eyes absorb her features and wished he had more time to entertain this cunning lieutenant. He would have enjoyed talking with her over dinner and lingering over dessert. A more primal part of him, one that he had thought had been long dead, wanted to see her smile and smooth away the crease in her brow.

"Don't you?" she asked, prompting a response with a slight twist of her head.

CHAPTER 3

"I do." Ethan sat across from Nora, relaxed and giving away little. The infernal man had draped himself over the artsy leather chair, where he managed to look powerful, in control, and dangerous. Hell, the suit he was wearing no doubt cost more than Nora made in a month. She didn't like how he looked at her as if he could peel away the years of experience on the police force.

"Can you tell me if Austin ever mentioned Mark?" She knew the standard lines would get her no new answers but asked them anyway hoping to crack through the polite mask of the powerful man in front of her. While he took time to pretend to think, she could tell it was all a show. He sat like a king in the corner office, commanding a view of the cityscape below.

"No, I don't believe they ever met, but if they did, Austin never mentioned it to me." A puzzled and concerned look clouded his face now. She almost couldn't hide her disgust. Men like him didn't even know what real concern would feel like if it bashed them on the head. They all just sat above the real world in their lofty stainless-steel towers, the rest of the commoners below.

"What about other people? Anyone ever bother him? Have an ax to grind?"

His light-brown hair swept over the side and reached the edge of his exquisite collar, displaying a temple a modeling agency would kill to get in their contracts. His cheekbones and strong jaw would have sent the best of them into fits. Now that she had gotten a good look at him, Nora was surprised he didn't have an equally stunningly beautiful secretary hanging around just in case. Nora didn't want to like him, or any man like him, but that didn't mean she couldn't call a spade a spade. He sat like Bacchus himself as he considered her question—beautiful and enjoying life as she never would. He pulled his hand up to his chin, revealing a Rolex, and pretended to think past the grief and through the years. Nora had to hand it to him, the guy knew how to put on a show in more ways than one. She continued to probe with her questions, looking for a way in, but damn him, he resisted. His features remained smooth like ice through her standard first round of questioning. She had hoped to find a crack, or make one, but still he continued, politely interested, unnerving in how much he focused on her.

That focus was what gave him away, she decided. When questioning others, Nora learned people never took notice of the person sitting in front of them. Too often they would focus on a fixture in the room, their eyes glazing over, blind as they remembered the person they loved. Ethan, much to Nora's annoyance, did nothing of the sort. In his presence, she found herself starting to look away, pretending to make notes on her phone, just to break the stare. He looked at her and nowhere else, his hazel eyes so cool, they were like ice.

"Can I take your cup?" he asked, nodding to the empty one she had forgotten about on the coffee table.

She stood, handing the cup over without making contact with his skin. "Thank you for your time."

"Please let me know if there's anything else I can do to help your investigation, Lieutenant. I'm afraid I don't feel like I've done much." His gaze still stared down at her, about a head taller, reminding her of a predator.

"Every little bit helps," she said, meeting his stare with one of her own. The ass knew precisely what he was doing, but she had been in the game long enough to stop giving a shit about what other people thought of her. The bastard was hiding a lot, and he had confirmed everything by saying nothing.

Nora reached in her wallet and pulled out a card, passing it over, again making sure to avoid touching any part of him.

"Here's my contact information. Give me a call if you remember anything."

It shouldn't have bothered her so much when Ethan held her card between both hands and glanced down at it, both front and back, but it enraged her, and no doubt that's what he wanted. He slid the card into his pocket and rocked on his heels, smiling at her, and then as if he knew they hadn't touched, stuck out his hand.

For the life of her, Nora wanted to leave it hanging there, but professionalism and a determination not to shrink from him had her making the connection. She steeled herself, but again when their palms met, he overwhelmed her. Nora did her best not to let it show, but the smooth grip trapped her hand, holding her in place, while his thumb pressed lightly into her flesh. This close to him, she could smell his cologne and see the stubble on his neck which, in the fading light, did not diminish his stunning features.

"I'll do that," he said, letting her hand go. To her credit,

Nora didn't snatch it back, but maintained decorum, giving him one polite nod before turning and walking toward the door. The whole of the office was bigger than her apartment back in Massachusetts.

When she thought she had put enough distance between them, Nora turned around and said, "I'll get your new contact information from your office."

Ethan smiled at her, his eyes twinkling with unspoken laughter. "I'm not sure where I'm heading, but when I do find out, I'll let you know."

Nora let herself out, cursing the lie.

CHAPTER 4

Ethan stood, rooted to the spot in front of the seating area he had never used, and watched Nora St. Clair shut the door behind her, the firm click the only sound in the large, dark office. She was one of many but somehow stood out. Just like Sarah. He shook his head at the thought.

Though he didn't look it, Ethan was approaching ninety years old and, over the years, countless people had walked in and out of his life. In business, especially, people came and went all the time, hopping from job to job, climbing the corporate ladder.

He pulled the cheap business card back out of his pocket and ran his fingers over the edge. Nora's golden eyes and firm resolve lingered in his mind. He wished like hell he had a different life and could enjoy what his brother had found back on Brightrock, but it was better he didn't. Better for everyone.

Brightrock's survival depended on him and his ability to seamlessly travel between the reclusive island and the outside world. He had become an expert at managing money, not only at navigating the changing tides of the market, riding out the crash of 1987, and then again in 2008, but knowing when and how to move money without suspicion. He had no moral disputes. His clients were family and friends who couldn't operate in the usual channels, and who still needed help. Without Ethan, his entire community could lose everything, and worse, become discovered, arrested, or killed for what they were.

Born in 1929, Ethan spent his childhood observing the worry and fear on his family's faces. His brother may have served in the navy, but Ethan served in other ways. He went to Wharton, learned about money, and now had dedicated his life to helping the people he held dearest to him, moving among the ordinary people, hiding in plain sight, never once letting someone get close enough to learn his secret.

Ethan pulled out his custom leather wallet and slid Nora's card inside, one sleeve behind a faded piece of ribbon and a four-leaf clover wrapped in delicate tissue paper. Though he would never be able to enjoy companionship, Ethan carried the memories of what might have been with him always. With that, he walked back to his half-packed desk and picked up the phone.

"Ethan, did the move go well?" Timothy Chappell always picked up when he called.

"Still moving out—but had some company."

"Is everything alright?"

Ethan filled him in on Nora St. Clair, imagining her still sitting in his office, wondering where she would be staying tonight. It would probably be cheap, and Ethan frowned at the urge to rush out, find her, and steer her toward the Plaza on his dime. He pulled a hand over his face. He needed more sleep, not that he would get it anytime soon. Sleeplessness was an occupational hazard for money managers.

Timothy sighed when Ethan had finished relaying the

questions Nora had asked him. "I knew this would happen eventually. We've been fighting off questions from the media ever since the explosion. I thought once they concluded their investigation, things would settle down." The fatigue of the modern world was evident in his accented voice. Everyone else had adapted in more ways than one, but his voice clung to the formality of England, clearly marking him as the loudest conservative voice on Brightrock's council of elders.

"Lieutenant St. Clair left without anything new."

"And you're leaving tonight?"

Ethan thought of her golden eyes, staring at him.

"That's right. She won't be able to find me again."

"Good, give me a call when you arrive in your new office. I want to review our holdings. The market seems shaky these days."

Ethan assured the old man again before ending the call. He finished packing the trivial office supplies that served a purpose and sealed the box. He checked the desk drawers, not out of sentiment, but to ensure no trace of who he was and where he was going remained. When satisfied, Ethan hit a few buttons on his phone, ordering a car. The few personal items he carried with him from life to life waited at the new apartment in the new city, already moved in days earlier.

Standing by the window, he took in the view from where he stood and admired it one last time. Part of his transient lifestyle meant that he would once again be starting at the bottom—a no one, nameless, with a skeletal résumé, just another hopeful ready to climb the corporate ladder. He knew he wouldn't be walking into a corner office on the top floor. It would be decades before he once again enjoyed this view, after years of acquiring new accounts while secretly managing more than others could even conceive, before the new firm realized his talent and skill. Starting at the bottom seemed safer. By the time he reached the upper echelon, the people with whom he had worked before would all be retired, and Ethan would be left waiting to repeat the cycle. After all, he had nothing but time.

Ethan pulled out her card and flipped it over in his hand a few times sliding the crisp edge along his fingertips. He shook his head to clear his thoughts and eyed the trash can by the window, flicking the card against his finger. If he threw it away here, it might link him to the investigation. Probably wouldn't cause suspicion, but better to throw it away elsewhere. He slid out his wallet and tucked her card inside.

A black Mercedes pulled up in front of the building far below, and with one last glance, Ethan picked up the small box of memories and left the expansive office behind him. As far as everyone else was concerned, Ethan Brooks had retired after a long career of steering through the markets and had left no contact information, no forwarding address, only polite well-wishes and a desire for change, hinting he would enjoy more sun in the Caribbean.

Ethan loaded into the Mercedes and tried to relax in the sumptuous comfort as the car sped toward the airport. On the way, all he could do was stare out the window and take in every anonymous face in passing, hoping to see one with golden eyes.

CHAPTER 5

Lizzy slammed her phone down on the cheap table in Bodo's Bagels. A few other people around her glanced up—students sporting T-shirts and hats from the University of Virginia, pausing their conversations before looking back down at their phones. Her blood pounded in her ears. Rage coursed through her veins. Timothy Chappell and the town council didn't give two shits about her and yet they controlled her whole life. She couldn't even do what she loved without being at the beck and call of the town council every time they got their panties in a tangle. It was so unfair.

She slammed her MacBook shut and stared out the window of the little diner-like space. Lizzy had just started her doctoral program, leaving the classroom for the first time in over three decades. She wanted to get better, improve her craft, and now she was being robbed of the chance to do just that, all because she drank the water. They owned her and always would for as long as she wanted to live.

When Ethan had told her the news—that she was going to need to change her identity, come back to Brightrock, start teaching all over again, and then reapply in a few decades—the air had left her lungs. Timothy Chappell could go screw off as far as she was concerned. Hot angry tears pricked at her eyes. Lizzy blinked them away, tightening her lower lip, refusing to cry over his bullshit. No one had questioned her about Austin, his new wife, or the crackpot bomber last winter. Ethan and Austin were her cousins, for God's sake. She never saw them outside the seasonal renewals. That she would even be involved in all of this was utter horseshit.

Lizzy's phone buzzed on the table, resolute despite her violence. She snatched it up, shoved her computer into her bag, and threw out the uneaten bagel, her appetite ruined. Driving to her meeting, Lizzy's thoughts raced. According to Ethan, she had maybe a month.

Timothy, the asshole himself, hadn't contacted her yet. Ethan had just been doing her a favor by giving her a heads-up only to receive her firestorm of pissed-off rage through the phone. She stopped the car at a red light, watching the other students jog across the road while a few strolled by in pairs. She drummed her fingers on the wheel, impatient. Lizzy hated all of them. None of them understood the freedom they had. They could choose to live each day as their own, cherishing the short time they had on this planet. Because of the bullshit nondisclosures, sacred pacts, and other weird ritualistic shit Chappell forced on everyone from Brightrock, she had essentially signed her soul over to the community in exchange for extended life. What everyone had failed to mention was the complete lack of ownership over your entire existence.

The light changed, and Lizzy drove through, sliding into a parking space when she reached her destination. She fumed the entire way to the office where she was meeting her professor to go over her most recent research.

As usual, Dr. Lin sat waiting. Patient and calm. An

English teacher for thirty years, the UVA alum had come back to his alma mater, earned his doctorate, and began teaching pre-service teachers from a comfortable tenure position.

"Lizzy, nice to see you," he said when she marched into his office, flinging her designer bag onto one of two empty red leather chairs. "What's wrong?"

"Nothing, just news from home."

"Oh?" Dr. Lin poured her a cup of coffee from the small Mr. Coffee machine he kept in his office.

"Yeah. It's nothing really."

"Takes a lot to upset you. I saw that recording of that one fourth period. Woof."

The fourth period in question was a colossal shitshow and part of her research on engagement in underperforming students. Because of scheduling and budget cuts, students who needed attention and would have benefited from a twenty-person class were shoved into a cramped classroom of thirty-two. The exhausted classroom teacher and teacher aide had almost worshipped in benediction when she had walked through the door to help as part of her clinical experience.

"So, tell me what's going on." Dr. Lin took a sip and waited, leaning back into his chair behind a desk drowning under papers.

"I just don't feel like I have any control in my life. I'd figured that by—" Lizzy paused, trying to remember the age she put on her application and hoped it was convincing. Dr. Lin nodded, prompting her to continue. "I just, I don't know, I figured by this age I could do what I wanted without people calling me from back home, trying to dictate my life."

"Ah. Families always have opinions. Try being Chinese and unmarried. My mother isn't happy." He cracked a wry smile.

"It's like they don't believe in me. Like what I want or need isn't even remotely relevant in the equations they're doing."

"Have you told them how you feel?"

"They wouldn't listen."

"Why do you need them to?"

Yeah, like she could tell him. "It's complicated."

"Trusts?"

Lizzy frowned and didn't take the sip she had been going for, instead holding the cup in midair.

"Excuse me?"

"I'm sorry if that's too personal. I shouldn't assume."

"No, no, it's fine. Why would you say trusts?"

"I couldn't help but notice your clothes and car. I assumed you came from money, and that might be an issue your family would hold over you. I apologize if I offended you."

"No, not at all. In fact," Lizzy took a sip now, taking the time to think through it. The comparison worked. "Yes, it's very much like that."

He nodded. "People find ways to control us. It's challenging. I wish I could offer you a solution."

She shook her head, staring at a coffee ring stain on a stack of papers. "It sucks the joy out of everything."

"What can you control?"

Lizzy looked up to meet his eyes. "What do you mean?"

"You said they're trying to control your life. You don't have any ownership. Try focusing on what you can control. Helps me whenever I fly." He took another sip. "Claustrophobic. Can't walk the whole flight, so I focus on moving my hand. It helps." He wiggled his fingers in the air.

Lizzy pondered that. There had been one thing she wanted, and she did have a month.

"I think that helps me. Would you mind if I made a phone

call?" Lizzy said, her hands now still with purpose, reaching for her phone.

"Not at all. I have nothing but time today."

Funny, she usually was in the same boat.

CHAPTER 6

Caleb let the heavy weight of the flak jacket hit the floor of his room in the compound. His muscles felt light without the burden holding him down. The tour around the oil company's property had been just as disheartening as always. He walked into the bathroom next to his small, sparse room and ran the shower, waiting for the water to warm, trying not to think of all the people who didn't have that luxury.

From everything he'd seen from his time in Iraq so far, the United States of America was indeed a paradise, a literal heaven on Earth. Here, there was no sanitation. Trash choked the dusty streets and pockmarked roads, while feral animals scavenged around on what little meat they could find.

He stripped and stepped into the shower, washing the dust off, letting the hot water run over his aching back. The stress of the job had clawed at him over the past six months. He didn't know how he would make it until the end of his thirty-day stay, but he had no choice, flak jacket or not. When the oil company had given him the option, Caleb had seen enough layoffs from the oil rigs in the Gulf to know he didn't have one. Most people would kill to take this job, but these positions were reserved for the engineers who played the game by saying yes and nodding all day long.

Caleb grabbed the shampoo, a luxury brand only in the compound, and rubbed his scalp back and forth, trying to stave off the headache. Money was no issue here. The shift had its perks and drawbacks. Like on a rig, Caleb and the other guys traded twelve-hour shifts running the compound for thirty days straight before another crew replaced them. Thirty on and thirty off made getting anything done at home almost impossible. He missed at least half of all his family's events and most of the major holidays. Days off were a no-go. The oil company had him over a literal barrel, but at least the money was good.

It was that thought that kept him going through the long, sad days, the endless lines in customs. Knowing his money paid for his grandfather's heart surgery and helped out with his cousins' school kept Caleb going. Good jobs were hard to come by, and prices had only gone up. A lot of times, when he went home, he felt like an outsider, like he didn't belong anymore, but he knew he was helping. Most of his family didn't know how they'd make it without his help. Besides, it wasn't like he lived with any of them. He'd been alone since getting his own place, and while other guys had photos of girlfriends, wives, and kids to share, Caleb had managed to make it to his midthirties alone. Every relationship he had cultivated never blossomed, no matter how hard he tried. After the last one had blown up in his face, Caleb figured he just wasn't good at the whole dating thing, and that was okay. At least he could take care of his extended family.

There was one glimmer of hope though. One person he had kept in contact with, if you could call trading a few emails back and forth contact. They had talked the whole way on the plane leaving Brightrock after Caitlyn's wedding, but he didn't know how to make it turn into more without it crumbling and hadn't heard from her in a while. He'd already emailed her twice without getting a reply. Should he reach out again? Did that make him look desperate? Probably. He had no idea what he was doing.

Caleb stepped out of the shower, killing the spray, and grabbed the towel, dragging it over his skin now raw from the heat. Checking the clock, he flopped down on the bed, grabbing the remote. Eleven hours until he was back on. The pace was grueling.

He had flipped through a few channels, casting the room in a blue, solemn glow, when the phone buzzed on the nightstand. Caleb reached over with a frown. Parrain, his aging grandfather, didn't usually call at this time, but he always picked up on a number from the U.S. Fear clutched in his chest as he answered.

"Caleb?"

The voice stopped him dead. He would remember that accent anywhere. He had only spent a few hours with Elizabeth in total, but her voice had fused to his brain, right next to images of her amused smile, and dark, wavy hair.

"Hello?"

He fumbled with the phone, clambering out of bed, standing in the darkness with nowhere to go. "Yes, yes. Can you hear me?"

A twinkle of laughter carried over the phone line. "Crystal clear."

Though Caleb had given her his number months ago, she had never used it. That she did so now seemed fortunate but odd. His instincts fired up when the silence stretched.

"Is everything okay?" he asked, clutching the phone, pressing it to his ear. He didn't want to miss anything. His dinner floated with unease in his stomach.

The sound on the phone was so quiet, he wasn't sure he'd heard it right until he heard it again. The soft sniffling sounded like air, dignified and ladylike, just like Elizabeth.

"What's wrong?"

She drew in a long breath as if steadying herself. Caleb hadn't ever held her, though he had thought about it every day since they met. Right now, he would give anything to wrap his arms tight around her and squeeze her into his chest.

"I think I need a vacation," she said in a burst of laughter that sounded like she was fighting back the tears.

"Okay. You can do that. Don't you have a break from school or something?"

"I don't care about that."

In the dark of his cramped room, Caleb frowned to himself. She had told him all about her doctorate program when they had talked on the plane from Brightrock, and most of their emails had been him asking her about it, and her explaining her research. Until she had stopped replying.

"What do you mean—?"

"Can I come to visit?" she asked, her voice small, punctuated with sniffs and puffs of breath.

Caleb frowned even more now. Something was wrong. "Yeah, I mean, of course. Uh...when do you want to come?"

"As soon as possible."

Caleb lurched over to the small desk and held the phone between his ear and shoulder while he thumbed through the pocket calendar with his schedule to be sure.

"Are you on a rig now?"

His heart dropped. He opened his mouth to speak but no words came. Lizzy didn't know where he was. Why would she? He had left after they had talked, and the emails had been light, mostly trading funny clips from the internet.

Whatever had upset her so much must have been something big.

"Caleb?"

"Uh...yeah. Sorry, the connection's slow or something. I'll be home in a little over a week. Can you fly into New Orleans? I'll pick you up."

Elizabeth sniffed again. Yeah, she didn't need anything else to worry about. There was no way he could tell her where he really was and add to whatever had happened. He got up and paced in the dark bedroom. The idea she was crying somewhere on the other side of the planet made him a frenzy of nerves. It didn't help that the situation was so bad she had called him, of all people. After all, they didn't know each other well and hadn't spoken in over a month.

"Okay, yeah, um, yeah, sorry, I'm a bit of a mess right now."

"Seriously, what happened? You're worrying me."

She sniffed again, breaking his heart with the sound. "I'm fine. No, really, I am. I got it. Just had a moment there. Look, I've got to go right now, but thanks for picking up and letting me ambush you." She laughed a little, the sound fleeting and cautious.

"No, no. I'm glad." He paused, wishing he knew what to say, and not for the first time. "I'm really looking forward to it."

"Okay, if you're sure."

"I'm sure."

"Okay, great. Thank you. I'll email you my flight info."

In the glowing blue light from the muted screen, Caleb said goodbye and ended the call. Standing alone in his room, his mind swirled with possibilities both good and bad.

Elizabeth, as he liked to think of her—she was just too elegant for Lizzy—hadn't seemed the type to need anyone, until now. Hearing her voice shake on the phone call rattled him. Caleb paced again, walking back and forth in the small space, compelled to act on something he knew nothing about and couldn't control. She was a world away from him now.

He slumped on the bed and held his head in his hands, pressing his skull, rubbing it up and down. Something really bad had to have happened. He sat up and cracked a few knuckles, staring at the ceiling to figure out what to do with her. Having the woman of his dreams fly into his life had never happened before. That kind of thing didn't happen to average guys like him.

He stalked back into the bathroom and threw the towel over the shower rod before stalking back to bed and sliding in between the covers, feeling their refreshing reassurance against his skin. The oil company could afford the best, but for all their sumptuous comfort, Caleb tossed and turned in the dark.

After an hour of wondering and speculating had passed, Caleb started to give in to sleep, comforted by the plan he had made and the knowledge he had thirty days to spend with her, or as long as she'd let him. He had to make it count.

CHAPTER 7

Two days later back in Massachusetts, Nora inched her unmarked cruiser along in the snarl of traffic heading toward the bridge. Orange cones funneled all of the cars heading for the Cape into one lane as everyone baked in the sun, the sound of the overtaxed air conditioner drowning out most of the horns. She cursed under her breath and propped her head up with her arm.

The fifteen-minute drive took forty-five minutes, marking the official arrival of the tourist season, which coincided with construction. After fighting her way around road closures and asphalt trucks, Nora swung the car into a parking spot and headed up the elevator to the briefing that had already started. After the meeting and instructions, she suited up and clambered into the back of the van with the others.

Today was all-hands-on-deck. Inside the van, everyone talked about the usual crap, but today Nora sat back and observed. She had to table her investigation on Austin and now Ethan Brooks, but something about him kept her coming back at the case to poke at it from a new angle, trying to figure out what she was missing. She had called his office to schedule a follow-up meeting, only to learn he was no longer working there and hadn't left any information about where he was going to next. The bastard had done just what he said he would. It'd be a miracle if she could track him down again, but she was her father's daughter and loved a good challenge.

Nora braced a shoulder against the inside wall of the armored vehicle as it approached the house—the body armor against her chest, the tactical gear weighing her down, the helmet heavy on her head. Relatively new, the fifth division of the Massachusetts State Police had been tasked not only with counterterrorism and criminal-intelligence operations but also opioid interdiction, the latter of which was today's mission.

The squat brick house sat on a patch of dirt, silent and sad. It had been the center of a drug ring for a while, producing some of the biggest profits on record through an order-by-phone program, set up by the two men and their trainees inside.

Officers had been driving by the area for days, tracking the movements, deciding what time would be best. Adrenaline raced through Nora's chest, making her twitchy. A thin trickle of sweat was already forming at the base of her spine under the Kevlar. The summer sun would be out in force soon, but the neighborhood remained quiet in the early morning. No joggers or people walking bright-eyed dogs. Here, pets were lucky to have a chain-link fence surrounding a yard with more grass than trash. Nora slid her gaze to an overturned, faded tricycle lying in an alley between two run-down houses; one of the wheels was broken clean off.

With a lurch, they pulled to a stop. All poured out onto the busted pavement and swept around behind the cars.

Detective Lieutenant Brown gave the order to follow toward the house, badges out. They couldn't wait long and blow their chance at surprise. Nora moved tight in with the people she knew closest, her finger ready by her Smith and Wesson, waiting alongside the barrel. The division needed to capture, not kill. They needed information just like they needed the drugs off the street. Passing a beat-up Kia and cheap Toyota, they ran up the cracked concrete walk, Nora close to the front, her back hunched, her partner, Manillo, right behind her. They moved in fast.

Sergeants Conway and Jagles reached the door first, slamming the ram against it once, sending shards of cheap wood flying with a crash, shattering the silence. Shouts from deep inside rang out. Nora ran in, sweeping down and to the left.

"Police!"

Confused yelling and the sounds of panicked shuffling echoed through the cheap walls. Shots followed. Sheetrock exploded into dust and rained down. Manillo dropped down behind a couch, Smith and Erickson each shouted from outside. Nora threw her body against the wall, pressing herself behind an old chair that smelled of vomit and piss, waiting for the barrage to stop.

The second that came was all she needed. Popping up, Manillo rushed the other wall, sliding alongside it to get to the back bedroom. Nora charged toward the dark hallway, her pistol raised.

"Police! Throw down your guns." Martin's voice called from the back of the house. Shots rang out with a pop, pop, pop. She hugged the corner, waiting for an opening.

"Come out with your hands up. You are under—Goddamnit!" Gunfire rang out again. The kitchen window exploded in a shower of glass.

"We need gas," Nora called into her shoulder.

Nora dropped low, raised the barrel, and pulled the trigger, aiming into the back bedroom. Screams echoed back through the dust, followed by more pops, though fewer in number.

From her point, she could see Erickson in the kitchen, shielding himself and preparing to aim. Nora leaned around the corner to look for an opening.

A thud hit her in the shoulder, right to the bone, hot searing pain slicing through her as she swore and grabbed at it. A barrage of bullets continued.

A heavy arm clamped down on her chest, hauling her back toward the front door through which she came, Manillo's swearing getting drowned out by the ongoing spray of bullets. Two more officers rushed in, returning fire in a barrage of deathly chaos until the heavy sounds of shotguns were all that could be heard.

Nora let herself be dragged out to the yard, knowing better than to get in the way. She tried to move her legs, but they buckled, and she got shoved on her back against something hard. Cracking an eyelid, Nora saw a patch of weeds in front of her face. The ground, she was on the ground.

A thick hand slammed down onto her shoulder, sending stars right into her skull, blinding her with pain.

Manillo stood above her, yelling at her, but for the life of her, Nora couldn't figure out the words he was saying. She felt light, floating almost like she was in a fog, and a faraway part of her brain regretted that she couldn't make out Manillo's words. Through the shield covering his eyes, she could just make out the vein that always popped out when he got real creative with the swearing.

He asked her a question and then shouted it again, making her head pound. She tried to nod a few times. More faces clouded her vision, all looking down at her from above, the sun lighting them from behind so she couldn't tell who was who.

"Don't you fucking die on me," a voice said.

The pain pulled her under as the sound of a siren wailed in the distance.

CHAPTER 8

Ethan stepped out of the glassed-in shower in a billow of steam and grabbed a towel. He had always loved broiling himself after a hard run in the early morning hours. Something about the freedom of running wherever he wanted before the world had woken up always soothed him with a sense of freedom and isolation. Normally, he'd dress for work and be out the door, but as it was Saturday, he had a chance to take his time and catch up on the new apartment.

The whole bathroom had sold him on the apartment. White marble and glass offset gleaming chrome fixtures which matched his taste, but the ceiling-mounted rainfall shower with wall-mounted shower body-sprays was a must to ease the aches from his days as a defensive lineman in high school and college. Back when he had been on the line, the hits had been just as hard, and the so-called padding left a lot to be desired.

Ethan ran a comb through his hair and reached for the Ralph Lauren aftershave which the new maid had left right where he had requested. He had to hand it to her and the movers. Everything was in place and unpacked just as he requested, down to the phone charger.

He pulled on a clean pair of running shorts and then a white waffle bathrobe and headed into the bedroom toward the new king bed. He dug around in the swishing sheets for his phone he had tossed into the rumpled mess after coming in from his run. He checked for messages, finding only one from his dad about the coffee he had sent a few weeks earlier for Father's Day. Ethan slid it into his pocket and padded out into the kitchen barefoot over the cool tile.

He tapped a glass panel on the wall in the dark living room. With a soft whir, the blackout drapes rose, and the blazing sun shot through onto the tile. He missed New York, but Boston was a beautiful city and still had apartments in towering glass skyscrapers, which he had become accustomed to. Ethan's main concern had been about security and location when he had purchased the unit, but it just happened that the most secure was also the most lavishly appointed.

The open concept layout and low furniture made room for the floor-to-ceiling windows to do their job, framing the morning cityscape beyond. Towering structures of glass and steel spiked up from the ground with the bay peeking in around them, shimmering in the morning light.

He turned on the coffee pot in the state-of-the-art kitchen and turned to study the furniture. All of the couches and tables were dark, sleek, and modern. He hadn't picked them out, didn't care what they looked like, preferring to rent furnished places so he wouldn't have to trouble with baggage in case he had to leave on a moment's notice.

The smell of Colombian coffee filled the space, and he opened the door to find the paper hanging from the doorknob. He skimmed the headlines, while grabbing the remote and flopping down on the couch he hadn't used yet. Ethan didn't make time for TV except on the weekends to fill the time. During the week, he always had on the business channel, but muted the sounds so he could study the numbers in silence. If he wanted something to fill the void, he preferred music.

The front of the paper was unremarkable. He stood, fixed a cup of coffee, and savored the first sip while leaning against the cold granite countertop. He tapped his fingers on the countertop and went to his wallet and pulled out the cheap card from Lieutenant Nora St. Clair.

He had kept it with him through the move and through the office day, pulling it out on occasion. He had done a quick search of her credentials, to find that she was a solid cop with a few big headlines under her name. Not that she'd care about that, he thought. Her golden eyes reminded him of a cat, hunting. He hadn't been able to get her out of his mind. As much as he had tried to focus on other things, Nora St. Clair kept coming back to him.

Ethan surveyed the apartment around him. After Sarah, he hadn't ever allowed himself to have a girlfriend or anything more than a one-night stand, and those he had given up years ago for the sake of security. Anonymous sex had never sat right with him, and getting close to anyone with the amount of lies he told daily seemed selfish and dangerous when his discretion protected everyone else on the island. His sacrifice made their life and financial security possible. He knew his place, but he also knew what he wanted when he saw it.

Ethan flipped the card over in his hand, studying it again. One corner was already bent from when he had looked at it all week. He flicked it again with his fingernail, stood up, and tucked it into his wallet before grabbing his cup and heading back to the couch. He flipped the remote in his hands and turned the channel to Boston's local news before picking up the paper again.

The news anchor nodded once to a woman in a bright yellow dress. "Thank you, Mindy, it's going to be a hot one out there today." He turned to face the camera as it refocused on him. "Alright, today we're going to look at how some reports show veterans at risk for homelessness and poverty, but first we turn to a breaking news story. Earlier this morning, the police raided a small house in Framingham uncovering the center of a drug ring. We're going to Philip now to get more details on this ongoing investigation. Philip?"

"Good morning, Thomas. Yes, today law enforcement officers from the 5th Division of the Massachusetts State Police raided this home behind me."

Ethan looked up at the screen and frowned. He stood and went to his wallet again, pulling back out the card to make sure he hadn't read it wrong. She was 5th division. He grabbed the remote and turned up the volume.

"As you can see behind me, officers have closed the scene while investigations are still ongoing, but suspects have been arrested under multiple charges and I have been told what they found inside was the center of a drug ring, including firearms and large quantities of opioids and other illegal substances.

Ethan stood and folded his arms. This would no doubt be another headline for Lieutenant St. Clair.

"Neighbors tell us the suspects inside opened fire on the police, and engaged in what one woman called a gunfight. No civilians were harmed. One suspect was shot and is currently being treated. One officer went down in the line of duty. Lieutenant Nora St. Clair was shot during the raid. Doctors have told us she is currently in critical, but stable condition."

The news hit him like a punch in the gut. He snatched his

phone and started to dial the number before stopping himself. She wasn't his family. This wasn't the bombing on Brightrock. This wasn't like before.

The news anchor moved on to another story, and Ethan flipped to another channel searching for more information. Finding none, he shook the remote in his hand before tossing it down on the chair and resumed pacing.

Ethan was agitated, restless. The apartment felt too small and too big at the same time. The whole place felt empty and hollow but confining. He needed to run again. To clear his head. Ethan shook off the robe, feeling hot, and walked into the bedroom to find a T-shirt and yanked it over his head before stomping into his sneakers. He went to tie the laces, but his hands were shaking. He scrubbed his face and tried to clear his head.

He had only just met her, so why did it feel like before?

Ethan stood slowly and breathed in through the nose, out through the mouth trying to calm himself. He pulled himself together and stepped out of his shoes. Surely this was just a reaction to the same events as before. Once he called his family and spoke to them, assuring his anxiety they were fine, he could go back to living his normal quiet life. He wished Lieutenant Nora St. Clair all the best, and the news said she was stable.

With a flick of his wrist, he texted his dad, got a reply, and slowly sank to the edge of the bed and hung his head, cradling his phone in his loose hands. He didn't feel any better. This wasn't about his family.

His reflection stared back at him in the dark, vacant glass of his phone. That's when he had an idea.

CHAPTER 9

Lizzy stepped off of the plane first, saying thank you to the flight attendant who had done a remarkable job of leaving her alone in the first-class cabin on the flight from Washington. To be fair, she hadn't needed anything other than alcohol, but the way she had asked for it had sent a message that the professional flight attendant heard loud and clear, then kept the champagne flowing.

Leaving the cool interior of the plane, Lizzy stepped out onto the jet bridge and walked into a wall of heavy, hot air. The smell of water hung like a fog around her as she pulled her leather carry-on bag behind her up the sloping tunnel. The hollow sounds of her shoes felt familiar to her ears. Ever since she had called Caleb outside of Dr. Lin's office, she'd been jittery. It wasn't that she didn't think Caleb would welcome her or that she would be too nervous. She had liked him immediately and would've pursued talking earlier had it not been for the bullshit NDA and cult-like secrecy.

Ethan calling her with the news had given her the chance to act. Time was ticking before Elizabeth Brooks ceased to exist, and she intended to have the best damn time of her life in those few remaining days.

Still, every time she thought of him, an unfamiliar feeling had crept up, rattling around in her ribs, keeping her up at night, and killing her appetite. By the time she had boarded the plane, Lizzy had been one hot, irritable mess. She hated the feeling of not being in control and had flashbacks to the night her parents had died when she was a little girl. Like then, Lizzy had felt out of control since Ethan had given her the news. The real self-destruction spiral had come when Timothy Chappell called her and left a short voicemail, requesting she return his call as soon as possible. She had done no such thing.

Lizzy marched out of the jet bridge and into the terminal. Jazz floated up in the cool building, the high arches like a cathedral of light, filled with art and little snack stands. While she hadn't traveled as much as Ethan, Lizzy liked to admire the small souvenirs in the shops, though she'd almost never had reason to buy one. Each little airport shop did its best to capture the flavor of the local culture, an appetizer for what weary travelers had to look forward to during their stay. The alligators and Mardi Gras masks filled the tables outside the stores but did little to calm her nerves of going past the security gate and meeting the man she couldn't get out of her head.

Lizzy sucked in a breath and marched forward, confident in the knowledge that if this didn't work out, she had her ID and a black American Express. Worst-case scenario, she would just fly somewhere else.

A crowd of people stood behind security. Some were waving goodbye to family and friends, while others stood, hands in pockets, keeping an eye out for their loved one's arrival. Lizzy's eyes went from face to face, scanning, anxiety rising with each set of eyes that didn't match the olive-green ones she remembered so well, until she saw him.

Standing there, calm as always, Caleb Broussard smiled at her, a bouquet of roses in his hands. He wore jeans, nothing dark or fancy, and a light-blue dress shirt rolled up at the sleeves. Walking toward him, Lizzy could see Caleb's smile broaden. She could've wept on the spot, and though she would regret it later she all but threw herself at him, wrapping her arms around him and holding on tight.

Caleb hesitated at first, but his arms came around her tentative and gentle, just like she figured they would be after their brief encounters on Brightrock. She leaned into his chest, smelling the clean soap on him and feeling the warmth through his shirt.

Caleb pulled her into him and held her. The dam broke and the tears she had been fighting streamed down her face through her waterproof makeup.

Lizzy clung to him, feeling the first real thing since Ethan had told her about her impending fate. She had just had a taste of freedom and didn't want to give it up. Leaving meant abandoning everything she had worked so hard for. It also meant giving up anything like this moment.

He was warm and steady against her cheek. She rested her head on his shoulder, where they fit together without any effort as if she had been carved from him. They stood, embracing, breathing in each other's presence while the crowd thinned around them. With great reluctance, Lizzy pulled back and wiped her face.

Caleb looked down at her, meeting her almost eye to eye, a welcome relief after being towered over by Ethan and Austin forever. Lizzy drank in the sight of his green eyes and thick, dark hair. He had a gentle way about him that made her feel safe. Calling him had been the right choice. Just like before, Lizzy knew in her gut she could trust him, and yet he wouldn't overpower her with his wants and wishes. Years of seclusion on Brightrock had her more than skeptical of outsiders, but Caleb was different. He had treated her differently from the moment they had met. He looked at her with admiration and respect, and truly listened. She glanced at him to find him watching.

"Now I'm really worried. What's wrong? What happened?"

Lizzy shook her head. She couldn't talk about it now. Couldn't get into it all, but Caleb's look of earnest worry and concern had her weeping all over again.

"Oh, no." He pulled her to him again, wrapping his arms around her shoulders and rocking her back and forth. The flowers he had brought for her crinkled at her back while he whispered sweet sounds in her ear she didn't understand. It sounded like French, but not anything she had heard before.

"Come on," he said, grabbing her bag and keeping an arm around her. "Let's get your luggage and grab something to eat somewhere where we can talk."

Lizzy nodded and accepted the flowers Caleb laid into her hands.

"I didn't know what was wrong—still don't, but I hope these help," he said. They were red roses with little purple flowers dotted throughout. She couldn't remember the last time a man had given her flowers. Now that Lizzy stopped to think about it, she didn't think she'd ever received flowers from someone she didn't share blood with. The weight of the years wasted, and the tenderness of his gift hit her like a shot in the chest.

"Oh God, I'm going to start crying again."

"Come on, let's get out of here, so we can talk. Let me get your bag."

"Just like last time." She laughed now through the tears.

"Did you bring the same one?" he asked, referring to the faulty bag he'd seen her struggle with on Brightrock.

Lizzy shook her head. "No, I threw that thing right in the trash the second I could. I did check a bag, though."

Caleb steered her toward the baggage claim, where he again picked up her bag with alarming strength. He walked her through the airport and into the parking garage where he loaded her into the cab of his F-150, taking care to open the door for her like a perfect gentleman. The inside of the cab was immaculate and smelled like him mixed with the faint smell of pine.

When he swung his arm on the headrest beside her to reverse out of the parking spot, a thrum went through her body. She loved the feel of being shepherded around by Caleb, which was a sharp departure from every other time she'd dated a man, not that she'd had much experience.

Back on Brightrock, thanks to her cousins, no one had really been interested, and those who had tried had been too bossy, self-important, or just plain egotistical. Since everyone knew everyone, there was no chase, no real dating on Brightrock. Instead, people just assumed since they had grown up together, they were stuck with each other, which set the bar pretty damn low. Why would anyone try when they thought they were an obvious catch in such a small pool of eligible men?

Caleb drove along with confidence down through the city. "We have a little time before we can check in at the hotel. You must be hungry."

"A little," Lizzy said, even though her stomach growled at the thought of food. She hadn't eaten much since the call from Ethan and was now starving.

"Have anywhere in mind?"

"Where do you like to go?"

Caleb thought for a minute while at a red light and said, "I mean, there's a bunch of places. Really, we have more options than I can list. Whatever you want, we got it."

"I want to know what you like. If you were by yourself, where would you go?"

"That's an easy choice," Caleb said, shooting a smile her way, which sent her heart tapping a little too fast. "I don't want to push, but I'm not going to relax until you tell me what's going on."

Lizzy crossed her legs and settled back into the seat as Caleb turned onto the main road.

"I'm sorry. I can't imagine how that must feel. I called you out of the blue, invited myself here."

"All of that's fine, but you've cried twice, and that doesn't seem like your normal running speed."

Lizzy let out a rueful laugh. "Damn sure isn't."

"That bad?"

Lizzy bit her lip.

"Sorry, I said I wouldn't push, but you're worrying me."

"It's fine. I'm fine. It's just—"

"Just?"

"I don't even know where to start."

"Let's play twenty questions."

Lizzy turned and looked at him. He returned the favor and shrugged. "At least it's someplace to start."

"Alright, fair enough."

"Is it school?"

"No." God, she wished it was.

"You aren't sick, are you?"

Lizzy shook her head and said, "Nope. I'm in perfect health." For someone who's almost a hundred years old, she added to herself. No need to drop that little detail.

Caleb let out a breath. "Okay, good, I was really worried you were sick. Okay, let's see. Is it a money thing?"

"Ha. Nope. I flew first class, so I'm good."

"Well, well, fancy you."

"Are you judging me?"

"No, I'm not surprised. You're too elegant for coach."

Lizzy opened her mouth and shut it again, stunned. He thought she was elegant?

"Family?"

Lizzy's heart seized in her chest. "Kind of."

"Parents?"

"Don't have any."

"Both of my parents are gone, but I still have my grand-parents. I'm sorry, I didn't know."

"When did your family pass away?" Lizzy asked, glancing over.

"A while ago. I was little. Died in a car accident. Other person was drunk. What about your family?"

"They died when I was little. Flu. My aunt and uncle took me in, so I was raised with my cousins, Austin and Ethan." Lizzy waited for a beat to gauge his response. People still died of flu, but not like ninety years ago. Caleb didn't question it.

"Oh, I know Austin."

"Of course. You were at the wedding."

"He's something else."

"He's a pompous ass, who is too smart for his own good."

Caleb smirked and then recovered. "How are he and Caitlyn?"

"Good. Happy, I guess."

"Good for them."

Lizzy shifted in her seat to watch Caleb. "Did you love her?"

He glanced at her and looked uncomfortable as hell. "Wasn't I the one asking the questions?"

"I'd like to know. We all thought you were. Why else would you go all that way?"

His mouth had a grim set to it. "She left without saying anything. I didn't know what had happened."

"You didn't answer my question." Lizzy held her breath, wondering why the answer mattered so much to her.

Caleb let out a sigh. "I don't think so. No. Maybe I thought I was or wanted to be. I wish her all the best."

"So you're not—"

"Upset? Jealous?"

Lizzy nodded.

"No, and you're deflecting. You said it had something to do with family."

"Yep." Lizzy tried to keep the bitterness out of her voice, but it still came through loud and clear.

"Did they do something wrong?"

Lizzy stopped and thought about it. "Nothing new."

"So, they're upset with you."

"Not yet. It's a control thing."

Caleb swung the truck down a side street and pulled off outside a little white building before cutting the engine. "Most of the time, families mean well." He paused and looked at her face. "But I can tell that's not what you want to hear right now. Let's go eat."

CHAPTER 10

Caleb held the door to the small white restaurant and watched as Lizzy walked inside ahead of him. He still thought Elizabeth fit her better, but he supposed he'd have to get used to calling her Lizzy as long as she was around him. He didn't want it to slip out, forcing him to explain how he'd thought of her every day since they'd met. That whole conversation would distract her from telling him whatever the hell had her calling him up, crying. His skin felt too tight with worry, and he really was trying not to push, but he had to know. Not knowing was driving him crazy.

He followed her inside the restaurant called Mother's and grabbed a menu but didn't read it. Instead, he watched her while she looked it over. In her black tights and white oxford shirt, her beauty knocked him on his ass just like it had before. Her dark hair and blue eyes turned heads and had men looking up from their food to get a glimpse, not that they could see even a fraction of her worth.

Underneath her perfect skin, his Elizabeth was intelligent, funny, and hurting. Before she had knocked the wind out of him at the airport crying, Caleb had seen the dark circles and a strained look on her face as she had walked over to him. She was thinner than he remembered. Whatever had happened must have killed her appetite. Even now, when she looked at the menu, Lizzy's brow creased with worry while she chewed on her perfect pink bottom lip.

Caleb wanted to put his hands on her again if only to knead away the knots he knew must be in her shoulders. He hated seeing her like this and felt a strong desire to make it right. He hadn't been able to breathe with ease after her phone call, and seeing her like this was not helping.

They ordered their food, which was old school Cajun cooking. Caleb never skipped crawfish étouffée and recommended the gumbo for Lizzy. They'd chosen a seat in the back room in a corner where they could talk.

"Can I ask you something?" Caleb said, turning to face her.

"Weren't we just playing twenty questions?" Lizzy teased.

"Fair point."

Lizzy took a sip of her sweet tea and leveled a sapphire gaze at him. "So shoot."

Caleb sat forward in his chair and folded his hands on the table. "You said your family had upset you."

Lizzy puffed out a breath between her perfect lips. He hated that damn worried look on her face. He wished like hell he could wipe those worry lines from her brow.

"Yeah, they want me to come home."

Caleb raised his eyebrows. "Like, leave school?"

Lizzy's lip quivered, and she swallowed before sucking in a breath to steady herself. "Yeah."

"I don't understand why."

"They don't think it's safe."

"The bombing. They want everyone from the island to come home." Caleb's eyes were solemn.

"Yeah, I guess. Circle the wagons."

"I'm sorry." Caleb meant it. Lizzy looked so unlike the strong, confident woman he had met before. She looked lost and alone. Hopeless.

"So why come here?"

Lizzy looked up from the table she had been staring at and looked at him. The corner of her mouth lifted in a playful smirk that looked much more like his Elizabeth.

"Last chance at freedom for a while. Gotta go somewhere, you know. Wanted to see if you were as cool as you were when we met."

Caleb laughed, and the food came. They dug in, breaking the silence only to comment on the dishes in front of them. The sound of spoons scraping punctuated the silence while they stuffed themselves to the brim.

"How's Virginia?" Caleb asked when he had scraped the bowl clean.

"It's nice." Lizzy ate some more gumbo and didn't elaborate. Caleb didn't like how quiet she was and wanted to make her smile. She saw this as her last chance at freedom, and it was up to him to make sure she enjoyed it.

"I've never been there myself," he added.

"Close to Washington, so that's cool."

"Have you taken a trip up there yet?"

"No, but I've been meaning to." Another shadow crossed her face, but she slapped on a smile and sat up to face him. "Anyway, I want to hear about you. Tell me something interesting."

"I don't know anything interesting."

"You don't know anything? I find that hard to believe."

"Well, I guess I'm not much different than you. I grew up in Louisiana, went to LSU, and now I work. All of my family is from here."

"Do you ever get tired of that?"

Caleb frowned. "What do you mean?"

"Having the same people all around you. Like doesn't that ever get on your nerves?"

"Sometimes, but I mean, I can't get rid of my family, so I just accept them and move on."

"But you work offshore, right? On the rig?"

Kind of. "Yeah," he said, surprised at how easy the lie came. Now was not the time to add anything to her plate.

"So then you get a break. It's not like you're with them every single day, right?"

"True, and then when I'm home, a lot of time they are busy doing their own thing, and I'm trying to catch up."

"I get that."

"I guess you don't miss your family," he said.

"They won't leave me alone long enough to miss them."

The question he had been wondering since they met popped out. "You haven't met anyone in Virginia?"

"Well, yeah, a few people. They're mostly cool. A couple jerks, but that's par for the course."

"So no boyfriends?" Caleb asked, feeling like he was in middle school again. He was pretty sure it was a no, but he felt like he had to have confirmation from her. She didn't act like she had someone, but still, it was hard to believe she was alone.

His question was met with silence.

"Did you seriously just ask me that?" Lizzy's face contorted into a grimace.

Caleb backed off, throwing up his hands. "I'm sorry, I didn't mean to—"

"That's why I'm here. I was hoping you wanted to date."

Caleb's mouth fell open a little, with his hands still in the air.

"Well?"

"Um, yeah. I mean yes, er...absolutely. I'd love to. Shit, if I'd have known I would've picked a different place to eat."

God, how stupid did he have to sound around her? He wished he could've been the one to ask her out, somehow find the words to tell her how much she meant to him. Instead, she'd just robbed him of the chance, and now he didn't know how to do this. He'd never had anyone ask him out before. Besides, his last attempt at a relationship had ended when his girlfriend had stopped calling after her parents' funerals and packed up to move over a thousand miles away without saying goodbye. To add insult to injury, when Caleb had visited to find out what the hell had gone wrong, there was a new man in her life, telling him to back off. All of it had done a number on what little confidence he had once enjoyed.

Now, to be presented with this opportunity, Caleb didn't even know where to start.

"So then, that settles it. We're going out." Lizzy sat back and nodded once with a satisfied smile before digging back into her gumbo, commenting on the flavor.

He sat slack-jawed. Sure, he had thought of her as his Elizabeth since seeing her on Brightrock, pulling her ridiculous suitcase, but he hadn't actually considered it would happen this way.

Turned out it was his lucky day.

CHAPTER 11

After eating at Mother's and driving around the city, Caleb had noticed the excitement in Lizzy's eyes and decided a night out on the town would do her some good to take her mind off her family troubles. She had said she wanted to visit Louisiana, and everyone needed to spend some time in New Orleans as far as he was concerned.

The first stop was one of the finest hotels. After a short drive over, Caleb passed the keys to his unremarkable, but clean, truck to the valet, slung his small duffle, and hauled Lizzy's bag up the steps of Le Pavillon. The bellman offered to help, but Caleb waved his hand in thanks and followed behind Lizzy who looked around in awe at the grand lobby.

"This is stunning."

Caleb couldn't disagree. The lobby was a masterpiece of marble and mirrors with columns that reached up to the vaulted ceiling. The perfume of fresh lilies in huge vases welcomed all the guests who milled around or lounged on plush, deep chairs that looked like they were fit for a French king.

Lizzy looked like she fit right in, a queen in her palatial surroundings, waited on by staff dressed in white ties and tails. She did a full spin and looked back at him with a smile filled with disbelief and wonder.

Her beauty radiated and filled the lobby like Caleb hadn't imagined possible.

"I guess it meets your expectations."

"Oh my God, this place is beautiful. I feel like I'm in a mansion."

"Well, good, I wanted you to be happy."

Lizzy stopped looking around and locked on him, her blue eyes boring into him as she broke into a broad grin.

"I love it." She tackled him again, wrapping her arms around his chest and squeezing. "Thank you so much for letting me come here. This is just the kind of adventure I need." She looked up at him with gratitude pouring out of her eyes.

"I'm happy you came."

"I wouldn't want to be anywhere else."

Caleb didn't know what to say, so he just smiled and watched as she walked around the lobby again, taking pictures. He pulled her luggage over to the reception desk.

Through an ornate window, a woman with a severe bun and bright smile looked up from her computer and welcomed them to the hotel.

"Thank you. Last name Broussard. I called last night."

The woman's long, painted fingernails clattered on the keyboard gathering his information. Lizzy popped next to him and flashed him another bright smile.

"Once we get settled in, we can go explore, right?"

"We can do whatever you want to do."

"Explore. I'm up for an adventure."

The woman through the window smiled at them both. "First time in New Orleans?"

"Yes, ma'am," Lizzy said.

"There's nothing like it. One of the best cities if you ask me. Food, music, like a party all year long. So, Mr. Broussard, it says here that you reserved two queens, would you like an upgrade to our king suite?"

Caleb froze and glanced at Lizzy, not sure what to say. She had said they were dating, but then he didn't want to assume—

"King, please." Lizzy glanced his way and winked. "We just started dating."

"Oh, congratulations! New Orleans is a very romantic city."

"That's perfect then!"

Caleb's face felt hot, and he didn't know what to say, so he just smiled and nodded while wondering how his life had changed so much in a week—from sitting alone in a small room on an oil compound in Iraq to watching Lizzy twirl around in a hotel in Louisiana.

They collected their keys and headed to the elevators with a bellhop the receptionist had insisted they use. Caleb listened to Lizzy chat with the friendly man in the elevator and down the hallway toward their room.

Her natural confidence struck him dead. He wasn't the best with words, never quite knew what to say, but Lizzy could jump right into a conversation with anyone she met, holding their attention, and making them laugh with a few quick jokes. She was stunningly beautiful, confident, brilliant, funny, and relying on him to show her around and give her the vacation of a lifetime. He watched her as the bellman gave her the tour of the room and asked her preference on where to put the bags. Caleb thanked him and passed him a five as the man left.

Lizzy flopped down on the sumptuous bed and sighed. "I feel like a princess."

"Good, that's what I wanted. So, do you want to—"

A knock at the door cut him off.

Caleb looked through the peephole and saw another woman from the hotel.

"Hello, I'm sorry to bother you, sir," she said when he opened the door. "I have some items, compliments from the hotel, to celebrate. May I come in?"

"Yes, please," Lizzy said, standing up. The woman picked up a tray from a cart in the hall and put it on the dresser. She then went back out and brought in an ice bucket and a bottle of champagne along with two glasses. She repeated the process, leaving a basket of fresh fruit and a small vase with a single red rose inside.

"I'll come right back with a vase for your other flowers, ma'am," the woman said, pointing to the roses Caleb had brought to the airport, now resting on the bedside table.

"Wow," Lizzy said when she had left. "Do you come here often?"

"Not really, but maybe I should," Caleb said. The last time he had been here was a wedding.

"Well, let me go freshen up and then we'll head out on that adventure. I don't want to miss a thing." She winked and shut the door to the bathroom, making Caleb's heart skip in his chest.

CHAPTER 12

The sights, sounds, and smells overwhelmed Lizzy. Unlike her understated, boring life, New Orleans thrummed with eclectic vitality. Lizzy strode across Jackson Square, the sidewalk lined with artists, a jazz band filling the air with a beat that echoed the city's easy-going and erratic tempo. Birds called down from the blooming trees in the fading evening sun. The air smelled familiar to her, briny like home, but the hazy quality brought down the speed, putting everything in slow motion. Tourists walked along the French architecture, darting into full restaurants where waiters in ties swooped through tables with elegance while holding trays filled with steaming food smelling of spice.

Lizzy loved all of it but couldn't enjoy anything as much as she wanted. Next to her, Caleb walked like his skin was too tight. Just like at Austin's wedding in June, his eyes darted around with suspicion. As they toured the city, Lizzy watched him out of the corner of her eye. Caleb didn't walk or stroll but almost stalked like a slow-moving bodyguard ready to pounce. Never shy before, Lizzy stole glances at his muscled forearms, exposed by his rolled-up shirt sleeves. She let her eyes drink in the sight of him. She wanted to know everything but couldn't find the words to ask. To be fair, he hadn't talked much on that first flight they had shared. He listened.

Worry that she had misread him crept up her chest, and she squashed it back down again like she had when she spoke up about the stupid room. Caleb had looked somewhere between alarmed and panicked when she said the words, "King, please," which was not the response she had wanted. Despite the spacious room being lavishly appointed, Caleb seemed nervous. Coming outside hadn't helped. She swallowed and slapped on a serene smile she hoped convinced him that her heart wasn't sinking with every step. She wondered if she had come on too strong.

They turned onto Bourbon Street and walked into a cacophony. Faded beads strangled the wires above, while music from opposing bars and restaurants tangled in the middle of the road. The crowd of tourists swelled around them both, as couples and groups walked both ways with various drinks in their hands.

"Looks like a party," Lizzy said over the crowd. As she kept walking, Caleb squeezed in closer to her, his arm pressing against her own, sending a thrill of contact down her body. All of her senses went on alert at his inadvertent touch. He hadn't expressed an interest in her, but that did nothing to quell what she felt for him.

"You should see Mardi Gras. This is nothing." His voice, low and like gravel, would have gotten lost had she not been hanging on his every word.

"This doesn't look like nothing. I can't imagine," Lizzy said.

She peered through a crowd of people clustered in front of her in the center of the street. A barefoot man and woman who both looked homeless beamed from the sidelines as a small feral child elicited cheers from the tourists around them. For all of the matted hair and old baggy clothes, Lizzy couldn't tell if it was a boy or girl, but a familiar warning bell sounded in her head. This child, who was decidedly not in school, darted around the circle, snatching up fallen palm fronds and weaving them into roses in a matter of seconds, presenting them to delighted tourists in exchange for tip money. Quick little hands, crusted with dirt, snatched the bill and repeated the show, with expert skill.

Back on Brightrock, Lizzy had never needed to call Child Protective Services, but as an educator, she had attended the mandatory training from the Commonwealth of Massachusetts. The amount of wealth on the island ruled out the possibility of students going without, but even if they had, Lizzy wouldn't have been able to call due to the nature of the island itself. Having a social worker from the outside investigate their students' home lives simply was not an option. Still watching the small child perform—there was no other word for it—made her itch to dial her phone.

The child performer handed a woman a folded flower before doing a series of flips, much to the delight of the crowd. Lizzy's purse slid on her shoulder, and she rolled her arm to tug it back.

Caleb shouted next to her and shot out a hand, clutching the arm of a similar, taller child. A few tourists turned toward them with interest, but most applauded the child in the center of the crowd, now doing a handstand.

Lizzy snatched her purse away, but the thin hand covered in dirt clutched her wallet. When she reached out to grab it back, the kid dodged her, despite Caleb's hold, his arm jerking with the frantic movements. Like an animal caught in a snare, the thin arm tried to wriggle out from Caleb's grasp, which tightened, the knuckles going white.

"Drop it." Caleb's voice was low, the intent clear.

The kid's eyes shifted left and right, fear evident in the wide stare. Caleb tightened his hold and leaned in close, saying something so low Lizzy couldn't make out what it was over the crush of people around them. The boy released her wallet to the ground where it dropped with a thud. Lizzy snatched the leather wallet back off the pavement, shoving it back into her purse, which she hugged to her chest. Caleb released the arm and let the boy vanish back into the crush of people.

Caleb watched him go, his face drawn in harsh lines, bringing out his age. Despite being rattled, Lizzy went to smooth his brow and had to stop herself, dropping her hand in midair. She didn't like the look on his face, but at the same time needed to know what had put it there.

"Come on," he said, wrapping his arm around her shoulder and steering her away from the crowd. Never one to let herself be guided around by a man, Lizzy took comfort in his touch and the closeness of his body.

"I'm sorry—"

"Do not apologize." He pulled her in tight, bringing her body into full contact with his own. "That was not your fault."

"I should've known—"

"Don't." He marched them both through Bourbon Street, asking a few times if she wanted to visit some of the nicer places. After everything that had happened, Lizzy couldn't bring herself to say yes. The magic had vanished.

"What did you say to him?" she asked when they were half a block away.

Caleb's mouth was a thin line. "Nothing much."

Lizzy stopped and turned to him. "No, I really want to know."

He sighed and propped his hands on his hips. "I told him we were local."

"That can't have been all of it."

"I may have mentioned the cops, but I passed him a couple of bills and told him to get a good meal for him and his brother."

"Oh, Caleb—"

He held up a hand to stop her. "I don't want to talk about it. I know that only encourages them. Let's just drop it. Everything else is in there, right?"

Lizzy rummaged through. "Yeah, looks like it."

He let out a breath. "Okay, good. Let's continue our tour. You still like coffee?"

"America runs on Dunkin."

Caleb shot her a real, broad smile, which sent her heart into full flip-flop mode. "I'm not talking about that, and they sure as hell can't make a doughnut like the place we're going to."

"And where's that?"

"Ever heard of Cafe Du Monde?"

CHAPTER 13

Nora stood at the top of the stage, feeling like a monkey on parade. All gussied up in her dress blues, with her arm in a sling, Nora looked out among the crowd of her peers while the Detective Lieutenant spoke about bravery, courage, and officers who put their life on the line for the community. A few cameras snapped, flicking a quick light over them. Manillo stood ramrod straight next to her, his wife and kid looking up at him from the front row, next to Nora's grandma and brother. Behind them stood Tom and Christine Harris, friends who had become family when her own dad had been killed on the force.

The ample meeting space doubled as the press conference room and event hall, the walls decorated with names of heroes from the Troop, some of whom had died in the line of duty. Her shoulder throbbed, reminding her of just how close she had come to getting a nameplate, not that she wanted one. When the doctors had told her just how complicated the repair had been, a sense of fear hit for the first time in a long time. She didn't know who she would be without this job.

Every cadet who entered the academy knew what was at stake, knew what the job required. Their mission to protect and serve could come at a price for any of them, at any moment. Years on the job showed Nora the truth of that statement a few times but experiencing it firsthand put things in perspective. Sure, she had been clocked in the jaw, but waking up with a bunch of bruises everywhere and her arm all wrapped up left an impression. If that hadn't done it, physical therapy had. She hadn't even started reporting to the shrink for processing, as was the procedure.

A round of applause drew her from her thoughts. She gave a polite smile as she scanned the crowd before shaking the hand of the brass on stage with her. Manillo stood in line, getting his hand clamped as well, at her insistence. The drug bust had been successful, with Nora's artery being the lone casualty on their side, and had helped to bring in a supply of fentanyl large enough to kill half the state, along with heroin and other drugs. Two of the leading dealers had been killed in the process. The cycle had been broken, for now, putting them in the lead of the ongoing war on drugs.

The festivities broke up, and a murmur of chatter filled the large room. Manillo hopped down the stairs to hug and kiss his wife before taking the toddler, who had started to grow bored, and hoisting him up on his hip. Nora made her way down the stairs and caught a glimpse of a tall man she hadn't noticed in the back by the door. His blond hair and amused smile lit his face and eyes as he watched her from the wall. Why was the bastard here? He had made no secret he didn't want to be found. Had something changed?

"Looking good up there. How's the arm?" Her brother Michael's thick accent cut through the noise. She still wasn't used to his deep voice and couldn't get used to the idea he was a senior this year.

Nora glanced back at Ethan, who smiled, nodded once, but remained against the wall. Good, he was waiting. She had questions.

"It's still on," she said, trying to ignore the fact that the damn thing hurt like a frigging bitch.

"Well, good. The throbbing means the blood is rushing to the area to heal." Gram nodded once, dressed in a light jade pantsuit, with a hat to match. In one hand, she clutched a pocketbook the size of Hyannis and held onto Nora's brother's arm for balance with the other.

"Well, it must be healing quick, but yeah, I'll be alright."

A voice boomed behind Nora.

"Good, we need you to heal up," Detective Lieutenant Brown said, shaking the hands of her brother and then grandma.

"She never was a good patient," her grandma said, shaking her head before turning to address Nora. "You heard him; you need to heal."

"Take the time you need. You can ride a desk until that shoulder comes back online. We need you at one hundred percent."

"Yes, sir," Nora said, watching as he chatted with her family before ambling off to congratulate Manillo.

"Ready to head to dinner? I want to get a table with the warm rolls before all the good ones are gone."

Nora glanced over her shoulder, hoping to still see Ethan waiting, and smiled to herself when he waved. Smug bastard.

"Sounds good. Can you guys go get the table, and I'll catch up?"

They parted ways, and Nora marched over to Ethan's direction, stopping a few times to shake the hands of a few fellow officers and various well-wishers.

"Lieutenant," Ethan said with a slight nod and smile. "Congratulations."

"I'm surprised to see you. I've been trying to call your office."

"You have?" His eyes lit with amusement again. Ass.

"Yes, they didn't have your forwarding address. Wanted to thank you for the flowers."

Nora caught the glance before he quickly masked it. Had she not been looking for the telltale signs, she would've missed it. The florist had been obstinate under her questioning of the origin of the biggest, most expensive bouquet Nora had ever seen. Now it made sense.

"I'm not sure I follow."

"You can pretend you don't, but I'm still saying thank you so I can walk away and not feel guilty."

"Why would you feel guilty?" he asked, a broad smile on his face.

"Raised Catholic. Pretty much my running speed. So anyway, thank you, but the department can't accept gifts."

"Still not sure what you're talking about."

Irritation bubbled in her chest. God, what about him got under her skin? He wore another expertly cut suit that could only be described as luxurious, the fabric lacking any sheen of the cheap ones available in stores. His jawline showed a hint of blond stubble, his lips curving.

"Why are you here?" she asked.

"I wanted to congratulate you on your bravery, though I'm concerned about that shoulder."

On his cue, the throbbing came back with a vengeance. "Thanks. I'm good, though."

"I know."

The deep tone of his voice caught her off guard and sent a thrill of interest into her chest, which she squashed like a bug.

"Right, well anyway, thanks for the flowers. I can't stay, but I need to follow up with you regarding my investigation. I have a few more questions." It was a bluff, but Nora needed to know more about what he was hiding. The investigator in her couldn't walk away.

"I can make myself available, but only for dinner." He smiled like a cat. Nora didn't like it.

"If you still have my card, tell me where and when."

"I'll see you tomorrow, Lieutenant."

CHAPTER 14

Lizzy climbed the steps to the lobby, her feet now aching and chafed from the walking. Her body demanded she march right up to bed, but she couldn't remember the last time she'd felt this happy, even with the pickpocket incident. She and Caleb had walked what felt like the entire length of Bourbon Street, soaking up the sights and sounds, stopping in a few places to share a drink or watch some karaoke after grabbing a few beignets and about a pound of powdered sugar at Cafe Du Monde.

Caleb opened the door for Lizzy. The scent of fresh lilies surrounded her in a refreshing perfume. She pulled her purse tight around her even inside the plush, golden lobby. Its weight was a comfort after what had almost happened. Thank God Caleb had noticed.

He walked tall and proud next to her, and despite being a bit quiet, she had complete faith he would do anything to protect her. The sight of him made the tension she'd been carrying in her shoulders for too long finally relax. Lizzy knew she could rely on him to be exactly who he was. There were no secrets, no games—just honest loyalty and kindness. That was part of the reason she was so drawn to him.

Inside the lobby, a row of long tables was covered in white tablecloths. Caleb turned to see what she was looking at and noticed the rows of silver chafing dishes laid out buffet style like at a wedding. The lobby swelled with the chatter of people dressed in everything from party clothes to bathrobes.

"What's all this?" Lizzy asked.

"Looks like one hell of a cocktail hour," Caleb said.

Drink dispensers were filled with milk next to jars of jelly and peanut butter. Lizzy reached out and opened a chafing dish to reveal slices of white bread all in rows. Her stomach growled, and she hesitated, unsure.

"Do you think this is for everyone?" she asked Caleb before looking around for someone to stop her. All of a sudden, she was starving, and she was going to help herself unless someone jumped out and stopped her.

"Looks like it's a tradition here," Caleb said, pointing to a small sign. "Years ago, a guest asked the chef for a peanut butter and jelly sandwich to eat late at night, in keeping a standing appointment with his daughter while he was away. The hotel liked the idea so much, they've hosted a nightly sandwich-making bar ever since."

"Hey, that's pretty neat." Lizzy made quick work of the sandwich while thinking about the story. Caleb followed suit, and they both headed for a corner seat with glasses of milk in hand.

Sitting down, Lizzy sunk her teeth into the white bread, savoring the familiar taste she hadn't known in years.

"God, when was the last time I had one of these?"

Caleb nodded and chewed a big bite himself. "There's something about it. Never gets old."

"I didn't realize how hungry I was. I don't know why. All I've done since landing was eat."

Lizzy chewed alongside Caleb and watched him as he ate. His muscles flexed under his shirt. What had been a neatly starched shirt had wilted with the heat and now clung to his body, making him look even more attractive. His dark hair and green bedroom eyes had been haunting her since they'd met back on Brightrock when her stupid luggage had broken. Since the moment she heard his southern accent, Lizzy had been hooked. She'd laid awake at night getting tangled in the sheets thinking of him, and now in the flesh, she couldn't fight the attraction anymore. Still, he was so quiet.

They finished their sandwiches and headed toward the elevator, which they shared with another couple. The silence felt awkward and made Lizzy's shoulders tighten.

They got out at their floor, padding down the narrow hall that smelled almost as good as the lobby. Caleb pulled the key out of his jeans and opened the door for her, revealing a perfect evening turndown.

Soft jazz danced through the room in the dim light. Two robes rested on the bed with the sheets turned down, waiting for them to slide inside. Lizzy was tempted, but as much as she liked him, she had been on a plane and walked more than she had in years in a thousand percent humidity. She'd be damned if their first night together she smelled like a dog.

"I think I'm going to hit the shower." She eyed him in the soft, golden glow from the bedside lamp to gauge if he would like to join in. Lizzy needed a proper scrub, but if he were interested, she wouldn't mind an audience.

"Yeah, of course. Whatever you need." Caleb sat down on the sofa and began pulling out the laces to his boots.

"I won't be long," Lizzy said, and practically jumped under the hot spray a few seconds later. She scrubbed, shampooed, conditioned, shaved, exfoliated, and gave herself the full treatment in the warm water, all the while considering how different her life was from last year.

Timothy Chappell and the rest of the town elders controlled her every move. Up until now, Lizzy had only gone to Boston and New York for supervised shopping trips, other than college, which had been years ago. Her entire life had been orchestrated, controlled, and managed. The word made her want to spit in the drain.

Maybe that's why staying in the same bed with a man she had met twice made her skin tingle in the best possible way. But she considered Caleb again. He was unlike anyone she had ever met. He was quiet, but strong, gentle, and smart. He treated her like a complete queen and hadn't asked a single thing of her for himself. Unlike Brightrock, where everyone had an interest in everything, Caleb seemed content to be there when she needed him, without pushing her to divulge information so he could swoop in and call the shots for her.

Lizzy finished up in the shower and wrapped herself in two large towels in the marble cathedral that the hotel called a bathroom. She cracked the door and caught a glimpse of Caleb.

He had fallen asleep on the couch, still fully dressed. Christ, he even still had his belt on. Lizzy slinked over to him, enjoying the feeling of just being in a towel near him.

Caleb was even more beautiful asleep. He had dark, long lashes which rested against his tan cheek, making him look much younger than his typical attitude and the way he carried himself allowed. Minutes before, she had been ready to strip down and jump on him, but now, seeing him like this, Lizzy's heart softened, melted, and she wanted to curl like a cat right into his side. But he hadn't showered or even changed.

"Caleb? Hey, you can jump in the shower now." Lizzy

reached out and laid her hand on his shoulder, surprised at the warmth radiating from him.

He sucked in a breath while his lids fluttered open. He looked around the room and settled on Lizzy, his eyes skimming down her body with a sleepy haze.

"What time is it?" His voice was hoarse. Man, he really must've been out hard. Lizzy hadn't stopped to think about what he had been doing before she arrived. If he had just gotten off the rig, he would be exhausted since he worked twelve-hour shifts for days straight. Guilt set up shop, and she bit her lip at her selfishness.

"Plenty late. Do you want to grab a shower? It's really nice. Good water pressure."

Caleb let out a laugh before sitting up and pulling on the back of his neck with a yawn. "I'm sure it's better than—"

He stopped cold and didn't finish his sentence. A look of concern crossed his features.

"Better than what? The rig? Yeah, I guess it would be. Those things don't look like they're built with luxury in mind."

Caleb sat on the edge of the sofa, his hands braced against the brocade fabric, watching her. She couldn't read his features.

"Come on. You look exhausted, and I know you can't be comfortable in that."

Lizzy grabbed his hands and pulled him to his feet. Her towel started to slip, and with her free hand she pulled the terrycloth together to keep from exposing herself. Caleb had caught the movement, too, and froze, looking at her hand concealing everything.

Lizzy stood in front of him, just inches away. This would be the perfect moment to lean in for a kiss, press her body into his, so their bodies held up her towel and nothing else.

She moistened her lips and felt her shoulders fall as she relaxed into his green gaze, which stared right back at her.

"I think I should go take a shower," Caleb said at last, breaking the magical silence between them.

"Yeah, okay. It'll make you feel better. Then you can come to bed."

Caleb looked over his shoulder at the bed and shifted on his feet. "Ah...I really don't mind sleeping on the couch. I mean, I don't want you to think that, you know—"

"I said I wanted a king bed for a reason."

A faint tinge of pink hit Caleb's cheeks. "Oh, well, you know, just in case you wanted to take things slow. I mean, I don't want to push you into anything."

"I'm the one who suggested it."

"Right." He stood before her and didn't seem to know what to do or say next.

Lizzy smirked at his dilemma. He was so cute the way he wanted to protect her feelings. Everything about him was so unlike the arrogance she had lived with for the last hundred years.

"Go shower," she said. "I'll open some champagne." Then she dropped the towel.

CHAPTER 15

Caleb stood slack-jawed as he watched Lizzy sashay toward the bottle of champagne. Just as he had imagined, her shape rivaled the statues of goddesses carved by the masters. Her elegant beauty was beyond anything he had seen before. There was something vital and healthy, like a glow from within that drew him to her like a magnet. Her skin was a perfect alabaster, except for a birthmark of some kind on her back near her ribcage. Looking at it in the soft lighting of the room, it looked like the wing of an angel, so formed he wondered if it was actually an old tattoo.

She glanced over her perfect, delicate shoulder and gave him a small smile. "I thought you were going to shower."

Shower. That's what he was doing.

Caleb walked into the bathroom, which was more of a marble palace. The shower had at least four jets, not counting the substantial rainfall one overhead that cranked on. In no time the room was filled with steam.

While under the spray, Caleb scrubbed and ran a razor over his face, chin, and neck. The day had been perfect. Well, except for her crying and still not entirely disclosing what had upset her so much. And not to mention the pickpocketing incident. But all considered, everything had gone better than he could've hoped.

He still didn't know what had brought her here or made her want to call him of all people. Yes, he had been enthralled with her, thinking of her every night, and looking forward to the few emails they had traded since they had parted ways at Logan Airport in Boston. Watching Lizzy walk away with a natural confidence that he envied still made his heart lurch in his chest, but what had seared it into his memory was when she spun on her heel midstride and toasted him with a Styrofoam cup of Dunkin. That casual intelligence and sexy, lopsided grin as she tossed her head back would be in his mind until the day he died.

But something was wrong. Wrong enough to make Lizzy take a leave of absence from her graduate school program and fly to Louisiana of all places, where she was excited enough to drive out past the swamps. Caleb got out, toweled off, and brushed his teeth, fast and hard.

Lord knew he wanted to skip the champagne and would kill to dive into bed next to her, but that didn't feel right. Of course, the minute he had what he wanted, he would have the Catholic guilt come on strong. Lizzy had been in Louisiana for less than twelve hours, which meant they had been speaking for less than twelve hours. Adding in the time they talked back on Brightrock, both when they met and at Austin and Caitlyn's wedding, Lizzy had known Caleb less than a week.

He spat in the sink and stared at himself in the mirror. More wrinkles than last year. Another birthday had passed last month, and he'd been overseas. Sure, the guys got him a cake, but at the end of the night, Caleb had lain awake in the small sterile room looking at the TV on mute. He had always wanted to be the guy everyone loved—the center of attention, the risk-taker, the popular guy—but he could never bring himself to make it happen. Even now, with the woman of his dreams lying naked on a king bed, going to her felt wrong. She was better than that—so much better—whether she knew it or not.

He pulled a hand over his face and popped a knuckle before pulling on a robe and opening the door, not sure how to find the words to tell Lizzy what was on his mind.

Lizzy didn't sit up from the bed where she was lying. Curled up under the covers, she snoozed with the light and TV still on. The unopened bottle sweated next to the roses he had bought her, now in a vase on the nightstand. A *Golden Girls* rerun ran on mute. Caleb picked up the remote and turned off the TV just as Blanche stormed into the kitchen to talk to Dorothy. He walked over and turned off the light, dimming it first, so as not to wake her with the click of the switch.

Asleep with her eyelashes against her cheeks, she looked exhausted and so fragile. A whisper from the vent above sent a shiver through her shoulders. He stepped over to the thermostat, adjusting it to make sure she wouldn't be cold.

Caleb padded over toward his bag and brought it into the bathroom. He pulled on shorts and an old T-shirt from college and crept out in the dark toward the bed. He eased the comforter and sheets back before sliding in. The second his weight hit the mattress, she turned over to face him. He could just make her out with help from the glow of the streetlights peeking past the drapes.

"You okay?" he asked.

She sniffed in response.

Caleb edged closer and pulled her into him, cradling her head on his arm. "It's going to be okay."

"I'm sorry. I'm a mess. I'm running from something and

using you as an excuse to forget everything."

The statement hurt, but at least they had both reached the same conclusion. "Everything is going to be okay. I promise."

"I wanted this to be nice and romantic. I wanted to get drunk and have the time of our lives," Lizzy said, before sniffing again.

"Who says we're not?"

"What do you mean?"

Caleb wished he had left the light on so he could still see her face, but somehow being in the dark made it easier. "Lizzy, I've been thinking about you every day since the day I met you. Lying here with you is perfect."

"Caleb?"

He held his breath, waiting for the letdown. "Yeah?"

"I feel the same way too."

He blew out the air and then started to laugh.

Lizzy let out a nervous laugh. "What?"

"Nothing. I'm just relieved."

"That's good."

Caleb propped himself up on an elbow. "Lizzy, I don't know why you're here."

"I don't want to talk about it. I don't even want to think about it."

"I understand. You tired?"

Lizzy was quiet as she thought about that for a moment. "I am, but I don't think I can sleep."

Caleb watched as she shifted, tucking both arms under her head.

"You've had a big day. Want some champagne? It'd be a shame to waste it."

"Sure."

Caleb turned on the lights and stood to open the bottle. He filled the glasses with the bubbly while Lizzy shifted up in the bed, rustling the sheets and hugging them to her chest.

"Here you go." Caleb handed over the flute and clinked his to hers. "To the present."

Lizzy beamed in the dim light. "I like that. More than you know."

They each took a sip while he crawled back in.

"I didn't realize you had clothes on. Does it bother you that I don't?"

Lizzy's dark hair tangled around her face like a halo of wild and untamed waves. Her face glowed with regal and refined beauty, while her big blue eyes watched him, assessing and waiting for his answer. With her head held high, the column of her slender neck ran down to her delicate collar bones and shoulders. With the white sheet tucked up against her chest, she looked every part of the goddess he believed her to be.

"Of course not. You're beautiful."

Lizzy beamed and took another sip of her champagne.

Caleb sat back down and grabbed the remote. "Let's just relax. You know what goes good with champagne?" he asked before taking another sip.

"Passionate sex?"

Caleb choked and sputtered champagne all over the bed, before launching into a coughing fit. Lizzy thumped him a few times on the back, while he gasped for air like a fish.

"You okay?" she asked, laughing.

"Yeah, good. I'm good." He coughed a few more times and sucked in a breath. "Just took me by surprise is all."

Lizzy smiled, her eyes still twinkling with laughter. "Not what you had in mind, huh?"

"I was going to suggest I turn your show back on and we snuggle."

Lizzy raised an eyebrow and tucked one corner of her mouth up into a small smile. "You know, Caleb. That sounds perfect."

CHAPTER 16

He would get hell for it later, Ethan thought, as he pushed the red circle on the sleek new phone in his hand. Timothy Chappell had been calling him at least twice a day, and while Ethan knew he had a sense of duty to the council back home, tonight he couldn't pick up. Not with what he was about to do. The guilt Ethan had been fighting all day came trickling back in like water through a leaky roof. No matter how he tried to patch his mind by thinking of something else, the wrongness came back. He shouldn't be here.

"Can I get you anything else, sir?" The sommelier poured a glass of Merlot the color of blood. Ethan couldn't see her well and wasn't interested in looking. The restaurant sat in Beacon Hill, hidden along cobbled streets and pristine brownstones. For the dinner service, the entire dining room glowed only with candlelight, small dancing flames twinkling on each table and in every sconce on the wall. The effect made him wonder about his parents. Even though the house had electricity and had for quite some time, Mom and Dad would turn out all of the lights, preferring to work by candlelight, as they found 'the new lights,' as they still called them, too harsh.

Timothy Chappell, who had arrived on Brightrock clutching a Bible while wearing a woolen doublet in a small boat heading for the New World along with Ethan's great aunts Tee and Mary, must have found the light bulbs even more painful than Ethan's parents. Guilt floated to the surface of his mind as he swirled the wine glass in front of him, waiting for his guest. The amount of change Ethan's life consisted of—Wall Street and offices—was nothing compared with what the elders had witnessed.

A group of couples laughed to his right, and Ethan looked out at the people around the dining room. Most were affluent, excited, and enthralled with the person with whom they shared small plates of expensive food, their faces lit by the candles in front of them, their hands dancing around while they shared their hopes, dreams, and secrets with each other. The door opened, a soft twinkling bell that no one noticed but him and the hostess who rushed forward.

Ethan stood on instinct and went to button his jacket but stalled out when he remembered he had opted to forgo the formality. From what little he knew of Nora, Ethan could tell she didn't appreciate anything that smacked of luxury. The hostess gave a quick nod and turned on her heel, leading Nora inside.

"Here you are, madam. Enjoy."

Nora murmured words of thanks to the hostess and sized up Ethan. He silently cursed the choice of restaurant. Though he'd wanted to treat her to something special, he wished there was more light to see her better. For some reason he couldn't get her out of his head; he wanted to know every swell of her body, needed to see them, despite already having it memorized in his mind.

"Thank you for joining me, Lieutenant." He went to pull out her chair, but Nora's hand stopped him.

"I got it, thanks."

"Of course." Her tone didn't bother him. In fact, after years of having women bend over backward to get his attention, he rather liked her firm independence. They sat down, and he handed her the wine list, only to be met with her raised hand.

"On duty, but thanks."

"You can't be working now." Ethan couldn't hide the disapproval in his voice. Her arm was still in a sling, an ugly mess of straps that restrained her arm and shoulder from any unnecessary movement. A thought crossed his mind, deepening the frown.

"How did you get here? I sent a car but was told you declined."

"I get myself around, and no, I'm not back on duty, but I'll consider this a continuation of our interview."

"I see," he said, leaning back and admiring her outfit. The dress suited her—plain black, with a neckline that revealed nothing and sleeves that ended just below the elbow. The simplicity spoke to her elegance and need for clarity. He wondered if she had her gun, and figured she probably did. The thought brought a smile to his lips. When he had asked her to dinner, he hadn't expected a yes and hadn't expected her to dress as she did.

"So, how did you find me?" she asked, direct and to the point when they had ordered dinner. Chicken for her and steak for him.

"You gave me your card."

She raised an eyebrow at him, the movement cool and hot at the same time, sending a shiver of interest over his skin again. The sight of her in the candlelight, holding a water goblet in one hand, even with her sling, was perfection. Her short golden hair framed her face, unadorned with makeup. Everything about her stood out as fresh, honest, and direct. She had no time or interest in anything fussy, and Ethan considered that she probably thought the whole place stood out as too much to her. He had seen her eyes widen at the prices, but it had only been a quick tell before her mask of professionalism slid into place. She didn't want him to see her reaction, but Ethan caught it, and it pleased him. If he had his way, she would be in the most beautiful restaurant on the east coast, though he had seen enough to gauge a place he hoped would exceed expectation while still keeping her comfortable.

"No, I mean at the ceremony. The invites only went out to the family and the department."

"How do you know I didn't try to contact you when you were in the hospital?"

"Someone would've told me."

"Are you sure?" Ethan enjoyed playing this game with her.

"Yes. So I guess you won't tell me. I could arrest you for stalking."

"But then we wouldn't get to try dessert and wouldn't that be a shame?" He grinned at her when the eyebrow raised at him again, studying him like he imagined she would one of her suspects, but then, that's how she probably viewed him.

"I suspect this mystery person, who I know doesn't exist, is also the one that went on to tell you what hospital I was in so you could send me half the flowers in Boston."

"You were on the news, and I thought the department doesn't allow gifts."

"We don't."

Ethan smiled as Nora's frown deepened. He could almost feel the frustration seeping out of her in waves. From her hard gaze, Ethan knew she didn't want to like him and didn't want to enjoy the dinner, and he savored proving her wrong on both accounts. It had been so long since he indulged himself the company of someone he enjoyed.

A waiter swept over with an array of bread, still warm from the oven. Nora glanced down at it but didn't move.

"Bread?" he asked, taking one for himself. He could almost feel her hunger, but she didn't respond.

"They're fresh. Let me get you some." Before she could decline him, he had given her a selection on the plate, taking care to butter each one so she wouldn't need to struggle with her arm.

"Thank you," she said. The words carved of stone sounded like a forced surrender.

"Of course," he said, picking up a roll and taking a bite in a show of good faith. Though he enjoyed the dancing intellect, he wanted her to feel more comfortable now that they were together alone.

He chewed, wiping his mouth with the napkin, aware of her eyes on his lips. Seconds stretched, but Nora looked down at the plate he had prepared and picked up a slice of cranberry almond, still warm and now soaked with melted butter. Bringing it to her own lips, Nora gave him a surprised smile when she took the first bite. Ethan could've cheered at the victory, and etched all of her features into his mind as a memory he wouldn't forget for the rest of the several hundred years he still had to go in his life.

"This ain't bad."

"It's certainly not. So, how is your shoulder? I want to know what happened. The ceremony talked a lot about bravery and general community help but didn't actually say anything."

"Yeah, they're good at saying nothing and making it sound like a lot," Nora said in a more conversational tone that gave Ethan hope.

"A lot of people have that skill these days," he said, picking up another roll if only to keep her comfortable and talking. He didn't add that he had personally become a master of that very skill to survive. The lie didn't sit well with him, and he pushed that thought out of his mind.

"Yeah, they don't want to get sued or offend anyone. Have to tiptoe around things."

"So, does that mean I don't get to know?"

"No, it's fine. Stupid really," Nora said before taking another bite. Without asking, Ethan reached into the basket and began to butter another slice.

"I doubt that."

She pulled a face at him, the kind that gave him an idea of what she might look like as a surly teenager filled with angst.

"Anyway, my division handles homeland security and drugs. This house had been at the center of a big drug ring for a while. We finally had what we needed to raid it. I guess you heard the rest at the ceremony, which, it's still weird you were there. Don't think I have forgotten that because of the bread and candlelight and stuff."

"Not at all. But that doesn't explain how your shoulder got hurt," Ethan pointed out. For some reason even he didn't understand, Ethan needed to know everything about what had happened to her. He wished like hell she hadn't been there at all but knew that he might as well have asked the moon to fall. The way she carried herself told him every-thing. She didn't have a job as a cop. She was a cop.

"It got a little ugly. They weren't happy to see us. Returned fire before we could disarm the threat."

"You make that sound routine." The realization bothered him.

"Not every day is like that, but yeah, shutting it down will stop the flow for a while. We got ahead of them there." On the last sentence, she stopped looking at him and instead stared into the flame as if she had forgotten his presence. The candlelight flickered in her eyes, bringing out their golden color, making them glow.

"You're very good at your job," he said at last.

"Shouldn't have gotten hit. Dumb."

"I don't think so."

Nora raised her eyes to look at him. The flat look in her eyes reached into his soul, showing him how much she had witnessed and survived. She started to open her mouth, but the waiters arrived, sliding in almost unnoticed with plates of food arranged with sweeps of sauce and clouds of potatoes.

Ethan murmured, thanked the staff, and stood.

"Bathroom?" Nora asked, sounding surprised.

Standing beside her, he picked up her knife and fork and proceeded to cut the chicken into bite-sized pieces, dragging the steel across the tender meat in a smooth motion.

Nora opened her mouth to protest, glancing both ways to see what other diners might think of this odd arrangement, though Ethan continued until the job was finished, lingering by her side a half second longer than necessary, before returning to his seat and replacing the napkin in his lap.

When their gazes met, Nora looked frustrated beyond belief, but like a queen, she righted herself, straightening her spine and picking up her fork.

"I hadn't quite thought about that yet. Thank you."

Ethan smiled at the admission, accepting it for what it was: progress.

CHAPTER 17

Nora stared across the table at Ethan. The candle between them flickered, casting a warm glow over his face, making him look even more handsome which shouldn't have been possible, but somehow was. His hair reached his broad shoulders and framed his strong jaw, clean-shaven today. Two women at the table next to Nora had been casting glances in Ethan's direction since she had arrived, and probably before. She had been ready to walk right out, but the damn man who she knew was hiding something hadn't taken his eyes off her once. The effect unnerved Nora.

She shouldn't even be sitting here in this restaurant, which was totally inappropriate for an interview. Nora would have felt more at home in an alley or some bar in a typical neighborhood.

Nora didn't want to like him. She didn't even want to talk with him. She just needed information, but despite every wall she built up and every obstacle she tried to throw at him, Nora had started to relax. She was screwed.

She had wanted to intimidate Ethan and get more information on Austin Brooks, who mysteriously died, though the obituary was slim, and the cremation records from the town were scarce. Something around this whole thing had struck her as odd, but then Ethan hadn't budged despite every question. It was his eyes that told her he enjoyed the chase and knew something worth knowing.

When the food arrived, Nora had felt a moment of panic, starting to reach for her fork and knife before realizing she still had her sling. Ethan cutting her food had felt too personal, too natural, and she didn't know what to do with the thoughts that ran through her head. Sitting there, staring at him, didn't tell her anything more, so she sat up straight with as much dignity as she could muster, thanked him, and picked up her fork and began to eat.

Any other reaction seemed silly and unnecessary, and judging by the bread, the entree wouldn't disappoint. Nora wanted to slap herself for even considering thinking about the food. If Ethan was trying to distract her, bribe her off with food and conversation, he had another thing coming.

"So what did the doctor say?"

The question threw her off guard, and she almost choked on the chicken Florentine.

"Excuse me?"

"I assume you went to the doctor. What did they say? Your shoulder," he added when she stared at him. Ethan's lips smiled upward at the corners, in another one of those bemused expressions like he found her entertaining. It might work on other women, paint him as charming and handsome, but it only pissed Nora off more.

"Yes, I went to the doctor. Things are healing, I guess."

He frowned almost like he had when she described the raid. "You guess?"

"Yeah," she said, moving bites of food around her plate. "Clean exit."

Met with silence, she glanced up to see him frozen, studying her, eyes intent and narrowed in her direction.

"Surgery." The word wasn't a question, but Nora didn't confirm or deny.

"Manillo pulled me out, but I stayed upright on my own until I got to the yard."

"And then?"

"What's with all the questions?" It came out harsher than Nora wanted it to, but she didn't want to get into how bad it had been, preferred not to think of it. Besides, it was none of his damn business.

Ethan's eyes narrowed into slits before he picked up his knife and sliced his steak. The noise of the restaurant around them amplified the silence between them. Nora studied him in the moment while she ate. The way he picked up his knife and sliced a small part of his perfectly cooked steak spoke of refined background. Having money was one thing, but learning how to cut a steak without scraping the plate didn't come with a larger bank balance. He brought the meat to his mouth without leaning forward and set his silverware down while he chewed thoughtfully and wiped his mouth with the napkin from his lap.

He had dressed impeccably and though she wasn't an expert on men's clothing, the tailored cut of his shirt and embroidered initials at his cuff sent a subtle message that would be lost on any of the men she had ever dated.

His eyes met hers. "I don't know what it is about you, but since you walked into my office, I can't get you out of my head. When I heard you'd been shot, I had to find out what had happened and where you were."

Nora stared at him. The candle danced on the table, while the murmur of the restaurant swam around them both sitting in silence.

"You're going to go back, aren't you?" he asked, never breaking his stare from her.

"What do you mean?"

"That won't be your last raid?"

She shook her head, transfixed on him and his low, soft words.

"Which means someone will try to hurt you again."

"Occupational hazard." God, his voice had some sort of hypnotic power over her. Nora knew that this was wrong, but for the life of her, she didn't want it to stop. "I swore to protect and serve."

"Right. You can't walk away from that, can you? I didn't think so," he said when she shook her head. He was right. Even though the injury scared her, and knocked her down a few pegs, how slow the healing process worked might kill her. Patience had never been her thing, anyway.

She continued to stare at him without answering. Ethan swore.

"Nora," he said her name like a desperate prayer. "Do you know what it is like knowing your whole family has been attacked? Calling their phones over and over, having them go straight to voicemail every time? Being in the dark while watching your home in flames on the news, knowing every person you've loved might be inside?"

She shook her head again. The pain on his face etched into lines she hadn't seen before, circles under the eyes. Nora didn't do a lot of post-emergency care, but she knew from experience that trauma weighed on the victims long afterward. Ethan clearly was locked in that very same battle.

"I'm sorry."

"Nora, I hadn't been able to get you out of my head and then one night I'm getting home late from work when I saw your picture on the news about that shit hole of a house. The yellow tape, the bullet holes, the white sheets covering bodies…"

"I didn't know."

He pulled his lips tights and kept eating. Nora had wanted this to be more of an interview or interrogation, but something about him had thrown her off, and she used the silence to reconsider her approach.

The meal surpassed the usual frozen or fast food she consumed blindly while watching TV most nights. The arrival of the waiter to clear the plates broke their silence.

"I think we'd love dessert. Care to share something with me?" Ethan asked her from across the candle.

The smart reply she wanted to say stayed in the back of her mind while the waiter watched for her response. Ethan's eyes laughed at her predicament.

"Sounds lovely. I like chocolate."

"Chocolate it is for the lady. Oh, and two coffees, please."

The waiter made a note and scurried off.

"How did you know I want coffee?"

"When does someone in your line of work not?"

"Are you familiar with a lot of cops?"

Ethan gave her a coy smile. "I can't say I am."

"Ever been arrested?"

"No, but you already would know that."

He was right, of course. His record was immaculate. Not even a speeding ticket, which made her even more suspicious.

"Tell me this then, how come you're the only one who is living off of Brightrock Island? Most everyone else is still there, it looks like. Why leave?"

"Work. I've always had an interest in business. Brightrock isn't what I would call huge for finance."

"But these days brokerage can be remote."

"True, but in my line of work it's helpful to be close to people with information," Ethan shrugged.

"You like to make money. I get that."

"Not quite. I like to grow money. I view it a lot like farming."

"Planting the seed?"

"And watching it grow, watering, and watching the conditions to make moves. I'm like a humble gardener providing for my friends and family."

Nora arched an eyebrow. "How noble. Why do I get the sense you're only giving me part of the story?"

He let out a laugh. "Is this where I'm supposed to confess I enjoy the city and a good cup of coffee? I imagine you're the same way. I don't imagine you on the farm in your retirement."

Nora shrugged. "Maybe. You don't know me."

"Oh, I think I do. You wouldn't be caught dead feeding chickens, knitting, and baking pies in a country cottage."

Nora felt herself grin despite herself. "Yeah, that ain't gonna happen."

He laughed right as the waiter set down the coffee mugs and began the artful pouring. Another waiter came and dropped off the dessert.

It was breathtaking, a chocolate confection artfully arranged with swirls of sauce and dollops of whipped cream, paired perfectly with the coffee that outed what they drank at the police department as a complete imposter. It was so damn good she didn't even mind going over the halfway mark and into his territory.

"Sweet tooth?"

"Funny, I don't remember the police academy mentioning that was a crime."

"If it is, Lieutenant, I'm guilty too. We can keep it a secret between us."

Nora covered her smirk with a sip of the delicious coffee. She would rather die than let him know that everything, right down to the little flickering candles, had been the nicest dinner with a man she'd ever had. She had no new information on Austin Brooks, but at least she had some on Ethan along with a killer dessert.

Nora tried not to squirm in her seat as Ethan swirled the pen in a smooth, fast motion, paying the check with no more than a blink of an eye as if he had done this countless times before and the price was inconsequential. With almost the barest shift in Ethan's head, a waiter wrapped the evening up. The nearby women glanced toward him when he stood, taking in a trim physique that knew how to dress and how to act, unlike their dates, who sat slumped around on their phones in ill-fitting clothes. He pulled out her chair, taking care not to crowd her, and as they walked away from the table, Nora felt an odd feeling in her chest, somewhere near regret that their time had now finished.

As they walked out of the restaurant, he stood behind her, but somehow managed to sweep past her to open the door in a graceful movement no other man had seemed to master. Like everything else, his natural grace suggested he was an old soul who had been at the game a long time, an action which didn't match his age at all. He reminded Nora of her dad and grandfather—each a former police officer taken before his time. Ethan carried himself like they had, like an older man, confident and at ease.

The summer evening air sat heavy like a haze in the night air outside. Couples clung to each other on the cobblestones, chatting as they waited for a table or walked by on the sidewalks lined with luxury cars. A sleek Mercedes idled by the entrance, the engine purring.

"How about a lift back home?" Ethan asked, looking down at her from his height.

Nora pulled a face. "That's a no," she said, though she did look longingly at the car behind her. How great it would be to just pop right in and rest her back, which now had moved past throbbing to actual aching pain.

"No handsy stuff." Ethan held up a hand. "Promise."

Nora sighed and shook her head. The dinner itself had been over the line, but to Ethan's credit, he hadn't actually done anything inappropriate.

"Alright, where's your car? I bet it's super fancy too."

He tilted his head and studied her. "Fancy too?"

Nora waved her good hand, almost knocking a girl in a miniskirt with her clutch. "Sorry, my bad," she said, snatching her hand back. "You know," she continued when they had stepped a little farther away from the entrance. "Your clothes, the place, your watch, the way you sign the bill with a little squiggle that's all elegant and shit."

His smile broadened. "Lieutenant, I think you're giving me a compliment."

"Yeah, don't tell anybody."

"Did I tell you that you look stunning tonight?"

"No, but if you did, you'd be lying again and it would piss me off."

"Me? Lie to you?"

"Bullshit," she said when he had the decency to pretend to look hurt.

He laughed at her again in a natural way before studying her with a twinkling look in his eye.

"If you touch me in the car, I'm going to twist your balls off so fast you won't know what hit you."

He laughed again and walked toward the Mercedes. "How do you know I'm not into that?"

"I'll make sure you don't enjoy it. Oh c'mon. You gotta be shitting me. You gotta driver?"

Ethan held up a hand when a man in a suit popped up out of the driver's side, apparently rushing to get to the door for his client. On Ethan's motion, the driver slid back in the car as if in a video being played in reverse.

"You should like this. Consider him a chaperone."

"You mean a witness."

"You can call him whatever you like, but I think his name is Will."

Nora stopped and leaned over the open car door that he held for her. "I knew you were an ass, but you should at least know the names of your damn servants."

He leaned into her again, the door separating them by only inches. "They don't like being called servants, and I don't know his name because I pay for the company and he's new."

Nora rolled her eyes and sat down on the seat, not wanting to be comfortable and irritated when she was. Ethan slid in, the supple black leather giving under his weight as he pulled the door shut. Without further instruction from him, the car started driving.

"Do you know where I live?" Nora said, eyeing the fancy water bottles in the pristine cupholders around her.

"No, but I have an idea."

"I'm not in the phone book."

"Good, you don't need to be."

"Yeah, I don't need creeps knowing where I'm at."

"I can assure you I've looked and found nothing. You can tell Will when we get out of the city. I've asked him to take the scenic route unless your injury has had enough?"

The concern in his voice struck Nora as genuine and hit her down in her core. She didn't like to be taken care of—thought any man who tried to do that in the twenty-first century needed to get with the program. In fact, she liked doing things on her own, and was proud of her record as a cop, never mind her TV dinner-filled home life. She couldn't bake a pie but was a hell of a shot, and that's how she liked it. Still, tonight had been... she paused and tried to find the right word before settling on great. He got her and wasn't pushing for anything more than she could give him, didn't want her to try and be someone else.

"I'm not giving you my real address just so you know that, and you're not getting invited in for a nightcap."

Ethan gave her a small smile that tucked one corner of his mouth up into his cheek. "I wouldn't expect anything less from you, Lieutenant."

CHAPTER 19

"More coffee?" A short, smiling woman in a pressed shirt and tie paused at the table, holding a silver coffee pot.

"Yes, please. Thank you, ma'am." Caleb shifted in his seat and watched as the dark liquid filled the delicate china cup, which was far smaller than the mug he was used to, but then again there wasn't much he was familiar with in this setting.

The dining room at Le Pavillon could only be described as jaw-dropping. Ornate moldings, a vaulted ceiling, a marble fireplace, and a life-sized portrait of a woman in a ball gown all conspired to make him feel very out of place with a pressed cloth napkin on his everyday jeans. Elizabeth looked at home in the grand setting and Caleb wouldn't have been satisfied if she had anything less.

He watched as she chatted with the chef at the omelet bar at what really was a buffet to end all buffets. She wore her dark hair up in a loose knot that begged to be plucked free. Her bright smile turned toward him, and Caleb's cheeks reddened at the realization they were talking about him. Elizabeth gave him a little smirk that made his heart skip a beat as he watched, back ramrod straight in the decorative antique chair.

Before they came down for breakfast, Caleb had listened in the hotel room as Elizabeth chatted with him while getting ready. All of it had seemed so natural, unlike any other relationship he'd known. She had brushed her hair and hadn't stopped talking about her research project through the closed bathroom door. When she had opened it, Caleb had nearly forgotten to answer when she asked him a question. In a light and loose peach dress that kissed the floor, Elizabeth looked like a spring goddess. Caleb had wanted to run his lips up every inch of her exposed arms before swiping his finger under the delicate shoulder strap. Her toes, painted a perfect pink, peeked out from under the hem where she wore gold sandals.

Now she glided across the ballroom floor toward him, holding a plate of what looked to be an omelet stuffed with a pound of cheese. He sprang to his feet and pulled out her chair, which brought a grin to her mouth as she sat down and allowed him to push her back in. He didn't always know what to say around her, but he knew how to act.

Elizabeth plucked up her napkin and draped it across her lap as if it was as natural as breathing. "The chef's very interesting. Been serving breakfast here for almost thirty years. Native to New Orleans too."

"Looks like she can make a hell of an omelet too," Caleb said, nodding to the plate. He picked up his fork and shoveled some more biscuits and gravy into his mouth, savoring the southern flavor he always missed when in Iraq.

"I'm going to gain so much weight here, I can already tell. God, I won't be able to eat for weeks."

"You're perfect and enjoying some food isn't going to change that."

Elizabeth held her fork midair before smiling with a faint tinge of pink blossoming on her cheeks.

"Well, thank you. Everything is delicious here."

They dug into breakfast, each commenting to the other about what they particularly enjoyed. Caleb sat, wondering if he had said the wrong thing again. He wasn't great with women, never had been, and Lizzy was next level. He had tried to do the right thing last night, but still wished he could've been smoother, known what to say.

The problem was that she deserved so much more. Elizabeth was perfection on God's earth. He couldn't even string two words together around her, and as much as he wanted to march back upstairs and fling her in that flimsy dress on the bed, he couldn't bring himself to do anything other than stare at her, tongue-tied with complete adoration.

Elizabeth brought her napkin to her delicate mouth. "Oh my God, I could not eat another bite, but I really, really want to."

"We can come back if you'd like," Caleb said, wiping his own mouth, following her lead.

Elizabeth laughed, the sound like a wind chime on a summer morning. "I'd love that, but I wouldn't be able to walk. You'd have to roll me around. Besides, I'm sure there are more places to eat. Where do you like to go?"

"I have a couple places closer to home, but nothing beats my Maw Maw's food." Caleb took a breath, hoping the next sentence didn't backfire. "I'd like you to meet them."

"I'd love to. Do you think they'd mind if I just popped in?"

Caleb imagined her crossing the threshold of Parrain's house, looking like a movie star. "No, I don't think they'd mind at all." He hoped his family and their humble life would be enough for her. Everything was neat as a pin, and the food was the best he'd ever had, but for someone like her, Caleb hoped everything would meet expectations. None of his family had yachts or mansions.

"I'd love to. Can we go today?"

Caleb cleared his throat and leaned forward, careful to avoid hitting the coffee cup. The last thing he needed to do was to spill coffee all over the place. "Well, I had mentioned I was picking up a friend, and they'd actually invited us to dinner today. We don't have to go if—"

"I'd love to." Elizabeth's face transformed and glowed with total joy. "I want to hear all about them. Do we need to leave now? I don't want to be late."

Caleb sat dumbfounded, feeling his head bob with nodding he couldn't control. She looked at him expectantly, and he shook himself and glanced at his watch. "No, we have plenty of time. I'm glad you're excited. Um, what would you like to know?"

Elizabeth leaned forward with her hands in her lap, her eyes bright with excitement. "Everything."

"Um, okay, I don't know where to start." Caleb shifted in his seat, unsure of what to make of her enthusiasm, but pleased he'd made her happy. He had told his family he wanted to see what she wanted to do, just in case she hadn't wanted to meet a bunch of Cajuns for lunch.

Elizabeth sat back in her chair like a cat with a bowl of cream. "Let's start with who will be there."

CHAPTER 20

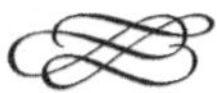

Lizzy watched as Caleb pulled off the highway and navigated the road until they were on a wide street lined with huge oak trees dripping with moss that swayed in the late morning sun. The single-story houses around them looked older but well-kept with flowers filling each bed and immaculate lawns that had been trimmed and edged.

"Nice neighborhood."

"It's old, but most of the residents have been here since the beginning, so it works."

"You mean, everybody knows everybody," Lizzy said, attempting a smile at how similar it felt to Brightrock, but then again at least these people could leave if they wanted. Her shoulders tensed at the thought of the clock ticking. She hadn't gotten a call yet, but she knew it was coming. As it was, she was going to miss the renewal ceremony. She hadn't asked the town council permission to leave Virginia and the rules stated they needed to know where everyone was at all times.

Lizzy's knee bounced in the cab of the truck. There

wasn't anything more the council could actually do to her other than what they were already planning. She knew too much for them to get rid of her. Because of what happened to Lizzy's parents, most of the members had a soft spot for her, which she had never really taken advantage of.

"Oh yeah, Maw Maw owns a few of these and rents them out. My aunts and uncles used to live in them when they first got married to save some money, you know?"

Lizzy nodded.

"Well, Maw Maw would cook, and she always made a lot, so she would box it up in those little Styrofoam containers, like the ones the restaurants have, and she would call for people to come to get some food, and then she'd pass it over the back fence to them."

"So, they lived directly behind her?"

"Sure did. Now they moved down the block after they bought a big house and renovated it. It had been vacant for years. Really pretty. They might invite us all over for coffee if we stay long enough."

Lizzy shifted in her seat, wondering just how much family she was supposed to be meeting at this dinner. He had said it was just the immediate family, but it seemed like he had a relative on every block they passed.

"There's the church where everyone got married and all the kids were baptized. Funerals too. I guess I should've just said, there's the church."

"Does anyone leave?" Lizzy asked, wondering why so many people would stay if given a choice.

"Sure, we have relatives farther up north and a few in Texas. People go to college, get jobs, military, stuff like that."

"But most stay here in Louisiana?"

"Yep. There's so many of us, it just wouldn't feel right to leave everyone else behind. We've known each other all of our lives."

Lizzy chewed her lip while she puzzled over that. She opened her mouth to ask if they had ever fought when Caleb pulled up to a perfect lawn in front of a big white house. The street in front of it was full of cars all parallel parked.

"I guess they knew we were coming. They saved the best spot for you." Caleb pulled into the short driveway, killed the engine, and looked over at her. Without the air conditioner blasting, the silence swelled in her ears.

Caleb turned to face her. "I don't have to mention the whole going-out thing if you don't want me to. I know that's kind of uh—"

"Unexpected?" Lizzy offered with a smile.

Caleb laughed and smiled. "I was going to say sudden, but I have to be honest, just your presence is going to make everyone curious. They're all really nice, like super nice, but don't be surprised if my aunts are all interested." He grinned and came around to her side to open the door. "You know how family can be."

Lizzy had to stop from snorting to herself. He didn't even know the half of it.

They walked through the carport and up the stairs. Caleb didn't even bother to knock on the glass storm door but instead held it open for Lizzy. A chorus of laughter cried out from inside.

The inside of the home was spotless. A dining room table draped in a tablecloth was set for ten to her right. To her left, a smaller kitchen table was set in the same pattern, but for four. Oh, boy.

"Well, hello, Caleb." An older woman with short, curly, dark hair in a crisp white shirt and pressed black pants came out of the kitchen holding a dish towel, her arms wide for a hug. A series of gold bangles dangled on her wrist. She enveloped him in a squeeze and planted a kiss on his cheek, leaving behind a hint of red lipstick.

"Hi, Maw Maw. How are you?"

"I'm fine, thank you for asking. You look good." Holding him at arm's length, she gave him a once-over of approval.

"Thank you. Maw Maw, this is Lizzy."

"Hi, it's nice to meet you," Lizzy said. She, too, was enveloped in a hug that warmed her to her bones. Maw Maw —she wasn't sure what else to call her—smelled like coffee, laundry soap, and light perfume. "Thank you for having me over for lunch."

"Well, of course. I fried some fish and fixed a little salad. Oh, and Caleb, Mrs. Carmichael—that's my beautician," she said to Lizzy, "brought the most beautiful watermelon back from Mississippi. I'll need your help cutting it."

"Yes, ma'am."

"Good. Lizzy, do you eat fried fish?"

"Sounds perfect."

Maw Maw clapped her hands together. "Alright, well good. I have some potato salad too, and Aunt Wilma brought a beautiful cake. So we're all set. Lizzy, when did you fly in?"

"Yesterday. Caleb showed me around New Orleans."

"Uh-huh, good, good." Maw Maw's shrewd eyes went from him to her, and her smile broadened. Lizzy got the same once-over treatment by Maw Maw. "I like that dress. So pretty."

"Thank you," Lizzy said, looking down at her light day dress. "You have a beautiful home. Caleb was telling me about the whole neighborhood on the way over."

"Oh yeah, the whole family lives around here. Been that way for a long time. Come meet the crew. They're in the den, visiting."

Lizzy followed in Maw Maw's wake. Caleb caught her eye and grinned.

"Hey everyone, Caleb and Lizzy are here."

About fifteen people all sat on couches and in recliners

around the room. Lizzy's head spun with all of the introductions and descriptions of who was who in Caleb's so-called immediate family.

"So how many are there in the extended family?" Lizzy asked one of the many aunts and cousins when she had sat on the couch. Caleb stayed in the back room to greet Parrain and the rest of the men who were talking. Caleb and Maw Maw had introduced her, before pulling her back into the room to sit with the girls, as she had called them.

Maw Maw eased into her recliner and rocked back while studying the ceiling and doing the math in her head. "Oh my God, let's see, at least forty-two when we all get together for Thanksgiving, but I don't know if that counts the new twins or not."

Lizzy's mouth went slack. "Good God, that's a lot of stuffing."

The aunts all laughed. "Oh yeah, but we wouldn't have it any other way."

"We don't know any better," added another aunt.

"That's very true. Most of us were born right here."

Lizzy leaned forward on the couch, interested to hear more. "Don't you ever get tired of the same people?" After a hundred years, the idea of a couple of hundred more was truly more than she could bear.

"Well, we all have our own houses," Maw Maw said with a laugh from her recliner. "And you see, we can't get together much anymore. Not like we used to. This one's working, that one is off doing something else."

A chorus of aunts agreed.

"Caleb tells us your family all live on an island off Massachusetts, so you must know how it is?" Maw Maw asked, changing the subject.

"Yes, but that feels too close sometimes." Especially when people lived for four hundred years give or take fifty, but she wasn't going to mention that little tidbit. "I've moved to Virginia to get my doctorate, but I think—well, I know—I'm going to have to move home again." Lizzy's heart broke again just thinking about it. It felt more like a jail sentence than a loving homecoming. The idea made her want to break out into a run to where no one could find her.

A chorus of quiet sympathy and understanding washed around the comfortable living room. "Can you continue your classes online?"

"Yes and no, but it's not the same."

Maw Maw nodded in understanding. "None of us old folks ever went to college— there wasn't money for that— but you must be so smart to get to that level. My God, can you imagine? She's going to be a doctor someday."

A murmur of approval agreed with her.

"I'm not one yet, right now I'm just a teacher."

"As if that's an easy job," one cousin said as she leaned back and folded her arms over her ample chest. "Kids are so disrespectful these days."

"You can say that again," an aunt agreed. "I see things on the news, and I wonder where the parents are."

Lizzy nodded. "I wanted to move more into administration and maybe be a principal, but now I'm not sure when that's going to happen."

"That's hard to have to leave in the middle," another cousin said.

Lizzy swallowed the lump in her throat and sucked in a breath to try to keep it together. They had no idea and yet seemed to understand.

"Your family must be happy you're coming home. I'm sure they missed you."

"My parents are deceased, but my aunt and uncle were thrilled, to say the least."

Maw Maw clucked her tongue. "Well, there's always more time."

Lizzy smiled a tight-lipped smile and nodded. They didn't know the half of it.

"I want to hear more about your job, but you must be hungry. Let's get the boys and go eat. I'm starving." Maw Maw eased out of her recliner while the other aunts slowly leaned off the couch and stood, but what they lacked in physical strength, they more than made up for in management.

With a flick of her thin wrist, and a few points with her arthritic finger, lunch was served, drinks were poured, and guests were seated in no time flat.

Parrain stood at the head of the dining table and raised his voice to get the crowd's attention. "Let's all say grace."

Everyone bowed their heads. Lizzy followed suit.

"Heavenly Father, we thank you for this food and for bringing Caleb safely home."

Lizzy peeked up at Caleb who looked worried and stood, watching Parrain speak. A pained expression was on his face as if he had just eaten something and was trying not to be sick. "We pray for his continued safety as he completes his work. May you watch over him and bring him back to us. We also thank you for this food. Bless us, oh Lord..."

Lizzy followed along with the blessing and watched the people around her from under her lids. All of them looked to be ordinary, hard-working people who loved each other dearly. Caleb stood next to her with his head bowed. His shoulders had relaxed, so his arms hung down where his hands were loosely clasped.

"And lastly, God bless the cook."

"Amen."

People shuffled toward their seats, and the meal got underway. Lizzy was torn between admiring the house around her, listening to the conversations, and eating the food, which was some of the best potato salad and fried fish she had ever had. Even the watermelon tasted better here. When Caleb had said the food at Mother's back in New Orleans had almost been as good as his family's, she thought he had been joking. He wasn't. If Maw Maw ever opened a restaurant, she would make a killing.

The conversation floated around Lizzy while people talked about jobs, children, and life in general. Caleb kept stealing glances at her. Whenever he caught her eye, he winked and grinned. Lizzy's cheeks warmed.

She wished she could stay here, she really did.

Lizzy sat in the den with an empty plate after being shooed away from helping with the dishes. She ran her fork along the porcelain to pick up any remaining crumbs of what had been the most delicious strawberry shortcake she had ever tasted. Caleb's aunts knew how to cook, and by the sounds of the laughter and the rushing water in the kitchen sink, they knew how to have a good time together too. Caleb had started to follow before being pulled away to look at some cousin's car in the garage out back. He had looked like he wanted to stall and not leave her but had given in to the peer pressure after she had smiled and waved him away.

"Mind if I sit here?"

Parrain, an old Cajun nickname for godfather, smiled down at her. She hadn't asked why he went by Parrain, even though he was Caleb's actual grandfather. Everyone here seemed to have a nickname.

"Not at all," Lizzy said, scooting over.

"Good. I was looking forward to meeting our special

guest. It's not often Caleb brings someone around to meet us old, country people."

He eased down, wearing khakis and a pressed golf polo. "Ah, that's better. So, you're from up north, huh?"

"Yes. A small island off the coast of Massachusetts."

"Caleb went up there after Caitlyn up and took off when her parents and that girl at the school died. Sad. Caleb went to see what happened. But, you know, we could tell that it wasn't going to be a good fit."

"Do you think he loved her?" Lizzy asked, aware of a tightness in her chest.

Parrain took a bite of cake, and pierced a strawberry with his fork. While he chewed, he shook his head. "Can't have two quiet people. Doesn't work."

Lizzy laughed. "Caitlyn married my cousin, and Austin's definitely not quiet."

"That's good. Navy man, right? Yeah," he said when she nodded. "Good. She was a little lost when Caleb met her. Nice enough girl but didn't hardly talk. Not the right fit."

"Lizzy, how do you take your coffee?" Maw Maw asked, peeking her head into the den.

"Oh, I can fix it—"

"No, you sit and visit. Cream? Sugar?"

"Yes, please."

Maw Maw nodded once. "Hun?"

"Thank you, babe."

Maw Maw darted back into the kitchen where the sounds of a coffee pot brewing and spoons tinkling in coffee mugs mixed with chitchat.

"Caleb told me you've been married for over fifty years."

"Doesn't feel that long."

Lizzy nodded, wishing she felt the same way. The last fifty years of her life had been a merry-go-round she'd been ready to get off. The same faces and events had rotated in and out of her life like the leaves on a tree. Stuck in the same place with nothing to look forward to but spring.

"It's been the best thing in my life. Really, it has." Parrain smiled as Maw Maw entered the room holding two steaming white mugs. "First it was just us, then our son came along, and that's when time really flew by. One day we woke up, and we were old."

"What are you up to now? Lizzy, don't listen to a thing he says." Maw Maw handed her a cup.

Lizzy accepted the coffee and thanked her. "He was just bragging about you."

"I got the better end of the deal. Y'all want more cake? Well, okay," she said when they shook their heads, "let me fix my cup, and I'll come visit too."

"She's wrong, you know. I got the better end of the deal," Parrain said after Maw Maw went back to the kitchen. "But anyway, how old are you? If that's not too personal?"

Oh, it was personal, alright, but the lie came as quick as ever. After telling it for so many years, Lizzy almost accepted it as truth and in a way it was. On her island, she was very young by comparison. "Thirty-ish." In reality, she was older than Parrain and Maw Maw, but the experience they had made all the difference.

"My God, I remember thirty. I had just gotten married and had one son, Henry, Caleb's father. Didn't have much money, so I worked the night shift, moonlighting—that kind of thing."

"Caleb mentioned his parents passed away. I'm sorry for your loss."

"I still think about him every day, and I will love him until the day I die when I get to see him again. Caleb is a blessing to us. Always was, but after the accident, he kept us going. Jeanette didn't even stop to grieve."

"That must have been difficult."

"Very, but she went to daily mass for years. She still does from time to time. Every morning she'd go at five, and I'd get up and have a cup of coffee and get ready for work. She'd come home, fix breakfast, and then we'd get Caleb up, and I'd drive him to school on my way to the repair shop. We knew he was smart, you see, and we had both just lost our only son, but he had lost his parents, and we had to take care of him. Routine is good for children. I believe that."

Lizzy nodded and finished her coffee.

"Well, anyway, we did that for years. Jeanette would pick him up from school and take him to baseball practice, then we'd have dinner together, watch the news. He never needed help with assignments. Smart, smart."

"You must be very proud."

"We are. He's an engineer. I can't believe that. My daddy didn't finish school. Had to drop out to work, no money for that you see and well, Jeanette and I never did go to college."

"But we made do just fine." Maw Maw came down into the den holding a cup of coffee and sank down into one of the recliners with a relaxed sigh.

"Yes, we have. We'd have more if we had gone to school, but we didn't know anything about that."

"Hey, you gotta make do with what you have. I may not have a big fancy house like other people, but my house is clean, and it's comfortable." She raised her hand and let it fall on her thigh with a slap. "That's good enough for me."

"Can't go wrong with clean and comfortable," Lizzy said, shifting on the couch to look at both of them.

"So Lizzy, what do you plan to do while you're here in Louisiana? Caleb going to show you the sights?"

Lizzy wasn't sure how much to divulge. Surely, a woman who went to daily mass would take issue with her grandson sleeping in the same bed with a woman he barely knew, even if they had just started dating.

"I think we're going to tour around. I told him whatever he liked, I wanted to see."

Maw Maw nodded while smiling. "Good, good. It's nice he has that schedule where you can come and visit and work doesn't interrupt. That's one good thing about where he's at now."

"He's tired, though, when he comes home, Jeanette," Parrain said, now pulling a toothpick out from his pocket.

"Oh, you talk about tired. That plane ride. I've only been out of the country one time, and that was enough for me. I can't imagine going back and forth like that."

"They take care of him," Parrain said, turning to her. "You know he flies first class almost all the time?"

"I didn't know that," Lizzy said, surprised. Caleb didn't seem like the first-class kind of guy, but she had never asked.

"Oh yeah, those oil companies take care of their people, but the flight is still so long it's hard to be comfortable. No, thank you." Maw Maw shook her head.

"He makes good money," Parrain said.

"It's a good thing too. We hope it stays like that."

"I thought we always needed oil," Lizzy said, setting her coffee cup on the table in front of her. A small green plant sat in the middle of a runner in multi-colored jewel tones. Maw Maw's house may have been older, but she had good taste.

"We do, but they lay people off all the time. No loyalty anymore these days. You're just a number," Parrain said.

"But they like Caleb. They're the ones who contacted him for this promotion. When was it, honey? I can't quite remember."

"Right before he went north, so what was that? October? November?"

"Something like that," Maw Maw said, nodding and waving a thin hand, so her bangle bounced around on her wrist.

"What promotion? I didn't know he got one."

"Oh yeah. A big promotion."

"A bunch of guys wanted to go to the Middle East, but they picked Caleb."

Lizzy frowned. "Middle East?"

"Oh yeah, he's been going to Iraq every other month since then. Thirty days on, thirty off. He's in a dangerous part too. I think they have bodyguards. He told me they have to wear a vest. Bulletproof. Just last week there was a car bomb nearby."

Lizzy felt her stomach drop out of her chest. Her face flushed with the blood racing around.

"That's only when he leaves the compound, but yeah. He tells us a few things when we ask," Parrain said, shaking his head. "He doesn't want us to worry."

Lizzy nodded and smiled her way through the rest of the conversation, but her head was spinning. How could Caleb not mention where he was working? She had overestimated how he felt. Embarrassment flooded into her again. She had misread this whole thing, then called him of all people out of the blue. She did the math in her head and with a sickening realization knew he had been in Iraq when she had called.

Now it all made sense. Lizzy had requested a king bed in New Orleans, expecting a night of passion. It hadn't added up when he seemed so distant and hesitant, but now it all hit with alarming clarity.

She had forced this situation upon him. Had she misread him? She thought he wanted more. Had she been wrong? Maybe he was just being polite. Had he lied? Maybe, she couldn't remember. Up until now he had been the most honest, kind, and humble person she had ever known. She had thought he was different.

Nausea swam through her gut, and the room felt too hot. Seeing Caleb come out of the kitchen, wiping his hands with a tea towel and walking into the den, Lizzy wanted to run and hide her shame. She was spending her last few days of freedom with someone who didn't feel close enough to tell her he had been in Iraq.

She shouldn't be here. This had all been a huge mistake. Maybe the biggest of her life.

CHAPTER 22

Caleb drove in the fading light to his house with Lizzy in the passenger seat, her face frozen like a mask he didn't believe. Everything seemed to have gone fine back at the house, and even Maw Maw and Parrain had swallowed her in two big hugs as they had left, with well-wishes and invitations for her to come back anytime. They had both given him a wink and a nod as he had hugged and thanked them. Once in the truck, though, Lizzy hadn't said more than one-word answers to questions he asked. The bubbly and confident person he had become accustomed to, now was distant and remote.

"I need you to talk to me."

Lizzy barely moved and gave no indication she had even heard him speak.

"Seriously," he continued, stealing glances at her while driving in the fading light, "I'm no good at the whole silent treatment thing. Did someone say something to you? Look, I'll just go ahead and apologize now."

Lizzy sat unmoved, staring out the window.

"Lizzy? C'mon, talk to me." He stopped at a red light and leaned over, throwing his arm behind the seatback.

"Why?" The look she gave him chilled him to the bone.

"Because everything seemed good at the house, but you're different now. What's wrong?"

"Why does it matter? None of this matters. In a few days, I'll be gone."

Alarm bells went off in Caleb's head. He slowed for a red light and turned to face her. "Hey, don't say that. We're dating, remember? Of course it matters."

"That's a lie. We're done. I'm calling it off. Shouldn't have come."

A horn blared behind Caleb, but he didn't budge. "Alright, stop. You need to tell me what's wrong because this is not the person you were this morning."

"You want me to tell you?"

The horn behind them blared again before the car blew past them with an angry snarl of the engine. Caleb didn't even flinch.

"Of course."

"I can't be in this enough for both of us. I thought you were interested. I made a mistake. I'll get a hotel tonight."

"No, you won't."

"Excuse me?"

"You heard me. I said no."

"You can't boss me around." Lizzy's voice took on a hard edge, which was an improvement from the flat, robotic voice she had been using.

"I want to know what's wrong."

"How come you get to order me around and demand answers, but I know nothing about you?"

"Wait...what? What are you—?"

"Oil rig, huh?"

Oh, shit. Caleb's stomach opened like a black hole and sucked his heart right inside to the darkness.

"If this is about my job—"

"You didn't think it was important to mention you were in another part of the world? Iraq, for God's sake."

"I didn't want to worry—"

"Your whole family knows, and then I look like an idiot when I try to talk about your rig only to find out I'm in the dark. Do you have any idea how humiliating that is?"

"I'm sorry, you're right."

"No, no. That's not enough. They said you had to wear a flak jacket and—"

"Yes, but—"

"—and you have a freaking bodyguard. Car bombs?"

"It's not for me—"

"I can't believe you didn't tell me."

"Lizzy, I'm sorry I wanted to—"

"Don't lie to me anymore." She snapped at him, her voice hitting him like a slap in the face. "If I meant much of anything to you, you would've told me. You would've called me. Said something instead of nothing. You kept me in the dark, Caleb. I thought you liked me. I thought I meant something to you."

"You do—"

"Shut up. I don't even want to hear the sound of your voice right now."

Caleb clamped his lips tight together, hoping to ride out the storm. When she didn't speak, he said, "I am sorry."

"Why are you still talking? I don't care what you are. You don't care about me."

"That's not true."

"Bullshit. Just cut the crap. I don't have the patience to deal with you anymore."

"Hey, stop—"

"Can you just drive the freaking truck, so we aren't sitting in the damn road?"

Caleb took his foot off the brake and drove in the stony silence. Minutes passed, and he tried again. "I meant what I said. I'm sorry, I should've told you."

"But you didn't."

"I didn't want to worry you."

"If you cared about me, you would've mentioned it."

"You called me, crying out of the blue—"

"Mistake number one."

That got him. Caleb jerked the truck to the side of the road and slammed on the brakes. "Alright, stop right there."

"Yep. Sure will." Lizzy pulled the handle of the door open and snatched her purse off the floor. "I'm out."

Caleb followed suit and chased her down. "Seriously, stop. I said I was sorry, okay? Why does it matter? You know now."

She rounded on him. "What the fuck did you just say?"

"It doesn't matter—"

Lizzy leaned into his face and hissed. "Do you have any idea what it's like to be kept in the dark by people who claim they love you? People who think they know what's best? I've been lied to my whole life about who I am and what I can do. I've been controlled, shoved away, kept like a fucking pet in a gold cage." She shoved a manicured nail into his chest. "You were supposed to be different. You were going to be the one to tell me the truth, the whole truth, and nothing but the truth, but you didn't."

"Lizzy, please—"

"Don't even say my name right now. I have been kept under lock and key, told when and where I can live my life, never trusted to make my own choices. I thought you liked me, but clearly, I made a mistake, so I guess they were right. Apparently, I have horrible taste in men."

Lizzy spun on her heel away from him, stalking down the street in the hazy twilight.

The blow she dealt hit right in the gut. "You can't just walk away like that."

Lizzy kept going, throwing up her hands as she walked. "And again someone tries to tell me what I can and cannot do. It's amazing how stupid I must be. I can't even walk down the street." Her voice reached a hysterical pitch.

Caleb jogged after her, reached out, and grabbed her by the shoulders. "I have thought of you day and night since I met you. Do not tell me that I don't care about you. Yes, I made a mistake. How many times do you want me to apologize? A hundred? Because I'll do it, but you're too damn thickheaded to listen."

Lizzy glared.

"I'm sorry, okay? I fucked up. I'm sorry."

She narrowed her eyes with suspicion. "Did you really think of me?"

"All the damn time."

"What did you think about when you thought of me?"

"I called you my Elizabeth and thought about how you looked so beautiful when you were swearing at your luggage on the beach."

"Your Elizabeth?"

"I didn't think Lizzy suited you. You were too regal, but now I'm starting to see the whole picture." He tried the ghost of a smile to make her laugh.

She shrugged him off and kept going.

"Alright, look, can we at least go somewhere else and talk this over?"

"Why? Sounds like there's nothing to talk about."

"Oh my God, I said I was sorry."

"You really don't get it, do you?"

"That I fucked up? Yeah, you've made that pretty damn

clear." Caleb propped his hands on his hips, wondering what he could say to get her into the damn truck.

"No, you obviously don't. If you did care, you'd get it, but then again, you don't care. You don't give a shit about me. All of this was a huge mistake—colossal. Total screw-up on my part. Sorry about that. Won't make that mistake again."

"Lizzy—"

"Don't use that tone with me. I mistook you for someone that gave a shit—"

"I do—"

Lizzy puffed up with air and let him have it. "Will you shut the hell up and listen? God, open your ears. If you really cared— not just thought about me, but really cared—you would've told me where in the world you were. I'm not important enough to be on your emergency contact list, but you were on mine." Breathing heavy, Lizzy stared at him like she was going to start screaming again or scratch his eyes out.

On the other side of the sidewalk, the screen door of an old house opened, and a woman in a robe looked out holding a wireless phone to her ear, watching them from her porch. She turned the porch light on and angled herself to get a better view in the purple twilight.

Caleb leaned forward and lowered his voice. "We're starting to cause a scene. C'mon, let's get in the truck, and you can yell at me all you want."

With great reluctance, Lizzy stomped alongside Caleb back to the cab, thanking him tersely with a shake of her head that fluffed her hair as he opened the door for her.

They drove a little more, not speaking to each other until Caleb pulled into his carport. The automatic light Parrain had insisted on installing popped on and welcomed them with total blindness. The flowers he had planted for her arrival beamed against the white walls of the house, their little burgundy and yellow flowers swaying in the evening breeze.

"Nice house," Lizzy said in a flat tone.

"It's okay." Caleb got the car door for Lizzy and unlocked the storm door and then the walnut door into his restored bungalow. "Belonged to a great uncle of mine. Bought it at the family rate. Been working on it when I'm home, but well, I haven't worked on it much. I guess you now know why." They stepped inside, and Caleb hit the light to a small chandelier over the kitchen table. With it, they could see almost everything from the small entryway, which still smelled of Pine-Sol from when he had scrubbed everything top to bottom for her. It opened up into the eat-in kitchen with a den off to the side and a hallway back to the bedrooms. Caleb set her bags down.

"You still should've told me."

He sighed and propped his hands on his hips. This was so not the way he had wanted this home tour to go. "I honestly didn't think you'd be interested. You have secrets you don't tell me. Why can't I have secrets when you still haven't told me why you're here? Doesn't that make you a hypocrite?"

He could've slapped her, and she would've looked less hurt.

Angry tears spilled over from her big blue eyes and down her cheeks. Caleb knew he'd fucked up again. He never had been any damn good with words, and this is why he usually kept his mouth shut.

Caleb stepped closer to her, closing the distance between them. Lizzy took a step back, then spun on her heel and shoved out the door, storming off into the night.

Lizzy flew out of the small house into a haze of thick humidity that clawed at her clothes and skin. The dark night glowed orange from an old light post across the street next to a church. The air hung heavy like the tears on her cheeks. Her shoes slapped against the stained concrete, echoing in the still night while a dog barked somewhere in the neighborhood.

She didn't know where she was walking and didn't care. Eventually, she'd call a cab, go to a hotel, and catch a flight somewhere else—somewhere away from Caleb. The thought of him hit her like a punch in the gut.

"Stupid. So fucking stupid," she muttered under her breath as she walked in the orange night. Shame ate away at her insides. She had been so eager for an adventure and so taken with Caleb that she clearly had made up this whole fantasy in her head. After all, who would go to the Middle East in this century and not tell someone important to them? His entire family knew, so it wasn't like it was some big secret. At least now she knew where she stood.

Lizzy let out a bitter laugh. Here she was on a strange

corner of two streets she couldn't pronounce under an orange light post. Neither direction meant anything to her. For all her time on the planet, she didn't know anyone or anywhere other than Brightrock. The one person she had called in crisis didn't value her enough to bother texting before taking off for another continent. Lizzy blinked fast so the tears would hurry up and fall so she could get on with being pissed.

All of the houses looked the same. The flat, squat structures with large roofs looked like nothing on Brightrock. Each had a covered porch. A few with gardens and some chairs in the front, ranging from expensive rockers to steel fold-ups that had seen better days. It seemed so peaceful and so foreign at the same time. She wondered what it would be like to have different people in her life, people that could come and go. After years of being trapped in a place she'd never felt she belonged, Lizzy wanted a front porch where she could feed stray cats and a community she could grow to be a part of.

Her phone buzzed in her purse. Lizzy dug around inside, hoping it was the cab company she'd texted moments ago. A screen door slammed from somewhere behind her. Lizzy kept walking in no direction other than to keep moving. Not looking at the number, she answered the call.

"Elizabeth, are you well?"

Her stomach sank even further into her gut at hearing the stiff, stuffy English accent.

"I am. How are you, Dr. Chappell?"

"Fine, thank you. I heard you weren't going to make the renewal and called out of concern. I've been trying to reach you for several days." The tone of censure in his voice told her more than she wanted to know.

"I apologize. I have been busy with school—"

"I called the University to have you paged but was told you had left on a trip."

"Yes, for research and to visit with a friend."

Lizzy closed her eyes while the pause stretched.

"No matter."

His words stung with truth. Lizzy's hopes and wants were no matter to him, more like a piece of lint on a sleeve requiring little thought and a quick pluck of the wrist.

"—as a precautionary measure. I know you'll understand. You are encouraged, of course, to revisit your studies under a new name after an appropriate amount of time has passed."

Her hand squeezed the phone, making the case squeak under the pressure.

"No."

"I beg your pardon—"

"I just applied. I've been working toward this for years."

"After an appropriate time has—"

Lizzy couldn't listen anymore. She held the phone away from her ear as she stopped in front of a house that needed some TLC and a good pruning. A dog eyed her through the chain-link fence. Lizzy empathized with him.

"—I suggest you come home within seventy-two hours."

"What? I can't—"

"You must, and as per your nondisclosure agreement, I will need to file a death certificate after that time. You won't be able to access your accounts and will lack all legal documentation." His curt tone made her want to cry and stomp on the phone until it shattered into a thousand shards of glass. "You won't be able to go anywhere after that, so it is in your best interest to cooperate."

Lizzy shook from head to toe with waves of anger. Through gritted teeth, she said, "Fine."

"Excellent. I appreciate your cooperation and await your return to discuss your new credentials." The propriety in his voice made her want to scream, along with the phony pleasantries he offered at the end of the call.

Lizzy stood there. Her impotent rage coursed through her body. Half of her wished he would kill her off, so she'd be rid of him and everyone else on that rock. Fuck their stupid water. If they wanted to annoy the shit out of each other until the end of time, so be it. She didn't hear the steps behind her.

A hand brushed her shoulder, and she shrieked.

"Calm down."

"Fuck off!" Lizzy stepped away from Caleb before she slapped him right across his face. Where was the fucking taxi?

"What's—?"

"Don't even start with me. I am NOT in the mood." Lizzy stomped away, marching into the darkness with no idea where she was heading. She didn't give a damn where she ended up anymore and if Caleb tried to stop her—

A hand pulled on her arm.

"I said don't fucking touch me," Lizzy said, whipping around to face him with a glare that made him hold up both hands in surrender.

"I really just want to apologize. I should've told you—"

"What?" She searched her scrambled brain before remembering why she was pissed before. "Oh, that? Yeah, you should've told me. Whatever, it's fine."

Caleb looked confused, like an animal waiting to be lunch, suddenly free.

"Yeah, I mean I screwed up. I'm sorry. I just couldn't find the right words or time. Um, are you okay? You seem more upset now than back at the house."

Lizzy blinked fast so the tears Timothy Chappell didn't deserve wouldn't fall. She had no control over anything else in her life, but she'd be damned if she couldn't save one shred of her dignity.

She turned away from him and swiped under her eyes.

"Woah, woah. It's okay. Shit, I don't have a tissue." Caleb patted his pockets and coming up empty, swallowed her in a bear hug, rocking her back and forth. The dam broke, and the tears flowed down her cheeks along with a few choked sobs.

"It's going to be okay. I'm really sorry. I should've—"

"It's not you." Lizzy sniffed and nestled in closer to his chest. He did feel really good all wrapped around her. No one had ever hugged her like this. She didn't think any hug would ever come close.

"Come back inside and tell me."

"No, I like it out here."

In the dark, the orange glow of the streetlight illuminated a small pool of light on the cracked sidewalk. Bugs danced around as if on stage under a spotlight. She could hear peepers and a dog barking a few houses over. The quiet of an American town at night settled around her like a childhood blanket, filling all of the voids inside, making her feel complete and safe.

"We can stay here as long as you like, but I have to say," Caleb leaned back and looked at her, "you're worrying me. Who was that on the phone? It's okay if you don't want to tell me—"

"One of the town elders from Brightrock, telling me I need to fly home in three days or he'll file a death certificate, canceling my ID and freezing my accounts. Fucking bastard."

Caleb froze against her, his hand, which had been rubbing her back, stopping halfway.

"But that's illegal."

"Yeah, he's been around for four hundred years; he doesn't get it."

Caleb took a step back but still held her in his arms.

"I don't care how old he is. That isn't right."

Lizzy laughed despite herself. "He doesn't give a shit about right and wrong. All he cares about is controlling everyone on Brightrock."

"I don't understand. Can't you just...I don't know, like leave?"

"I wish."

Caleb stood in the night on the sidewalk, speckled with weeds and cracks. The glow from the lamppost behind him gave him an ethereal appearance, almost like that of an angel. Maybe that was why Lizzy took in a breath and let it all spill.

"I can't leave."

"Why? If it's money, I can—"

"Oh no, it's not that. Well, unless he closes all of my accounts."

Caleb looked more concerned by the second.

"I can help you, whatever is going on, we can fix it. Figure out a way—"

"I'm not like you."

"You mean southern?" Caleb looked hurt and a little offended.

"No, for God's sake, I'm almost three times your age."

Now that shocked him. He blinked twice trying to do the math and coming up empty.

"No—"

"Oh, yes. I drank the secret water from the secret spring, and now I don't age like the rest of the world. By doing so, I got myself trapped on the island, and Timothy Chappell and the rest of the council of elders can control my every move whenever they get a hair up their ass." Lizzy threw her hands up into the night, hoping for some prayer that would buy her freedom.

"You can't mean this. When were you born?"

"Try about a hundred years ago."

Caleb opened his mouth and shut it, before trying again. No sound came out the second time either.

"So, let me get this straight."

"Go for it." Lizzy folded her arms and let her head loll to one side while she waited for him to catch up.

"You were born a hundred years ago."

"Yep."

"You drank this secret water or whatever."

"When I turned eighteen. They called it a graduation ceremony, but by the end, it was too late to leave. They give it to kids while they're too young to understand what they're signing up for," she added, her voice laced with bitterness.

Caleb narrowed his eyes while he processed what she was saying.

"Okay, right, so you drank this magical water."

"Every season."

"Every season, and now you don't age."

"Correctamundo."

"Like a fountain of youth?"

"It's not eternal, more like a renewal thing, hits the brakes on the crows' feet, at least for a bit." Lizzy stretched her neck to the other side. Breaking all of her vows and nondisclosures felt liberating and had lifted her mood considerably. She watched while Caleb worked it out.

"So, you go back every season and don't age as fast."

"Bingo."

"And if you don't return, they'll close your accounts and say you're dead, trapping you." Caleb frowned again like he truly didn't like the idea of it. She'd kill to have a moral code half as strong as his. "Why do they want you back so bad?"

"So I don't spill the beans."

"But didn't you just do that?"

"Yep. Not like it changes anything. You're just one guy, and they'll just write you off as crazy. I'm surprised you're still listening actually. I would be back in the house if I were you."

Caleb started to shake his head and then stopped. His eyes went wide, and he sucked in a breath through his nose.

"The bombing. Caitlyn. Holy shit, does Caitlyn know?"

"Yep."

"And Austin...so he? That means Caitlyn now—"

"Yep."

"So, she can never leave?"

"Not without permission. Going to be a long four hundred years if you ask me, but then again, she's in love." Lizzy picked a piece of lint off of her sweater. "I hear couples are usually happy with the arrangement. It's the singles like me that want out."

"You know too much to leave." Caleb's voice held a note of sadness as the understanding of her predicament dawned.

Tears started to well up. She had been pissed, but she was trapped. Totally dead in the water.

Lizzy opened her mouth to speak, but her voice cracked on the first try. Caleb stepped forward and wrapped his arms around her. With her mouth against his chest and the tears streaming down, she said, "I wish I could just stay with you."

Lizzy walked into Caleb's house and tossed her phone onto the kitchen table. The phone clattered and skittered across the polished surface into a bowl of fake fruit no doubt from Maw Maw.

The sound of the storm door slapped shut behind her. Caleb shut the wooden door behind her, throwing the deadbolt. All of it seemed so normal.

"Listen, I know you mentioned the whole water thing, but I was going to tell you, you can stay here as long as you like."

She blinked and looked up at him. Even though the point was moot, the meaning behind the gesture still felt the same. "You mean that?"

"Course I do. We're dating after all. I mean, if you still want to after finding out where I work." Caleb looked down, sheepishly avoiding her eyes. "I understand if you don't want to." He looked up and met her eyes with his own, the twin emeralds with dark lashes pleading with her. "But I would like that."

The whole conversation seemed ridiculous after what she had just told him, but Lizzy stared at him anyway. With

Timothy Chappell's phone call still fresh in her mind, the reality was, she couldn't, but the idea of staying here with him tugged at her heart like a primal calling to something right. Still, life wasn't that simple, even without her massive, complicated big-ball-of-mess life. "Won't your family—I mean, they seem pretty old school, which I totally get, like there's nothing wrong with that. Shit, I'm pretty old school, older than most you know, but like still, I can't imagine the idea of you shacking up with someone would go over well."

Caleb shrugged it off. "Maw Maw likes you. She'd love for you to hang around forever."

Lizzy sniffed the rest of her tears away and wiped her face as more tears rolled down her cheeks. She wished she could throw her arms around his neck and demand a ring and that he ask her properly, but taking a sip of water when she was eighteen almost eighty-two years ago prevented her from doing any of that. Lizzy wept and held her head in her hands. Heavy arms came around her and held her close.

"Sorry, I'm just a wreck," she said after sniffing away more tears.

"It's okay. You're allowed to fall apart." Caleb wiped her tears away with his hand, which was as gentle as a kiss from a butterfly. "And I got just the thing to put you back together."

A few minutes later, Lizzy stood in a steaming shower, letting the hot water race over her head and down her back. Her fingers had pruned, but she still wasn't ready to get out.

Right now, she wanted to hate Brightrock but couldn't. She hated Timothy Chappell for boxing her in with his conservative ways. He always would be the biggest and loudest vote on the town council, and though Lizzy's Aunt Tee and Aunt Mary didn't mind going head-to-head with him, she knew they quietly agreed with him on this matter. The rules were simple. No one left the island. The only exception was Ethan, the argument being, of course, that to stabilize the island's finances and allow them to live in secrecy, they needed a skilled money manager who had connections with the outside world.

Lizzy didn't fit that bill. In fact, because she was herself, the rules had always been a little stricter. From the moment her parents had died, Lizzy had been under the watchful eye of Aunt Katie and Uncle Fred, but also Timothy Chappell by proxy. Most people on Brightrock rarely spoke to the intellectual founder, but because Lizzy was the island's only orphan, she had always been treated differently. The adults in the community rallied around her after the traumatic loss, peppering her with gifts and advice everywhere she turned, but all of it had come at a price. Lizzy had never been able to swim out quite as far as anyone else or get away with behavior in school like the others. The only conclusion she could draw had been inspired by the sage words of Laurie Michaels, the school's librarian and counselor.

After Lizzy spent a few aimless years writing a book and enjoying researching the topic—which had been encouraged by Timothy—Laurie had encouraged her to apply to Brown to become a teacher and make use of her interest in ancient Rome and Greece. Once she had her degree, Lizzy was hired in no time flat, but was continuously denied promotions or off-island professional development. Other teachers were able to attend workshops and classes on various topics around the country during the summers with little issue, but Lizzy had always been denied approval.

Back then, Lizzy had only been teaching for twenty years. Now it had been almost three times as long. She had finally gotten the approval to travel to Virginia for her doctorate in education. The move had been a long time coming, and the council had run out of excuses to keep her pinned down. For God's sake, she had felt like Rapunzel.

Finally free, Lizzy had soaked up as much as she could. She loved her aunt and uncle dearly and missed them, and her little apartment over the Two Scoops Ice Cream Parlor with its view of the Atlantic. But there was just something about finding a new place in Charlottesville and being out on her own to explore the world, meeting new people.

That's how Caitlyn had been hired. The council had taken a risk, and a few months later, the oldest and most significant building on Brightrock had gone up in flames. Lizzy had no idea if the two were related, but a lot of people thought so, which meant the entire thing had been her fault. She should've just stayed in her apartment and been happy with her boring, dull, never-gonna-change life.

Lizzy faced the spray and let the water run over her face until it started to turn cold. She killed the shower and wrapped herself in two towels, one on her head and one around her body, before applying every type of lotion the department stores could sell.

Looking at her reflection, Lizzy's own blue eyes stared back at her. Her pale skin didn't have any lines, despite years in education, thanks to the secret she had just screamed in the middle of a street. She looked paler than usual, and a little thinner too. Without her dark mass of curls now hidden under the towel, Lizzy looked regal, confident, and elegant. An educated and experienced woman who should be in control of her own future, but that couldn't be further from the truth. As much as she wanted to control her life, she had absolutely no authority.

That was if she still wanted access to the water. Sure she still had to go home and clear up credentials, but if she really wanted to leave—

Lizzy cut the thought off, too shaken and too emotional to entertain the notion further. She finished her skincare, flipped her head, and shook out her curls, running her fingers through the dark and tangled mass with some oil. She had packed a few negligees and other sultry items, but too tired to care, she pulled an old T-shirt over her head and shimmied into her comfiest pair of undies.

She left the bathroom, bringing a cloud of steam with her into the hallway. She padded down to the kitchen, holding the wet towels.

Caleb was at the kitchen counter, still in his jeans looking every bit the respectable boyfriend in the middle of wiping down the counter. He stood transfixed and did a slow sweep of her from head to toe with his eyes.

Maybe she had underdressed after all. "I, uh, wasn't sure where to put the towels."

Caleb took them and tossed them into the back room with the washer and dryer where they landed with a splat.

"Come here, you." Caleb wrapped his arms around her and held her close, pouring love into her bones like no one else had before. "I'm sorry."

"I am too. I just...I just can't handle any more secrets. I hate them."

"You got it. You want to know something about me? Just ask. I'll tell you. I promise."

Lizzy nodded against him and sucked in a breath, swallowing the tears. "I don't want to go home. I wish...I just wish everything was simpler."

CHAPTER 25

Caleb didn't know what to think about everything that just had happened outside. What he did know was that the woman he had thought about every night was standing in his kitchen looking like a wet puppy in need of a hug. The small chandelier shone down on her like a spotlight on a tragic figure.

The worst part was the hug hadn't made the problem go away. As much as Caleb wanted to fix everything and wished like hell he could wave his hand and wipe away all of her fears, he hadn't even fully understood the issue.

"Did the shower help?"

Lizzy kept staring off into space, those big blue eyes looking at nothing in particular. She gave a little shrug and then nodded.

"Good. Maw Maw always believes a hot shower can fix a lot. Deep sleep too. And a good meal, but we've already eaten."

Lizzy didn't seem to be listening, but she sure as hell wasn't about to start talking, either, so Caleb kept going. After all, his worst secret was already out, so he didn't have much to lose. "I think I have just the thing. It always makes me feel better, at least."

He eyed the clock on the stove as he pulled down two bowls from his cabinet and cracked open the freezer to pull out some of Blue Bell's finest ice cream. He rummaged around in the drawer to come up with his ice cream scoop buried at the back and made quick work of serving both chocolate and vanilla in both bowls. He didn't know which one she would like better, and now was not a good time to ask.

"Why don't you go sit on the couch and find something for us to watch?"

Lizzy kept staring off, but after a minute nodded and padded for the den on her bare feet, with her perfect pink toes.

A few minutes later he was eating ice cream, watching baseball with Lizzy snuggled up against him. The Braves were on, and the ice cream had lived up to expectations, and that was saying something.

"When did you move into the place above the ice cream parlor?" He took his spoon and dug in for another bite.

"Moved out from my aunt and uncle's place once I started teaching when I got back from Brown."

"How long have you been teaching?"

Lizzy looked down and picked at a cuticle on her thumb.

"That long, huh?"

"You know you're taking this whole my-crazy-girlfriend-is-damn-near-immortal thing really well. Are you sure you aren't like a serial-killer psycho or something?"

Caleb glanced down at her for a full three seconds and started laughing.

"That's not helping your case, buddy."

"Well, what do you want me to say? I'm no Casanova, but like calling BS was going to calm you down? I'm not an idiot.

Besides, either way, there's nothing we can do about anything tonight, so what does it matter?"

Lizzy stared at him with those big blue eyes in a way he had always dreamed she would.

"Go ahead, eat up," he said when Lizzy eyed the bowl in front of her. "A hot shower and ice cream, that'll fix a lot of evil right there. I brought a couple Cokes too." He popped open the tab of the can, hearing the fizz, and passed it over.

Lizzy hesitated and then brought the drink to her lips. "You're going to make me fat."

"Bone is for the dog, meat is for the man."

Coke sprayed everywhere. Stuck somewhere between a coughing fit and laughing, Lizzy reached out for a napkin to blot her soaked shirt. Caleb jumped up and came back with a rag while she sat giggling on the couch. He moved the flowers he had brought her at the airport, which had ridden home in a drinking glass in a cup holder and now sat in the center of the table, and wiped down the oak.

"I can't believe you just said that." Lizzy cracked up again.

"I mean, it's true." Caleb could feel his ears turning pink but grinned despite himself. Lizzy wasn't crying anymore. Well, maybe she was, but at least it was for the right reason.

Lizzy wiped her face and leaned forward to grab the spoon. "What the hell, right? I can just diet when I get back home." She took a bite of ice cream, considered it, and then took another. "On second thought, I could just eat until I'm as a big as a house. Not like there'll be anything else to do." Lizzy slumped into the couch again.

"Well, I could come and visit, right? I mean, I did that before. Sal and Alex's place was great."

"Yeah, there was a whole thing about that. Wanted to shut it down because you were causing suspicion. We aren't supposed to be friends with anyone off the island."

"At all?"

Lizzy shook her head and ate more ice cream. "Nope, so I'm afraid this relationship of ours just got a lot shorter."

"Well, there's not a rule against me coming, so I'll come."

Lizzy froze and looked at him, an assessing look in her eyes that studied him. "Would you come to Brightrock? You know...permanently?"

The hairs on his arms rose, and the quiet seemed to get louder around them as if what they were speaking about were an unholy summoning of something humans should never discuss.

"I would have to give up my family?"

She nodded. Caleb knew his answer.

Her lips formed a thin line of a smile, while her eyes shimmered with tears. "I didn't think you could. You're a good man."

Caleb didn't feel like one.

"You could always stay here. Live with me. I'm gone sometimes, and I'm still fixing the backyard up, but—"

"If I leave, I don't get to go back to Brightrock. Ever. It's exile. I'd never see my aunt and uncle again."

"So, no water?"

She shook her head.

He shifted uncomfortably and put his spoon down in the bowl of melting ice cream soup.

"I don't want to sound ignorant, but—"

"No, please ask away. It's a weird subject. Not too many experts on it." She let out a bitter laugh.

"Are you...is it like those zombie movies?"

Lizzy raised a perfect dark eyebrow. "How so?"

"You said you're one hundred, right?"

"Look pretty good for my age, don't I?"

"You're the most beautiful woman I've ever seen."

Lizzy's lips parted, and a sly smile grew across them.

"Do you really mean that?"

"Yes. I can't believe you're sitting in my den, eating ice cream. I haven't been able to get you out of my head since I first met you."

"Do you want me out of your head?"

"Not at all."

A pink tinge kissed Lizzy's perfect cheeks. She swirled her spoon through the melted cream and smiled to herself.

"So I don't want to be dumb, but what happens if you don't drink the water? Like if you stop?"

Lizzy's smile ran off, and she bit her lip. "I'm not really sure."

"You're not going to turn into dust or anything? Like, you know, in *The Mummy*?"

"Well, I've missed a renewal before when I was at school, and I haven't dried up yet." She held up the back of her hand and studied it. From where Caleb was sitting, her skin was perfection.

"What do you mean you missed one?" He leaned forward, not sure what to expect.

"We have to go back quarterly, and there's this whole song and dance that we go through, but yeah, I didn't go. Figured if I did, they might not let me leave, so it was better just not to go." Lizzy glanced back up at him.

"Is that going to hurt you?"

She shrugged. "So far, so good."

"No one has ever done this before? Just stopped?" This conversation was making his chest tight with concern.

Lizzy rubbed her elbow and pulled one leg in to rest on the other knee. "Not by choice. I think there was one guy— way before my time—who was exiled. We never heard from him again, but I think I heard a rumor that when they researched him, he had lived a normal life."

"But you're not sure?" Caleb's breath burned in his chest.

He watched for her answer, searching her face for any visible sign of decay.

"No, but like I said, so far so good."

Caleb let his breath out in a slow sigh, relief washing through his body. "So, if I understand you correctly— and I'm not sure I get any of this, but—"

"You're doing a pretty good job. Austin said when he told Caitlyn she freaked out and drove away into the night. Tire squeal and everything."

"I don't know if I'm crazy or dumb, or how much I really believe, but let's say you can live for what would be a normal life span without the water—"

Lizzy nodded and took another sip of Coke.

Caleb held his breath for a moment. "Would you like to live with me? Forever?"

She looked up at him through dark, tear-stained lashes. "I would love nothing more."

Caleb's heart swelled. He pulled her close to him and kissed the top of her head. "Then it's settled. You can just stay here."

Lizzy pulled back away and looked up, confused. Sitting there in his arms, she looked so small and vulnerable. He wished he could make all of this go away for her and whisk her someplace beautiful with palm trees and sunshine.

"But my accounts and my paperwork. I need to—I don't have a choice. I have to go back."

"Oh yeah, I know. We'll take care of that, and you can wrap up whatever details you like. I'll go back with you."

"Really?"

"Of course. I have another twenty days of freedom. I wouldn't want to spend it with anyone else."

Caleb cupped her face in his hand, searching her eyes. Commercials droned in the background. He had vowed never to say these words again, but nothing had ever felt more right in his life.

"You're my Elizabeth, and I love you."

With that, Caleb touched his lips to Lizzy's for the first time.

CHAPTER 26

Lizzy couldn't remember the last time she had been kissed. On Caleb's couch in his den, she leaned into his soft lips, marveling at how gentle he was with her. His touch was so light if she hadn't been paying attention, she might've missed that he'd kissed her.

She pressed into him, exploring his chest with her hands, feeling the taut muscles underneath the shirt. Everything about him was quiet and gentle, yet his body was strong. For all of Brightrock's cult-like atmosphere, she had never met anyone as loyal as Caleb Broussard, and she doubted she ever would again.

Their hands roamed, explored, and kneaded each other through their clothes while they kissed. Lizzy snaked out her tongue to taste and moaned a little to give Caleb some encouragement. He gave in, and their mouths melted together.

She pulled him on top of her, and they fell back into the couch, the weight of his body bearing down on her, but as if he could read her thoughts, Caleb propped himself up and let her breathe. Breaking the kiss, he pressed his lips to her jaw and nibbled down to her collarbone murmuring compliments on the way down. The stubble of his beard rasped along her skin, tickling her and making her squirm beneath him.

"You're just as perfect as I thought you'd be."

"I have pretty good skin for an old woman." Lizzy started to laugh, but Caleb grazed his teeth on her neck behind her ear, dragging out a sigh from within her.

"You are not old," Caleb said into her ear before continuing to nuzzle his way along her skin. Lizzy let his love wash over her while she sank into the couch, making her muscles tense and relax with each breath. She tangled her hands in his dark hair and pulled him closer and harder to her, shifting herself to allow him more access.

His hips locked right into place with her own. A hard ridge rested on her core, sending a wave of heat down to her most sensitive point. He had so much power but was so gentle and slow with her. Lizzy rolled her hips for him to get a move on, only to have Caleb stop his progress and kiss her wanton mouth.

"You smell sweet," he said at last when he broke the kiss to let her pant with want.

"You stopped kissing me."

"I don't think I can stop."

Lizzy frowned and watched him. "Why would you?"

"I don't want to rush into anything, make you feel pressured, but you're more...just more—"

"More what?"

"More everything than I had ever hoped for."

Lizzy let a slow smile spread over her face as she ran her hands up his arms and down his back where she tugged at his hips, drawing him into her core.

"I want everything."

Caleb's lips were parted as he panted. His eyes were dark,

his thick hair tousled in all directions thanks to her greedy hands.

"Everything? You're sure?"

"I've never been more sure of anything." She reached up and pulled him back down, rising up to bring her mouth against his.

They twisted and tangled on the couch until Lizzy couldn't take it anymore. Reaching down, her fingers found the hem of his shirt and tugged upwards.

"I want to see you," she said in a hoarse voice. "All of you."

Caleb got the hint. He rose up, and in a flash, sent the shirt hurtling across the room where it fell into a crumpled heap. His muscles strained out from his chest, showing his strength. Biceps and pecs bulged as he bent down to work on her mouth again.

"Do I get to see you?"

"Only if you really want to," Lizzy smirked at him. Caleb didn't return the gesture and instead pulled the T-shirt off her. Still leaning back, she admired the view, running her hands over his smooth skin, feeling the barest dark hair on his chest. Caleb's face melted into adoration as he smoothed the fabric away from her skin and down her arms, pinning her.

Caleb sat back and stared with a wide smile.

"You're stunning."

"Come here and kiss me."

"Gladly."

They tasted, probed, and explored each other, falling into a rhythm together. Lizzy arched her back to press her chest into Caleb. Her nipples pressed against his chest, and she said his name like a plea for mercy.

He propped himself up over her again and looked down, grinning.

"You're more beautiful than I ever imagined."

Lizzy pulled him down to her mouth and arched into him again. Caleb was a quick study and had her writhing and panting with moans of need as his mouth worshiped her breasts, sucking on each nipple. His hands kneaded and drove her wild.

Gasping for breath, Lizzy wiggled against him, but without success. He had her pinned with his hips between her legs. She was on fire, and the ridge of his jeans against her panties made her want to scream.

She was drenched and craved his touch.

"Caleb, please."

Her eyelids closed as one hand left her breast to travel south and explore her hips, gripping her butt and then coming around to the front.

A skillful finger pressed against just the right spot, making her jump and try to jerk away, but he held her fast. He drove her wild, and without even being fully undressed, Lizzy was on the verge of coming when Caleb stopped and pulled away.

"What the hell are you doing?"

Caleb scooped her up in his arms and carried her out of the room, his eyes narrowed to slits. "Taking you to a proper bed."

He shouldered open the door to the dark bedroom and laid her down on his grey bedspread before climbing on and claiming her mouth with his own.

"Too many clothes," Lizzy said against his mouth while clawing at his waistband.

Caleb pulled back and shucked off his pants and whatever had been under, and went right back to work on her mouth, neck, and shoulders. Shivers skated over her skin from the rasp of his jaw.

The blunt head of him nudged her hip. Lizzy found his length and closed her palm around him, pleased when he froze and strained with pleasure. She let her finger glide up his shaft, feeling him twitch with need. A slow smile spread across her face as she kissed him now and continued the slow, aching pace. His hips pressed toward her in a silent beg for more. One she was happy to oblige.

Lizzy lowered her head and worked him with her mouth. Hearing Caleb suck in a breath, she did it again, adding a graze of her teeth.

"Please." Caleb's voice, a low, hoarse prayer, empowered her to take his length into her lips.

She worked him with her mouth rocking back and forth in a slow rhythm of pleasure. Caleb's body strained under the pressure of pleasure as she licked and lapped every inch, sucking slightly and creating a pop when she came up for air. Lizzy angled her head to watch him as she worked him into a frenzy.

His head was thrown back into the pillows with one arm thrown behind him to hold on to something. The muscles in his neck bulged with the effort of keeping control under her power.

Eyes that had been closed opened to watch her. His lips parted as he panted for breath, watching her pump up and down along his shaft.

A vibration of energy coursed through his body as he started to lose what little control he had. Lizzy released him with another pop and looked up with a small grin. She was about to say something smart when Caleb rolled her on her back and growled, "My turn."

He planted a hard kiss on her before nestling his shoulders between her legs, creating a space for himself. He looked comfortable, like a man who wasn't going anywhere for a while.

That was the last coherent thought she had.

Caleb drove her wild. Lizzy oscillated between clinging

to him and trying to squirm away from the intense pleasure as it consumed her. She went from begging him for more to pleading with him to slow down. Caleb left her just shy of the release she craved.

Her legs shook, and she clung to his shoulders, desperate for some relief. Caleb wouldn't give it to her. When she was on edge, he pulled back and sat up, leaving her panting and watching him, drenched.

"Oh my God, you can't stop."

"Not planning to." Caleb leaned over to the bedside stand and, with a flash of a packet, sheathed himself in a condom.

Lizzy wriggled down toward him, baring everything to him for the taking as if she was on a platter, ready to be eaten alive and happy for it.

"Hurry."

Caleb planted his arms on either side of her and lowered himself to her, kissing her mouth hard. The fire inside her burned, wanting the most primal thing she could need from him. Her legs buckled as he tried to slow down the raging pace between them.

"Now. I need you now." Lizzy propped herself up on her arms and met him halfway, kissing him hard, spreading her legs, feeling the blunt tip of him against her slick core.

With one thrust, he was home. Lizzy cried out and Caleb froze, looking down, concern flooding his features.

"What's wrong?"

"Nothing, just been a while. Oh, God, you're huge."

A smile spread, and he rocked his hips into her, slow at first and then as she settled in, he sped up to drive her toward release again.

Lizzy grabbed his shoulders, pulling him down to her, her nails digging into his skin. Chest to chest, Caleb drove them both, sending them higher and higher on the climb. Every muscle tense and taut with passion, Lizzy hung on as Caleb pounded into her again and again, driving her forward in an unrelenting pace fueled by a passion she hadn't known before. Desire coiled in her and she hovered on the edge, stuck somewhere between wanting to hang on and begging for a release. As if he sensed her need, Caleb pulled up and pistoned into her, shaking the bed.

The last thrust sent her flying, and as she shattered into a million relaxed bits, Lizzy felt every muscle in her body melt into her bones as she floated out of her body and down to the bed for what felt like an eternity distilled into a frozen moment in time.

Caleb's breathing was hard and slow as he collapsed on her, exhausted from his own passion. Together they lay entangled with each other for what could've been minutes or hours, Lizzy wasn't sure. Their breathing slowed and they held each other as one being existing in tandem as if they were always meant to find each other.

His body was still on top, but Lizzy didn't feel crushed. Caleb stroked her hair and murmured words she didn't have the energy to follow. Some in English and others were in French, just barely under his breath so she could hear him speaking but had no idea what he was saying to her. The soft patting of her hair on the pillow felt so lovely. Lizzy couldn't remember the last time someone had played with her hair.

She didn't know how long she lay there listening to him, but for the first time in her memory, Lizzy knew what it felt like to be loved and truly cherished. In the dark night of the bedroom, she opened her eyes and felt a tear slide down her cheek as she studied the ceiling fan above her. Lizzy would've loved to stay with him and be normal. At least this way she had gotten what she wanted during her taste of freedom. The problem was she wasn't sure if she was strong enough to walk away and give it all up.

Maybe Timothy Chappell had been right. Perhaps this is

what he was trying to protect her from. If the people of Brightrock didn't know how good things were on the outside, they wouldn't leave, yet if they knew, they were a danger to themselves.

Lizzy felt another tear slide down her face, and right when she wondered how much of a mistake she'd made, Caleb's hand swept over her cheek, wiping her tears away again.

Letting him go was going to kill her.

CHAPTER 27

Nora waved goodbye to the bubbly secretary at the physical therapist's office and shoved out through the door to her car. Tossing the keys up and down, she flung open the door and threw herself behind the driver's side, a grin on her face. She fired up the engine of her Mustang, swung back and sped out of the lot, hitting the gas pedal a little harder than she meant to. It felt so good to drive again. It had only been a few days, but she hated not being in control.

Navigating traffic, Nora stretched her arm, now free from the sling, again feeling the soreness setting up shop from another grueling session. She'd been pushing it at home, treating every exercise like a religion, and pushing herself a little harder with the weights and resistance bands each time. They had been happy about her progress, and though she still had to return for the foreseeable future, Nora was close to getting released from medical leave and back on the job.

In the seat next to her, Nora's phone buzzed beside her wallet. Seeing Ethan's name pop up almost tempted her no texting rule, but she waited until she reached a red light to glance at the screen. Smiling to herself, Nora hit send to her response and punched her blinker to head in a different direction.

Ten minutes later, Nora pulled into a cute little coffee shop near the city. Ethan stood outside, wearing a stellar navy suit, the blue shirt open at the collar, looking down at his phone. Nora zipped into a parking spot on the road.

"You don't like Dunkin?" she said, walking over to him.

"I love Dunkin."

"Then why are we here?"

"You don't branch out much, do you?"

"Nope."

"You should."

"Why mess with perfection?"

"Lieutenant, you need to stop and smell the roses more often."

"I do."

"When is the last time you drank out of something that wasn't Styrofoam?"

"How do you know I don't have a reusable mug?"

Ethan smiled at her. "Just a feeling."

"Uh-huh." Nora looked up at the little place, the pretty tile work, the wall of plants, the artfully arranged reclaimed wood, and the intricately decorated menu with chalkboard lettering.

"Let's give it a try."

Nora sat down across from Ethan, watching again how he moved, taking the time to thank the barista individually and smiling as he entertained a little baby whose mother was trying to juggle her phone, purse, and a screaming toddler while waiting for her coffee. A few college girls had ogled him, which pissed Nora off, even though she told herself she didn't have anything to do with Ethan and it shouldn't. She tried to sort out her feelings and frowned when she couldn't quite place her finger on what exactly she was thinking.

Nora looked up when Ethan set the latte mug in front of her.

"Why is there a heart in this coffee?" she asked him once she had finished studying the design in the foam.

"I thought it was nice."

Nora looked up at him and blinked twice.

"Yours has a leaf."

"Yes, yes, it does."

Nora stared at him, trying to hate his natural smile, the one that told her how much he found her amusing. He held the cup to his lips and took a sip, taking care to wipe his mouth with the napkins he had also brought.

"You always are frowning around me."

"No, I'm not. That's just my face."

Ethan barked out a laugh, his eyes shining bright when he looked back down at her. The damn man looked like a frigging movie star. Nora fought the urge to roll her eyes.

"I'm glad you responded to my text." Ethan said the words while looking into his mug of coffee. His eyes met hers in the silence that followed.

"I wanted to question you again since we didn't get too much further at dinner."

"I invite you to coffee, and all you want to talk about is my brother. What about me?" Ethan held up his hands and put out his lip. "I'm feeling left out."

"Uh-huh. So you want me to ask you things?"

"I'd like that."

"Where are you working now?"

"Not sure I can say," Ethan spoke the words as if they were just discussing the weather, leaning back into his seat and crossing one ankle over his knee.

Nora raised an eyebrow. "Okay, where are you living?"

"Are you interested for personal reasons or business?"

"Just answer the question."

"I have an apartment in the city."

"Care to be more specific?"

"If you have a warrant or other motivations, perhaps I could be persuaded."

"I'm not interested in playing games with you like this," Nora said, throwing up her hands.

"I'm answering your questions, but maybe you're not asking the right ones, Lieutenant."

Nora glared at him over her coffee. "You're pissing me off."

"Should I take a turn then?"

"Fine. Shoot."

Ethan leaned forward and looked severe. All joking had left his voice, his eyes focused and serious. "How's your shoulder? What did the doctors say?"

Nora shrugged her right shoulder. The bad one was still tender. "Lots of questions. They're mostly happy. Just got out of physical therapy today. I'm getting stronger, but they're predicting months until I'm back to where I was."

"What kind of questions are they asking?"

Not the kind of questions you want to talk about, Nora thought to herself. "Just routine, I guess."

"Therapy." It wasn't a question.

"Yeah, I guess. Nightmares and shit like that."

Ethan made a noise in his throat and nodded once, giving her space to continue.

"I mean routine stuff. The bullet went clean through, just nicking the artery. They think my adrenaline being high caused all the blood spurting, which is why I passed out, but yeah—"

Nora stopped and glanced up. Ethan held his mug in

midair. "I had no idea," he said, his voice so quiet she could barely hear him.

"Yeah, um, Manillo dragged me out and tossed me on the ground before slamming his big hand against the wound. I passed out pretty soon after that."

Ethan sat across from her, stony-faced. He put his mug down with a slow, mechanical movement.

"You could've died."

"Yeah, I know. On the shitty lawn of a drug house." The words came out harsher than she meant. A shiver crossed her body as she remembered waking up in a cold sweat in the middle of the night with that same thought for what must have been the hundredth time since it happened.

"I'm so sorry," Ethan said, looking at her.

Nora shrugged again. "It's the job. I'll be going back in at the end of this week. Light duty shit. But in a few weeks, I'm going to be back in business."

"What do you mean going back this week?" Ethan said across from her, his brow furrowing low as he glared at her, trying to follow her excitement and clearly not getting the same result.

"Doc says I should be good to go."

"You gotta be shitting me."

"Why? You gotta problem with that?"

Ethan swore and looked down into his mug, his hands cupping the warm white ceramic, cradling it with the kind of care Ethan brought to everything. He opened his mouth like he wanted to speak but closed it and shook his head.

"Why do you care?"

Ethan stared hard into the coffee. "I shouldn't care, but you already know how I feel about you."

Nora felt her mouth go dry but shifted in her seat and looked up at him. Her stomach fluttered at the memory of him telling her to stay safe in the light of the drop off point she gave him the last time they met. He agreed to drop her at a well-lit restaurant only when the Uber arrived, and she assured him the drive to her house wouldn't be long. When she had gone to get out of the car, Ethan had opened the door, held it open for her, and tipped the driver. Nora had been ready to stop him right in his tracks if he so much as touched her elbow, but he kept his distance, giving her no reason to fault him.

Instead, she had thought about him all night, which was no doubt what the smooth bastard wanted her to do. Nora had lain awake in her bed, wanting to toss and turn, pinned to the sheets by her sling, staring at the ceiling, trying to forget his voice and the way he looked at her.

She had told herself that technically he wasn't a suspect, and technically the investigation was concluded, though she'd be damned if she didn't get to the bottom of this. Still, the way Ethan looked at her kept her awake at night, wondering what it would be like with him in her life.

"I'm never not going to be a cop." Nora looked up at him, making the declaration clear.

"I know." Ethan looked sick as he said the words.

"If that bothers you, go get your panties in a bunch somewhere else because I am what I am."

He laughed, but the smile didn't hit his eyes.

"You have a problem with me?"

"I don't know."

"You seem to know everything else. Of course, until I ask you a question."

His fingers twirled the spoon on the edge of the saucer.

"I'm not used to letting things go."

"Uh-huh. Sure, a powerful guy like you. Rich too. I bet that's a real kick in the ass."

Ethan smiled more, the skin around his eyes crinkling, revealing the weary look Nora hadn't noticed before.

"I'm not used to being worried someone in my life could die, as you said, on the shitty lawn of a drug house."

"Well, to be fair, it wasn't really a lawn. More like a patch of dirt with some weeds."

He took a sip, his cufflink glinting in the afternoon sun streaming through the large windows in the cafe, and drew in a breath.

"Yeah, I've never had to worry about someone I care about getting shot. Austin was in the navy. That was the only exception."

"I knew about the navy from his records, but the dates don't match up. There's no way he could be your brother. Those pictures were from at least the forties."

"Pictures?" Ethan frowned now, focused on her like a laser.

"On the floor of Mark Schmidt's house we found every picture of Austin from the internet in the last twenty years. He never changed one bit."

Ethan shifted in his seat, trying to look relaxed, but the deadly focus in his eyes gave him away. She had his attention.

"There were more pictures. Most with Mark's old man in the navy during the forties. One showed a picture of a guy that could be a dead ringer for Austin, but of course, that's impossible. I think ol' Schmidty was hitting the sauce a little harder than normal. Wrote a couple of notes about not aging on Brightrock. Crazy shit. You should've seen the sermons lying around too. None of it made any sense."

"Do you think he had my brother confused with someone he knew, or his dad knew?" Ethan asked.

"Probably, but I feel like there's more to it. If that's the case, why didn't he go after just Austin? He tried to take out the town during a town meeting for chrissakes. I feel like there's more to the story. Then your brother dies."

"I can see why you're determined to get to the bottom of it. I wish I could help you."

"Does that mean you know anything?"

Ethan took a sip of coffee and pulled a face. "About a drunk's religious fantasies? No. I do know I don't want you getting shot again."

Nora took a sip of her own fluffy drink and almost choked. He cared about her. She hadn't made it that far in three relationships, all of which were just convenient ways to work out some urges along with the stress of the job. Most were with other cops, not in the same troop, but who knew enough about the business to not want to form ties.

"I'm fine. I'll be fine. Look," Nora said when he didn't look convinced, "I can take care of myself. I didn't make rank for my personality, though I'm sure that totally helped, but yeah, I got this."

"You won't have full strength for months."

Nora waved a hand. "I've been going to therapy. Working out, putting in the time with the weights. I'll be fine."

"What does your grandmother think about all this?" Ethan asked.

"She's a big believer in getting back out there."

"And your brother?"

"Same."

"Did they talk to your doctor?"

"You know, when I agreed to dinner and to coffee, I thought I'd get to ask you questions."

"How about dinner tomorrow?"

Nora's breath caught in her throat. This was starting to get out of control.

"I don't know if that's—"

"You can ask me anything."

Nora sighed. "This isn't a good idea."

"Tell me about it." The edge in his voice caught Nora off

guard, her vibes perked up at the sound. She waited for him to continue, taking a long sip of her coffee milk confection.

Ethan crossed his arms and bore down, staring a hole in the floor, looking like he might blow up, but was trying to get himself together.

"I don't know what it is about you, but I find myself compelled."

"Compelled?"

"You know what I mean, Lieutenant." He sat up and leaned forward on the small table, his broad shoulders dwarfing the little round piece of reclaimed wood. "I don't know what it is about you, but I need you to take care of yourself. I could barely handle seeing you in a sling. I know this is your damn job, I respect the hell outta you for it, but I don't have to like the idea of a bullet ripping through someone I—"

A fire engine rolled down the street, siren blaring, ceasing all conversation in the cafe and on the street outside.

When Nora looked back at him, Ethan looked exhausted. Nora leaned into the table, so their faces were only inches apart. She smiled.

"Don't worry about me. I'm a big girl. And I'm a badass."

CHAPTER 28

Ethan thanked the waiter who poured sparkling water into Nora's glass before his own. She still declined any kind of alcohol, on the pretense of this being some sort of interview, and he hadn't liked drinking in front of her last time. She could call it whatever she wanted to, but spending time together was starting to become a habit, something that thrilled and interested him.

She eyed the candle on the white tablecloth while the old school voice of Dean Martin swam through the haze of diners enjoying company, conversation, and calamari. All of it reminded Ethan of his first time in New York back in the fifties, when he'd heard the songs for the first time live and never forgot them. People today had no idea what good music was, and Ethan knew in his gut that for the next three hundred years or so, he'd never get sick of Dino singing, "Ain't That a Kick in the Head."

Like last time, Nora had declined the car he offered, and instead grabbed a rideshare. When he had gone to greet her at the curb, she stepped out and might as well have knocked him flat. A different dress, this time, clung to her curves, outlining her healthy, lean body. He questioned her about her shoulder, but she just waved her hand blowing his concerns off like a stray piece of lint.

"You don't need to butter my roll," she said from across the table, glowing in the candlelight like a Madonna. "I can lift the knife." She smiled at him, her eyes dancing with amusement.

"I like doing things for you." Ethan swiped some extra butter over the ciabatta before placing it on the white plate and sliding it over to her.

"Why?"

"It makes me happy."

"I don't need you to do this."

"You've already said so."

"No, but seriously. I'm not some idiot chick who needs someone to get her a glass of water every time she turns around."

"I'd love to get you water."

Nora rolled her eyes and looked across the restaurant, shaking her head in frustration, though the small smile still stayed in place, dry humor shining in her eyes.

"When do you go back to work?"

"Tomorrow."

Ethan almost dropped his knife on the table.

"You can't be serious."

Nora sighed, exasperation clear in her voice. "We've been through this, don't go all He-Man woman protector on me now." She turned to face him, her head tilted slightly in a way that suggested she was annoyed she had to keep stating the obvious. "Badass cop, remember?"

"And that's why I like doing things for you. I imagine you don't let many people butter your roll."

"If that's not a euphemism for sex I don't know what is."

"Well, I didn't think we'd talk about that so soon, but if you insist."

"No, no." She held up a hand as if to stop him. "Not going there."

Ethan smiled to himself. He'd very much like to go there with her and explore this woman warrior and watch her moan with pleasure. He felt heat begin to rise at the thought of him undoing her careful mask of irritation, and seeing her in a full, passionate spread beneath him, begging for more.

"If you're having a fantasy, I will walk out right now."

Ethan snapped himself out of it and drank a full gulp of ice water to clear his thoughts and slow down some of the throbbing need pushing against the belt of his pants.

Setting the water down, Ethan stared at her across the table, letting some of the heat show in his face. "If you leave now, you won't get answers or food. That would be a shame, wouldn't it?"

"Ass."

"Guilty as charged," he said, raising his glass of water while Nora sat, arms folded, glaring at him from across the table.

He loved this back and forth; couldn't get enough of her. When he wasn't with her, Nora plagued his thoughts. At work he'd been lucky to be in a moderately low position under a new name starting from the ground up, operating on autopilot in a cramped office, while running his hands over Nora's firm body in his mind.

The obsession startled him, and though he knew he had to take it slow if he wanted to be with her, the familiar fear kept creeping back into his brain. He hadn't allowed himself to get this close to anyone since Sarah. That thought alone stopped all urges on a dime like a bucket of ice had splashed over him. He had never been one to cheat on someone he loved.

"You alright over there, big shot?" Nora's voice cut through his thoughts, her brow low as she studied him.

"Yeah, of course. Why?"

"You changed for a second. Got something on your mind?"

"No," he lied, pushing out the memory and hating himself for it. He carried the past with him every day, as a loyal servant to tradition, but the past wasn't welcome here. Nora consumed him like no one else in fifty years. Out of respect for both Nora and Sarah, Ethan knew he couldn't bring himself to touch her other than a polite handshake, but the temptation burned day and night, whether as embers or a full blaze; he couldn't stop thinking about his cop as he had come to think about her, texting her at least once a day to ask about her shoulder.

Nora nodded once and leaned forward, both arms on the table. "You said you could tell me about yourself."

"I thought you wanted to talk about Austin."

"Yeah, but you don't, so let's order dinner and start with you."

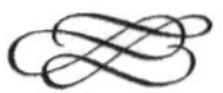

CHAPTER 29

One excellent meal later, Nora picked up her spoon and dove into the rich mountain of ice cream that swirled around a dense chocolate cake on the plate between them. Dinner had been a master class in Italian, and she knew she shouldn't be getting dessert, but then again, who turned down ice cream? Ethan had a few bites but set down his fork, declaring himself too full to continue. He sipped on coffee, watching her with the same heavy-lidded look he always had. He reminded her of a tiger in the zoo, only acting friendly for now.

They had chatted about him, but she hadn't found out much. He managed funds, had been doing it for a while, didn't have many close friends because of work, didn't have a car, didn't have a pet.

"What do you have then?"

Ethan raised one eyebrow at her. "So direct?"

"Occupational hazard."

His eyes went to her bad shoulder, as Nora had taken to calling it, and that's when she saw it. The mask of happy contentedness slid away as Ethan stared through her, not seeing anything around them anymore. His smile dimmed from the handsome lopsided grin, down to a thin slash across his face. In his silence, the restaurant seemed to get louder, couples and groups chatting and laughing, while ice rattled in glasses and forks and knives scraped plates.

"Time," he said at last, still not meeting her eyes.

"Excuse me?" Nora said, trying to figure out where he was going with this. His features told her that he was giving her his first truly sincere answer, the foothold into a dark cave she'd been trying to find since first meeting him in New York.

"I have time. A lot of time to kill."

"Most people would say that's a good thing."

He gave a rueful laugh.

"They have no idea."

Nora took another bite of the dessert in front of her, swiping up the last few bits before dropping the spoon on the empty plate.

"What do you do besides visit your family and work?"

Ethan frowned, still in some other world, looking at something only he could see.

"Nothing really. I read a bit. Watch some movies."

Nora nodded, but he didn't see her, so she lowered her voice, shifting into her professional tone so as not to rouse him from whatever memory he saw.

"What worries you?"

Ethan sat silent.

"Ethan?" she prompted, wishing she had Manillo there to help her. He always did better in these situations, but she was on her own.

"My family. Letting them down. Losing them."

"Like Austin?"

Ethan frowned again, at her suggestion. "Yeah," he said, but Nora would've bet her badge he was lying.

"How could you let them down?"

"Money. They all rely on me to watch and grow their money."

"You're bound to be pretty good at it. Farming, remember?"

"If I'm not, they lose everything. College funds for my cousins, retirement money for the town council. Money toward medical bills. It's all on me."

"I understand. I give a lot of money to my brother. He's a smart kid. Graduating this year. Applying to every school, but money's tight. Grandma's doing okay, but she doesn't have that kind of cash. Plus, I've got these family friends. One, he's kinda like my dad. Stepped up when Dad was killed—"

"I'm sorry for your loss."

Nora shrugged. "It was a long time ago. Made me want to be a cop like him. He always said I was like a dog with a bone, and I'd be good in an investigation."

"I can attest to that."

Nora smiled. "Yeah, well, his medical bills are out of control, but he has too much pride to let me help. His wife, Christine, bites my head off any time I even suggest it, but I can tell they're feeling the pinch. I know what that feels like." She took a sip of water, wondering why she revealed so much, wanting to take it all back. "What about your family? They can't go somewhere else?"

He shook his head.

Nora frowned. "Tell me why that's a problem. Wealth management or whatever rich people call it."

"No, they won't trust anyone else."

A warning went off in Nora's head.

"Why don't they trust anyone?"

He opened his mouth to draw in a breath when a hand swept down over the table. Ethan blinked a few times, and his smooth mask slid back into place as he smiled up at the waiter, leaning back into his chair and rolling his massive shoulders back as he straightened his spine. Nora stopped herself from ripping the tray out of the waiter's hand and throwing it toward the bar.

"Let me clear this plate out of your way. More coffee, sir?"

"Uh, yeah, sure. Thank you." For the first time since she'd met him, Ethan seemed rattled.

The waiter poured with the skill of an artist, right before another one came with a tray of additional cream and sugar, which Ethan declined.

When they were finally alone, Nora leaned in. Ethan didn't say anything, but watched her, brow furrowed as if he was trying to figure out the answer to her question. For a moment she thought he might apologize, which would make her feel like an ass, but he didn't. Instead, Ethan reached down to a dark corner behind him, pulling out a large box, wrapped in white paper with a single red ribbon tied into a bow.

Nora sat back and almost dropped her glass, setting it down too hard on the table, so another couple stopped chatting and looked over.

Through gritted teeth, she said, "We can't accept gifts."

"I know," he said. "This isn't a gift."

"Looks like one to me."

"Consider it a donation to the force."

"Madam?" the waiter said to her right.

"Ah yes, thank you," Nora said, leaning back. The waiter filled her glass and ran a little piece of metal over the tablecloth, sweeping away every crumb in a fluid motion that resembled a complicated and elegant dance.

"Did it really need a bow?" she hissed at him when they finally left.

Ethan didn't answer, but merely smiled and nodded. "I need you to open this, Lieutenant."

"What if I refuse?"

He sighed. "Why are you being so difficult?"

"It's my job."

"You're good at it."

"I know."

Ethan let out a bark of laughter and a smile that would've melted another girl's heart, but Nora remained steadfast. This gift was over the line.

"I think you'll like it." When she didn't move, he leaned over and said, "It's for your shoulder. To help you heal, although I have mixed feelings about this myself."

That caught her interest. As much as Nora didn't want him to see any weakness, her shoulder throbbed with the activity of the evening, and she was already running down and couldn't wait to sleep, the exhaustion tugging at her resolve. She also had therapy in the morning, which she didn't want to go to, but she needed to get back to one hundred percent before she actually went crazy and needed a different type of therapy.

"If you don't like it, you don't have to take it."

Nora glanced down at her throbbing arm and looked back up at him. "I may need a little help."

The slow smile in the candlelight made him look even more stunning than usual, and Nora considered he was by far the most handsome man with whom she had ever shared dinner. Hell, even if he had been butt-ugly, the dessert would have made the trip worthwhile.

"Happy to oblige, but you have to pull the tissue paper. Otherwise, it won't be a surprise."

"I'm not seven."

"When it comes to surprises, I am."

"I'm sure you're full of surprises."

He grinned a diamond white smile at her, while he pulled the ribbon away through slender fingers, taking time to thread the satin intricately while looking at her. He dispensed with the paper and stood again, bringing the box, which was larger than she realized, and laying it on her lap.

"No gifts."

"Never," he said, lifting the cover.

Nora gave him the eye one more time before she pulled the cloud of tissue paper back and gasped, which would've pissed her off if she had noticed anything but the sleek black metal in front of her. The body armor plate sat in the tissue paper like lingerie. Unable to stop herself, Nora went to lift it with her good hand, bracing herself for the struggle and finding the material lighter than she had expected, only slightly heavier than her own, but better quality and thicker material.

"It'll fit into your vest, and these bits can attach, so I'm told," Ethan said, reaching over to hold up the shoulder straps.

Nora ran her hands over it, in awe. "This is stronger than what the tactical guys get. This is the lightweight version, too, isn't it? I've heard of this. I didn't think this was even for sale yet."

"I persuaded them."

Nora snapped up to look at him, finding him giving her another stunner of a smile in the candlelight, although this time he glanced down, sheepish at having been caught so happy at her reaction.

"Ethan, I—" Words failed her as she stalled out. The department bought the best they could, but this had to be far beyond what she made in a month.

Nora ran her finger over the extra shoulder protection, jointed to allow for movement and flexibility.

"I've never seen anything like this."

"The shoulder bits are custom."

"What?"

"They're custom. These bits can attach but won't get in your way. You'll still have full range of motion."

Nora sat and blinked at him, while figures spun around in her head, the total climbing.

"I'm sorry," she said, leaning back into her chair while still unable to take her eyes off the sleek powder-coated steel. "I can't accept this. This is too much. I'll never be able to pay you back."

"I don't want your money—"

"I can't accept this gift. I'm sorry. Thank you, but there's just no way. This isn't right."

Ethan sighed again, his shoulders slumping. He ran a hand over his face and looked at her, studying her in the light. Concern shone in his eyes. Closing them once, he glanced down before reaching across the table, taking her good hand in his palm. The contact froze her, suspending time. She wanted to snatch her hand back, but he didn't grip her, didn't crowd her. His touch felt light and warm, though she could see the muscles in his forearms peeking out from under his sleeves, hinting at how strong he was.

Nora glanced around the restaurant to see who might be watching.

"Don't worry, they're very discreet here. No one knows you or me."

For whatever reason, she nodded, accepting his word. She had never trusted someone so implicitly and knew she shouldn't, but something about him told her that while she might not have the truth, he wouldn't hurt her. His gift certainly proved that.

Ethan leaned in, the smell of his cologne reaching her senses, drawing her in even more.

"I can't have you out there in anything but the best."

Nora shook her head. "I need to know something."

Ethan looked at her, his hazel eyes tired as if he hadn't slept in weeks.

"Yes?"

"Why all of this?"

"How do you mean?"

"If you're not going to talk to me—or tell me anything worth hearing—why are we doing this?" Nora waved her hands around the restaurant. "You keep promising me answers, and yet we seem to always end up at dessert with me knowing nothing new."

"You should know I care about you."

Nora's stomach dropped again, but she refused to process the feeling, forging ahead using momentum as fuel.

"But then why don't you tell me anything?"

"You haven't asked the right questions."

"And what would those be?"

"Lace or leather?"

"Oh, for God's sake. This is what I'm talking about. Every time we start to talk, you either dodge the question or flat-out lie."

"Lieutenant—"

"And you can cut that crap out right now. I don't have time for all this fancy shit. Are you going to tell me stuff or not?" She was rattled now. This had all been a mistake.

"What do you need to know?" Ethan asked, exasperation clear in his voice.

"You know what? Fuck it. I'm out of here." Nora shoved away from the table and marched toward the exit. Ethan cursed in her wake and reached for his wallet presumably to pay the bill, but that didn't slow her down. She had bigger shit to deal with than someone who was trying to play her feelings. Been there, done that.

She shoved through the door and onto the sidewalk. The

restaurant was another fancy place, this time down by the harbor. The smell of salty air, heavy in the twilight, felt good on her skin after being shoved into the tiny booth of a minuscule table in the back of the crowded restaurant.

A hard hand clamped on her good shoulder. In a flash, Nora twisted around, spinning her arm free, pegging him with a cold stare, stopping herself short of grabbing him by the shirt and hauling his linebacker ass against the bricks.

"Don't ever fucking do that again."

"Then don't walk away from me."

"Let's get one thing straight," Nora said, squaring off with him, so they were nose-to-nose. "I will walk away from you any time I damn well please."

A drop hit her shoulder, and then another one hit her head.

"It appears to be raining," Ethan said as the drops smacked the sidewalk faster and faster.

As if on cue, somehow summoned from thin air, a black Escalade pulled up alongside them.

"Want a lift?"

Nora glared at him and turned on her heel, marching away in the opposite direction.

Another curse, and then Ethan's fast footsteps followed.

"Don't be this stubborn," he called out after her.

"Now you're just egging me on."

"Nora, shit. Nora, stop."

"Why?" she said over her shoulder. The rain came harder now, pelting the concrete around them, the sky heavy with clouds that turned twilight into night. Tourists ducked into awnings as the first echo of thunder rolled into the city from the nearby harbor.

"Come on, just get in the car."

Nora turned to glare at him and then spun back around.

"You're right," Ethan called after her.

"Always am," she tossed over her shoulder at him.

"I'm not telling you stuff."

Nora smiled to herself as she kept walking toward the corner in what was a fast summer rain, threatening to become a downpour at any minute.

"I'm sorry. I'm just trying to protect my family."

"You should get in your car."

Ethan swore and jogged in front of her, walking in step alongside her when she didn't stop. His hair was soaked, and his wet shirt clung to his chest, outlining muscles Nora hadn't seen the likes of in a while.

"If you come with me, I'll tell you something you want to know."

"Like what?"

"Stuff about Austin."

Nora stopped and turned to look at him. "Why should I believe you? You keep dangling this carrot in front of me."

"What do you have to lose?"

Another roll of thunder, louder and closer, bringing more rain. The headlights of the black Escalade cut through raindrops, making them shine like shattered glass. Apparently, the driver had followed them at a crawl, traffic jam be damned.

"Fine, but this is your last shot."

They ducked over to the Escalade, where Ethan held the door and all but threw her in, slamming it shut behind him. The driver didn't pay any attention but instead navigated the streets clogged with red lights, honking horns, and unprepared tourists. Inside, smooth jazz played softly on the radio.

Nora pegged him with a hard stare. "Well?"

"You're unbelievable. Would be great in business."

"Not my thing, and you're stalling again."

Ethan tied back his hair, pulling it into a tight hold at the base of his neck, showing off those cheekbones, looking every bit the mystery man she was struggling to figure out.

"Austin knew Mark Schmidt's dad, or at least was close to him. Something like that, I can't remember."

Nora frowned. "But that can't be possible."

"What do you mean?" Ethan asked, looking at her with a cold gaze, studying her reaction, waiting to see what she said before judging the weight of her words.

"His dad was in World War II."

Ethan's face didn't flinch. Instead, he watched her, waiting for something but damned if she knew what.

"Mathematically, that isn't possible."

His face could've been carved from stone except for the muscle in his jaw which was now twitching as he clenched his teeth. "Yeah, I must be wrong. There's no way that's possible."

He turned away from her and looked at the back of the seat. His face was drawn, exhaustion creeping into the lines, making him look older than he was. Nora felt the urge to apologize for pushing him so hard. She opened her mouth to speak when he beat her to it.

"I don't know what to do about you." His voice was barely above a whisper. Even exhausted with whatever memory he was trying to process, Ethan looked stunning. By far the most handsome man she'd known outside of TV and movies. He looked like some superhero—or supervillain—who could snap his fingers and reveal a hidden lair with sumptuous luxury.

Though Nora knew better, she had thought about him too. She had told herself that all of these visits and interviews were just that, but he knew as well as she did, she was on medical leave, Mark Schmidt's case was as good as closed, and the world had moved on, no longer interested in the island Ethan came from. Still, something told her there was more to the story. She needed to find out, wanted to know, and for the first time, realized that what had been pure curiosity had become an all-encompassing quest for knowledge, not just about Brightrock, but about Ethan, the mystery man, who seemed just as intrigued by her. This drive went well beyond trying to live up to her dad's expectations, and into something much more.

"Ethan…" Her voice sounded far away like it wasn't her own. As if she was detached from her body, Nora saw her hand rise and land on his arm, skin meeting skin, exposed by his sleeves that were rolled up. The connection felt warm and real. He was all muscle, strength coursing through his veins. The back of the car was dark, illuminated only by lights from passing cars. She leaned toward him, and he met her.

Their lips met in a brief, faint touch, so light Nora wasn't sure what had happened or how it happened, but the instant contact was made, she needed more. Nora pulled back and glanced at the driver, who hadn't noticed a thing, when Ethan took her hand and held it between his own. He put his lips against her ear and murmured something she couldn't make out.

In the dark of the backseat, Nora felt free as she let her hands roam over his chest and neck while her mouth melded to his. What little thought remained fled the scene as his tongue jutted out into her mouth and his powerful arms pulled her close, taking care to avoid her shoulder, cradling her with his body, bringing her into his lap.

CHAPTER 30

Ethan pulled her closer still, the flames of desire rising up and bringing him to a height he hadn't experienced before. He didn't just want her—he didn't know what he'd do without her tonight. Nora pressed herself into him, her arms coming around his shoulders. His fingers clung to her back, pushing her against him as their mouths tasted and explored.

He had wanted this since he first saw her.

The urge to throw her on the seat next to him rose—the driver would be discreet, but Ethan wanted to savor her, despite how hungry he was for her. In the dark of the back seat, her lithe body, still damp from the rain, surged against him. He ran his hands along her back, stroking her and memorizing every inch of her strong curves. She was perfect. Her mouth soundlessly plunged into his own, taking what she wanted for herself as if he had put himself on a platter.

"Oh God," he said, his voice barely more than a breath as she pulled away for a second, still halfway in his lap, her hip hard against his cock, which was pulsing with need.

Her breathing heavy, he tried to search her features in the dark and found he couldn't.

"You're perfect," he said, his voice again more air than sound.

Nora silenced him with her mouth, which he eagerly accepted. She was like a fire, all-consuming, with the power to drive him to the edge. He happily let Nora take the lead, cupping her ass when she wrapped her hands around his neck, rising up over his lap. Her mouth tasted like chocolate and didn't stop, making no sound as she pressed her body against his, her own need evident.

Ethan had to stifle a groan when she stopped for a moment and rearranged herself over him, her legs straddling him in the pitch black of the back seat. Doing anything else would be stupid, however much Ethan wanted to strip her of her dress and replace the fabric with the cover of his own skin.

Her dress rode up on her thighs, bringing her core right against his throbbing length. Her hands now left his hair and began rubbing his chest, traveling south, until a finger ran over the tip of his cock, making his whole body twitch in response. With one free hand, Ethan exchanged the favor and ran a thumb over her nipple, licking up the sigh that escaped her lips between kisses.

A siren outside the window reminded him they were in a car with someone else, but Nora didn't break her rhythm, her tongue twisting with his own while her fingers traced circles around his head, pushing him to the edge. He didn't think he could take much more.

"Baby, stop," he breathed into her mouth, taking care to make no sound.

"Why?" she murmured back, doing the same thing while her hand played with the zipper of his fly.

Damn good question, but as much as he wanted her,

Ethan wanted her in a bed for their first time, under him, over him, writhing and resplendent where they could lie together without the cover of darkness.

"Wait until we get home."

Her hand slowed. "I don't know if I can do that." The tone of her voice sounded almost sad. The effect was immediate. All his protective instincts fired up, wanting to shield her from whatever had just happened.

"Why, baby?" he said in a whisper pulling back and running a hand over her hair, smoothing it back. "What's wrong?"

"This isn't right. I want you, but this isn't right."

Ethan's heart broke with the words he knew to be true. "I want to see your apartment, but if you don't like that, we can head to mine."

Nora eased off him, but his hands stayed around her, cradling her body in his lap.

"I'll do whatever you want," he added.

"Ethan—"

"Whatever you want."

"I don't know what I can give you. The last time I was in a relationship it all went to hell."

Ethan's body tensed at the idea of someone hurting her and a surge of anger and possessiveness came in a wave. "Well, I can promise you—"

Nora shook her head. "I don't like promises, for a variety of reasons that I'm so not ready to get into now. My job—"

"Don't worry about me. My job is to make you happy, to take care of you."

"I don't need you to."

"But I will anyway."

The passing light of a car lit her face, so he could see her golden eyes glowing, wide and gorgeous. She looked like a

Celtic warrior filled with passion and innocence at the same time.

"Nora, I think I'm starting to love you."

"Please don't."

"Why?"

"I can't handle that kind of pressure."

"It's not pressure." His voice would be hoarse with the whispering. "And I can't help it."

"I can't let you come to my place. I'm not ready for that. Not yet."

"Will you come to mine?"

Nora paused, holding her breath. Ethan's chest felt like it could burst on her answer. Not since Sarah had he brought someone into his personal space, but now he had to have her there. Not having her felt wrong, and all of this felt right. His careful world he had controlled for so long, now had been undone by this one cop with golden eyes, and God help him, he needed to have more of her.

"No. I can't."

Ethan nodded once and planted a hard kiss on her mouth, which she returned, now more hesitant than before. She slid off his lap, but curled against him, under his arm where she fit perfectly, their bodies molding together as if by design.

"We'll be heading to her apartment," Ethan said to the driver, who had been circling.

Nora rattled off her address and glanced up at him, a shy smile on her face. Her black V-neck dress had plastered to her with the rain, outlining every inch of her perfect body that he'd hoped to see tonight.

They headed out of the city toward the suburbs when Nora pointed him in the direction of her apartment complex.

"I'm honored you trust me with this knowledge," Ethan said, his lips brushing her damp hair.

"You're not getting a nightcap." Nora's voice still had the harsh edge that intrigued him, but now sounded softer and more hesitant.

"I know."

"I can't trust myself around you, and I can't cross a line. My job—"

Ethan shushed her, not wanting to hear the reasons they couldn't be together.

"I know you are who you are. Taking you out to dinner is more than enough for me."

Nora glanced up at him, her eyes flashing in the passing light of the overhead streetlamp shining through the window.

"Thank you. I don't like being shut out, though."

"Investigator until the end."

"Yeah, I am."

"But?"

"I do like this."

Ethan luxuriated in that statement and pulled her close to him. Against his chest, she felt lean and petite, but still a fighter in her own right.

"I do too."

"This is so wrong, though. On so many levels."

"Why must you insist on bringing up the bad stuff?"

"Because it's the only thing keeping me from doing something I'll regret in the morning."

"I'd make sure you wouldn't regret it."

Nora laughed. "Yeah, no thanks. No amount of alleged awesome sex is going to be worth losing my badge."

"Alleged? I feel attacked."

"Well if the shoe fits—"

"And you wouldn't lose your badge. We'd be doing nothing wrong—"

"I think this is my stop."

Ethan held the door for her and stood facing her under the yellow streetlamp. He could see a rippling reflection of her apartment building's standard red brick in the puddle at his feet. The landscaping needed attention, and the windows had more towels and bedsheets than actual curtains.

"Is this a decoy address?" Ethan asked.

"No, and you're not getting my unit number."

Ethan frowned at her.

"Don't start. It has good security. Badass cop, remember?"

"Nora—"

"Thanks for the meal," she said, walking back toward the main entrance. "It would've been better with answers, though."

Nora pulled the car into her normal space at work and hit the stairs two at a time with a grin. She felt so good to be back, but that wasn't the only reason. Her evening with Ethan had put a smile on her face and left her wanting more.

As if on cue, her phone buzzed in her back pocket, a subtle reminder about him and how much he thought about her during the day. Smiling to herself at the memory, Nora strode into her department to a chorus of cheers.

Manillo leapt out from behind a shitty filing cabinet with a wide grin. "Surprise."

"Ah, shit, guys," Nora said, beaming herself. It felt so damn good to be back.

"Welcome back."

"How's the shoulder, St. Clair?" Price walked over, carrying a cake that looked like a child had drawn all over it with red icing.

Nora patted her shoulder once. "Rock steady. I can't believe the cake made it this long in this office."

"Don't worry, it won't make it through lunch," Manillo

said before everyone started roasting each other to bouts of laughter from the group.

Her phone buzzed again while she cut the cake, as was the rule in the department; he who gets cake cuts cake. While she ate and listened to what had happened while she was out on medical leave, Nora wondered in the back of her mind when she could get away to read her texts. Ethan had kept her up half the night, while they traded messages about nothing after they'd already had a forty-minute phone conversation about stupid commercials.

"What are you smiling about?" Manillo asked when they were back by her desk, which was covered in welcome back streamers and banners. "By the way, you got a present. Big box, heavy, must be expensive." His eyes went over to the white box with the red ribbon on the corner of the mess.

A quick glance had told her exactly what was in that box. How Ethan had managed to get the custom armor delivered without everyone knowing what was inside was yet another mystery. "None ya."

"Ouch," he said, grabbing his chest. "Shots fired. I can't remember the last time you told me that."

"Yeah, well, there has to be some mystery. You going out today?"

"Maybe. I have some reports to do and a briefing later. We'll see. Why?"

"Want company?"

"Not you with that shoulder. You know the rules."

Nora rolled her eyes. "I'm fine."

"Uh-uh. Desk duty for you."

"Go be pretty somewhere else," she said, shooing him out the door with a grin that he returned while sauntering out the door.

Nora waited in the quiet, listening to the familiar sound of the air conditioner running overhead, savoring the aroma of stale coffee and old carpet, smiling at her cheap computer on her desk covered with random papers and reports.

She slipped her hand into her back pocket and pulled out her phone, checking the text from Ethan.

Are you wearing your armor?

No, but I have it in case I have to go out, she answered, waiting for the response.

I hope it makes you think of me against your skin. I'd protect you myself if I could.

Well didn't that just send a shiver of delight down her traitorous body.

Yes, want to meet after work?

Thought you'd never ask, he answered.

Nora shoved the phone back into her pocket and read through her email, deleting most of what was there, as it related to things that had either happened already or never had anything to do with her in the first place. When she had finished, Nora headed toward the meeting with the shrink, as was the protocol for reentry. Most of the time, she needed to answer just a couple of standard questions to screen for trauma and other shit that had no business banging around a cop's head while on the job.

When do you want to meet? she typed while walking.

Right after work, but I have to leave tonight to go out of town.

Nora frowned to herself and typed back, glancing up once to smile at a few people in the hall.

Where are you going?

Need to run some errands. I'll be back soon, just a quick trip.

A cold pit set up in Nora's stomach, making the muscles tighten, turning the cake into a lump of unwelcome sugar. She reread his text again and again while rounding the corner to the shrink's office.

So you're not going to tell me? Nora hit send and hated

herself for even replying. Before meeting Ethan, she would've never felt the need to text a man back pushing for answers. She had learned that lesson the hard way right out of the academy. Now, all of Nora's relationships had revolved around one rule—she didn't need them. Replying to Ethan felt like she had let herself down, falling into her old habits of being too available, waiting to get hurt, vulnerable. What made it worse was that as she watched her screen, holding her breath for an answer, the cake rolled around in her stomach along with a feeling of regret.

I'll be back in a few days. Just a quick trip. If you must know, I'm going to visit my parents.

Nora read the information again and again.

"Lieutenant?" The receptionist looked at her through the window holding up some clipboard. "You'll need to fill this out."

Nora thanked her and took the clipboard to go sit on a cheap chair in the depressing waiting room. No wonder people needed a shrink when they came in here. The old magazines, gray walls with peeling wallpaper, and chairs that looked older than her gave a rough first impression.

Once inside Dr. Martha Lewis's office, Nora always felt better. The interior of the office had been updated with pastel colors that somehow all blended together. The good doctor matched her interior environment and looked like the type of person who did yoga, drank tea, and listened to cultured, soft music. Nora hadn't wanted to like her, but after only a few minutes, she found Martha to be rock-steady and smart. The woman also liked running and kickboxing, which she and Nora had bonded over. Nora stared at a skinny chick on a magazine with a perfect smile under the words, "The Magic of Self-Care," when she felt her butt buzz again.

Why didn't you answer me?

Nora's fingers practically flew across the glass of her phone.

You want an answer? Funny how life works, isn't it?

Clicking send, she rolled her eyes, and though she turned her attention back to the mindless task of circling numbers of a scale she didn't care about, Nora couldn't get a bad feeling out of her gut.

"Lieutenant St. Clair? She's ready."

Nora thanked the receptionist and walked back into the cloud-like office, where everything ran in perfect order, unlike the rest of the department. If there were offices in heaven, Nora pictured them like this one. She smiled and shut the door behind them before turning on a little white noise machine, which had always managed to make Nora tired. Martha sat down without making a noise, her hands folded. Plants adorned her office, each thriving in its own corner, looking chic and orderly. Seeing the plants had always given Nora a sense of peace.

"How are you?" Martha asked when they had sat down and reviewed her answers. "You look well."

"Does that mean I looked like garbage before?" Nora said with a smile that Martha returned.

"Not at all. You look particularly well."

Nora didn't shift in her seat, but the urge was there. Whenever she was in Martha's office, she always had the feeling the doc could read her mind, pulling all the secrets out until she confessed and confirmed.

"Must be all the rest."

"It suits you."

"Yeah, I guess. So, when can I go back? We good?"

Martha shifted her gaze away from Nora's face and down to her notes. Nora had to stifle a sigh of relief. She watched the older woman review her records, holding a perfectly sharpened pencil as she wrote in an elegant script. Her pants were a soft purple that matched her scarf and jacket. Each nail was buffed and polished to perfection. Nora curled her fingers under out of reflex. She couldn't remember what they looked like, or when the last time she had looked at them was.

"Your physical therapy report is good. They say you've been pushing it. Adding more weight. Doubling the reps."

"Yeah, want to get back into the game."

"I know, but if you push yourself too far, you know that this could have lasting consequences."

"I understand. I listen to my body." At least sometimes she did, but then she ignored it anyway.

"Well, I think everything looks good on my end. I'm going to close your file and then you'll just be waiting on when PT gives you the final thumbs-up."

"Awesome. Sounds great."

Martha didn't move.

"I'm interested to know what changes you've made since we last met." Martha shifted in her seat and looked at Nora, her blue eyes intrigued and curious.

Nora knew she was assessing, but at least with Martha, it didn't feel like she was in some kind of Petri dish.

"I mean, same old, same old."

"Sleeping more?"

Nora had to stop and think. "I guess a little."

"Drinking more water?"

"Not that I know of."

"You just seem relaxed."

"Well, I don't know what to tell you. It must be all of this time off."

At that moment, Nora's left cheek buzzed with an incoming text to her phone in her back pocket. The new chairs in this office amplified the sound in the silence.

Martha raised her eyebrows.

"It's nothing."

"You can check it. It's okay. I understand."

Nora shook her head. The last thing she needed was the doctor getting an eyeball of some weird muscle twitch that unraveled all of her secrets.

"No, it's fine, but I do need to get going." Nora stood, and so did Martha.

"I'd like to see you back in a month."

"Wait, I thought you said you'd closed out my file."

"Yes, but I feel like a follow-up to check in would be good. Sometimes trauma side effects can pop up later. In the meantime, keep doing whatever you're up to. It suits you."

Nora thanked her and left on that note without another word. She also fought the urge to pull her phone out until she was in the safety of her office.

I don't like it when you're unhappy.

Nora's fingers hovered over the glass. She didn't like this feeling of the need to respond. In truth, she didn't like being unhappy either. She'd been much more comfortable when her life had been boring and predictable, at least as predictable as a cop's could get. Nora didn't like having to answer to someone else, but the feeling to do so was there, urging her to keep the conversation going. Determined to avoid just that, Nora put her phone away, but within five minutes, she'd pulled it back out.

Then tell me why you're leaving now all of a sudden or you can keep your coffee. She felt like a bitch typing it, clinging to a man who refused to give answers to anything. The reply was almost immediate.

I have to visit my family. I already told you that.

Nora wanted to push. The investigator in her wanted to ask questions and demand he give her some answers. Another part of her, one that Nora refused to acknowledge, felt disappointed he wouldn't be around to visit.

She shoved up from her desk and paced, tempted to kick something, but didn't want to draw attention to herself. The cops in the department were a bunch of old ladies when it came to gossip. Once you told one person, the whole crew knew five different versions of it within one shift.

Pissed at herself for even being in this position, Nora shut off her phone, shoved it into her pocket, and sat down at her computer. Clicking a few buttons, she called up the file on the investigation from Mark Schmidt's house. Nora leaned in and started reviewing everything from the dead man's house, including the photos of Austin Brooks. She reviewed everything for hours until she had to admit defeat and leave with no more information than she had started.

CHAPTER 32

Ethan got out of the Escalade, leaving his packed suitcase behind with the driver who knew to wait for him. The blue sky above, green grass, and fresh air were a welcome break from the sticky, humid concrete jungle. He walked toward the two-story building and admired the trees and landscape, having seen it from the first planting. With every visit, Ethan had watched the bushes and trees grow to maturity.

Ethan tried to stagger his visits so that he wouldn't be remembered, taking care to avoid the same shift or the same day. He came no more than four times a year as he felt that was the most he could manage without being noticed. When he did come, he changed his name or the nature of their relationship just in case her family ever caught on.

He pushed through the front doors, taking the time to nod and greet the residents sitting outside or in the hallway. Walking up to the desk, Ethan did the usual check-in and let the nurse escort him down to the room he had visited so often over the past few years.

"So have you known Mrs. M for a while?" the nurse asked him as they walked down the hall.

"My father went to school with her, and they were very close for years." Ethan removed his jacket and draped it over his arm as they walked.

"That's sweet. I'm sure she'll be glad for the company."

"How has she been?" Ethan always asked the same question on every visit, each time worried about the answer.

"Pretty good. Has good days and bad days, but who doesn't? Mostly good though." The nurse pulled out a badge and held it against the pad to unlock the doors to the memory care unit within the nursing home.

"How are her bad days?" Ethan asked when they were inside, where the smell of fake-lemon-scented industrial cleaner overpowered anything else.

"Quiet. She doesn't engage, but most of the time, she'll say a few things. Hey, Mr. March."

An older man with a walker shuffled down the hall with the determined focus of an Olympian.

"Morning," Mr. March answered to both of them, not looking in their direction.

"Where are you off to today?"

"I have to feed my chickens."

The nurse stopped and turned toward Ethan with an apologetic smile. She put her hand on the man's walker and one hand on his back. "I'm just coming back from doing that."

Mr. March turned and faced her, his smile brightening with surprise. "You did?"

"Yeah, I took care of it for you this morning. They're looking great."

"Did you check the water?"

"Yes, sir. All topped up."

"Well, I'll be. Thank you so much."

"You're more than welcome. Are you okay to walk by yourself?"

"Oh, I need the exercise. It's good for me."

"Okay, well, you let me know if you get too tired. I'll come back and walk with you in a bit."

The nurse turned and gave Ethan a smile. "Mr. March was a farmer in his old life. Never gave up the habit."

"Do you have chickens?"

"No, we've thought about it, but we're stretched thin as it is. It's easier to keep the moment going for him." The nurse swung into a bright room at the end of the hall.

"Mrs. Malcolm, you have some company."

Sarah Malcolm sat in a blue recliner facing a window that looked out onto a butterfly bush. A few bird feeders and houses swayed in the autumn breeze. Her gray hair was cut short, close to her head. She wore a blue sweater that matched yellow pants and sat with her hands folded in her lap, relaxed and at peace. Sarah didn't turn around while the nurse murmured things about the weather and what the kitchen was serving for dinner. Sarah's eyes remained fixated on the birdhouses outside the room.

The nurse gave a smile and a quick nod before leaving them alone. Ethan stepped forward, wishing he could bring flowers or leave things in her room. The birdhouses had been a risk, but no one seemed to mind or even notice a stranger had sent them with orders to be placed outside Sarah Malcolm's window.

Her almond-shaped blue eyes, faded with age, watched the window, admiring the pleasant view of the garden. Ethan pulled a chair over to the rocker recliner and sat down to join her.

"Sarah?"

There was no response.

"It's Ethan."

Had he not been watching, studying her features, he would have missed the small muscle twinge above her eyes. Her eyebrows dipped as if unsure she had heard him correctly.

"I'm here."

Ethan reached out and took her hand, so small and delicate like it had been when they were in college. He could remember holding hands with her before, sitting on the green. She hadn't been a student, but instead, a local girl whose brother went to school there.

One day, Ethan had been walking to the library when he saw her sitting by a bush with her hand outstretched, a piece of meat in her fingers. He had stopped and learned of the litter of kittens living under a hedge Sarah had spotted after a recent visit with her brother. The pair of them had grown close, talking about everything from finance to history to hopes for the future. She would wait for him after every class. He would be eager to get to her.

Ethan had fallen in love one day at a time, watching her laugh in the sun, her golden curls gleaming in the light, bouncing with an energy that never stopped. Sarah had been his first date, his first kiss, and his first dance that meant something to him. She had wanted more, wanting a family, a house, and a future. So had he, but Ethan also knew better.

Before going to college, the seniors on Brightrock had to visit with the town council in the middle of the night for the special graduation prayer service. What had started as a routine turned into a ritual that had changed everything. Ethan walked in the old meetinghouse, the one that Mark Schmidt had destroyed, thinking he knew everything, and had left shaken to his core with the life-extending water flowing through him, marking him as different forever.

Sarah had stopped waiting. Even today, Ethan remembered the pain in his heart when she told him she was getting older and couldn't wait forever. He carried that memory every day, and until recently had never even considered being with another person.

He had sent cards over the years to her and her husband, kept all of the baby pictures, which turned into communion pictures, which turned into graduation pictures, wedding pictures, and then back to images of babies, but this time grandchildren. Because he hadn't changed, he stopped seeing her in person, preferring to speak on the phone from time to time, catching up and still finding comfort in the sound of her voice.

When her husband died, Ethan had gone to the funeral, paying his respects to the man that loved Sarah as he couldn't, sitting in the back alone. He had watched as she cried, tears falling down her cheeks with her daughter and son around her. He had started calling more after the burial, checking in once a month, talking for an hour. Several times Sarah had wanted to see him in person, meet up and talk about the good old days, but Ethan couldn't allow that. Not until recently.

The first sign something wasn't right was when she started repeating the same story. The second sign was her starting stories and forgetting where they were going. Ethan knew where it was going. Her mother had been taken away by the illness. Sarah had told him about it during one of their annual Thanksgiving talks long before she had buried her.

Like her mother, Sarah started asking for family members that were long gone, asking Ethan if he still knew about the cat from their time together at college. He had wanted to mention something to her doctor but knew it wasn't his place and had to trust her family to care for her in her most vulnerable time. When Ethan had called on Thanksgiving a few years ago, her daughter picked up and let him know the news, kindly giving him the address to the memory care facility.

Ethan had known this day would come, but hearing it had rocked him, throwing him off balance and flinging him into a deep well of desperation where he was powerless to do anything. He had rushed to Milford, Connecticut the following week when he was sure her family wouldn't be there and sat with her to visit. For once, he had been damn grateful for his anti-aging curse.

Sarah had smiled when she saw him still as she remembered. Her seeing him as a memory instantly transported them both to a time in college. She looked so frail and unsure, but her smile remained the same as she stood to greet him. Talking with her freely refreshed Ethan, melting years down to nothing. He could be open with her like no other. If she passed anything along about him, it wouldn't matter. The sad truth of their realities had presented a rare opportunity to share this time together before the window closed.

On the walls of the small room, smiling pictures of her children and grandchildren, now grown, looked out at him, each representing a life well-lived. Her hand in his own felt small, the bones visible under the skin. Like his last two visits, Sarah didn't speak. He wasn't sure she knew many words anymore. So instead they just watched the gifts Ethan had sent. Though he couldn't leave evidence of his visits in her room, the facility had enjoyed large anonymous donations along with general endowments for the improvement plan.

Ethan sat and admired the butterfly bush, holding Sarah's hand in comfortable silence, cherishing the moment when his mind wandered back to another pair of eyes who wanted to know about him. Nora reminded him of Sarah, but instead of pushing him to commit, she posed a larger threat, looking for answers he couldn't give her, probing, questioning, and assessing. Ethan squeezed Sarah's hand, smiling when she squeezed back in a silent goodbye.

CHAPTER 33

"Yeah, well, you can bite my ass." A drugged-out woman, fueled by rage and an extensive cocktail of prescription pills lunged back at Nora, who ducked just in time.

"Not interested," Nora said, grabbing one arm and hauling her toward a pair of officers to bring her into holding for the night.

"Good move. You can't get clocked this soon after being on medical leave." Manillo walked over in the shitty supermarket's parking lot sporting a helluva bruise on his cheek with a few scratch marks from some killer sharp nails. He shoved his hands into his pockets.

Nora shrugged. "So far, so good. Ready to roll?"

"Yeah, I gotta write all this shit up, and it's like the last thing I want to do. Kid had a birthday."

"Want me to take it?" Nora said.

"I'd feel guilty. I'm behind, like epic."

"It'll make me feel useful. I'm still on light duty. You've been doing a lot of the heavy lifting around here. Seriously, go home. I'll take it."

"You sure?"

"Are you going to keep asking or just go home?"

Manillo picked up a crushed beer can from the hot, cracked asphalt and tossed it in the back of his cruiser. "You know what? Suit yourself. If you're sure—I mean, I can stay if you're not up to it."

"Stop, get outta here."

He held up his hands in defense and headed to his unmarked car in retreat. "Adios."

Nora headed back to her own car and drove back to the station in the dark, letting her mind review the events of the day. Ethan had texted only once at the beginning of the day, letting her know she was on his mind again.

He had been on his trip for only a day, and yet her mind had abandoned her, wandering to think about him. She didn't want to worry about him. Didn't want him on her mind. Frankly, the whole thing pissed her off. She'd been much happier when she didn't have to occupy her mind with anything but work.

As if on cue, her phone rang in her pocket.

"Bout time you called me," she said, answering without looking.

"Um…Nora? This is your grandmother."

Shit, shit, shit.

"Oh, hey, Gram. What's up?"

"I haven't heard from you." The tone of voice was one she remembered from her teen years, even though the strict woman had ruled life with a keen eye and air of disapproval. "Wanted to let you know that our number hadn't changed and to remind you that we're invited to have dinner with the Harrises."

"Oh." Shit. "Yeah, I know. When is that again?"

"Tonight. You know, I don't know what's going on with

you. I tell you things, and you never seem to keep track. I think I need to get you a notepad."

"Jesus, Gram."

"Don't take that tone with me. It's not my fault you can't keep track of your social engagements."

Nora wanted to pound her head on the steering wheel.

"Alright, well, fine."

"Good. Also, I wanted to ask you, if it was convenient, I don't want to put you out, but do you think you'd be able to swing by Stop and Shop and bring dessert?"

"Yeah, I guess. What do you want?"

"Well, something light would be good. We don't need to get too fussy."

Nora finished up the call and thought about the drug addict sitting in jail tonight, and whether or not Nora would want pie or cake, before she got out of the car, stalking through the humid to get to her office.

Her phone buzzed again almost an hour later, and this time Ethan's name popped up with another sweet message that warmed her heart but said nothing about where he was or what he was actually doing.

Just thinking about you in uniform. I bet you look beautiful.

A smile twitched at the corner of her lips, but she didn't respond, focusing on finishing up the report and sending it off, making sure to copy Manillo.

You wearing my armor?

Nora glanced behind her, but she was alone at her desk, and no one would know about her texting. No one gave a shit when other people texted spouses and kids, but she still wasn't comfortable with the whole thing.

No.

Why not?

Not in the field.

How was your day?

Long, not over yet.

Anything exciting?

Nora thought about Ethan's response to her dodging a pissed-off swing from an addict.

The usual. You?

Silence. In the space between his answers, doubt grew roots and spread around her body, setting up shop first in her stomach before seeping in her hands, causing her fingers to clench. Minutes ticked by. Nora checked her phone and rechecked it. Nothing.

Turning back to her screen, Nora called up her old files and flicked through some information reviewing the information on Austin Brooks.

While her phone sat on silent on her desk, Nora settled in and scoured the information, looking for cracks. She wanted Ethan, had already spent two fantastic evenings with him, but he was lying.

By the time she was done, Nora's shoulder had more than enough, and a throbbing ache had set up shop in the center of her spine. Pulling some notes into her bag, she shut down her computer and called it a night. Walking back to her car, she pulled out her phone to find another message.

Visiting a friend I haven't seen in a while.

Anyone I know?

No, but she reminds me of you.

Nora raised her eyebrows and started the engine, rolling down the windows and setting the air conditioning to freeze.

Care to share why?

We used to date.

Uhhhh, not sure that's a compliment.

It is. What are you doing? I wish I was with you.

Where are you?

She sat watching the screen, and minutes ticked by. The air blasting out of the vents went from hot to ice cold. The phone sat dark. A familiar feeling of unease trickled over her skin. The gut instinct of a cop roared inside of her until she couldn't ignore it any longer.

With a curse, Nora killed the engine and stomped back inside to her desk. She pulled out the case file from what she had seen at Mark Schmidt's house. Going back to the beginning of why she first started looking at Brightrock in the first place, Nora pulled up the pictures she had taken of all of the printouts from Mark's old house, which had since been bulldozed and turned into a park.

Nora shuffled through the papers, looking for clues she might have missed.

"What did you know?" she asked a printout of Mark Schmidt's ID from two years ago, studying the files. "What did you find out about Austin?"

She flipped back and forth between pictures of Austin at the only school on the island. Wrestling coach at states, a quick photo snapped in the middle of the match. Blue ink circled a splotch on Austin's forearm, which Nora hadn't noticed before. She opened up her computer and clicked through her files to find the digital copy, enlarging it until she could get a good enough look at what appeared to be some sort of burn scar or birthmark.

Nora leaned forward, flipping through all of the printed photos, now scanning for blue circles. Mark hadn't left a single word or note as to why he was after Austin, other than the useless religious ramblings about devils, but this circle she had just noticed was a link she hoped like hell led to somewhere.

She made a mental note to call the librarians again, try to ask them if it meant anything. Nora had interviewed them before in hopes of finding a possible motive, but neither had noticed anything out of the ordinary, as Mark had only shared he was trying to find a long-lost friend.

On her second pass through, Nora saw it. The stack of papers fell out of her hand and shuffled on the desk. Muttering another curse, Nora shuffled through, searching for what she had thought she saw when she pulled an old navy photo out. The image was a little blurry and looked to be from World War II or something similar. Nora made another mental note to have a historian try and take a peek at the picture to identify a date and place, but it wasn't the content that caught her eye.

The man on the right had a striking resemblance to Austin, but the timing was all wrong, which is why initially Nora hadn't noticed a small blue ink circle on the man's fore-arm, where she could just make out the shadow of a blotch on the inside of his arm.

Scrambling now, Nora pulled up her computer files flicking through the lengthy list to find the match. Her phone on the desk buzzed next to her. She flipped it up briefly, hoping it was Ethan. Nora pressed ignore when she saw her Grandma. She'd call her back in a bit.

Nora opened the image on her screen and pulled the wrestling photo from a few years ago, alongside the one with the sailors. She zoomed in on the arms. Both had blue ink, both had a blotch, and both looked like the exact same person.

All of the breath left her lungs as she whispered, "What the fuck?"

CHAPTER 34

Nora's hands shook the entire way across town, through Stop and Shop, and to the Harrises'. Even the Boston Creme pie riding tight in the passenger seat did little to calm her nerves.

The photographs from Mark Schmidt's house suggested Austin Brooks had been alive since serving in World War II, which was impossible. When Nora had done a little digging into the records, the social security numbers matched and would've appeared normal unless you paired them with the candid newspaper shot from a high school state wrestling match a few years back. Austin hadn't aged one bit.

Nora had turned the possibilities over in her head a thousand times and still came up empty. Whatever was going down with Ethan's brother involved a major cover-up, one that messed with government records at the highest levels, which the last time she looked, was frowned upon, to say the least.

As she pulled into the Harrises' modest neighborhood, Nora tried to ignore the silence from her cell phone. Ethan had texted a few times but consistently refused to answer her questions about where he was and what he was doing. Her fingers twitched on the steering wheel as she itched to get back to her research and dig up some answers.

Nora pulled behind her grandma's Buick and hopped out, grabbing the pie and jogging up to the door. If she was lucky, she could duck out without issue in an hour. She'd hear about it from Gram later, but it wasn't anything she hadn't heard before.

Nora knocked twice and heard a familiar thick New England accent call out, "Door's open."

They'd known the Harrises for most of her life, as they lived next door to Gram. Tom Harris had been her dad's best friend practically since birth until he'd been killed in the line of duty. After that fateful September day, Tom had stepped seamlessly into the role of surrogate parent, doling out dad jokes and praise often.

"How the hell are ya?" Tom, wearing a Pats shirt, enveloped Nora in one of his giant bear hugs that always managed to make her feel like a teen at her dad's funeral.

"I'm alright." Nora held out the pie for inspection. "I brought pie."

"I like pie," Tom said, taking the dessert from her and holding it at arm's length so he could see without his glasses. "Oooh, this'll be a great addition to my cholesterol."

"You should have lemon in your tea," Gram called from the other room. "Cuts down on the fat."

"I hate lemon, and I like fat!" Tom called back in a voice too big for his tiny two-bedroom home. He winked at Nora and shut the door behind her. "How's your arm doing?"

"Out of the sling."

"Light duty?"

"You got it."

"Don't push yourself or you'll end up back on your ass," he said, pointing a finger in her direction.

Nora followed him into the dining room. "Yeah, yeah. I know. Hey, Michael."

"What's up?" Michael got up from a dining room table too big for the tiny space and came around to give her a hug. His green eyes were the same as their mom's, and though he was only eighteen, he carried himself like an adult, but then again, that's what grief did to a person.

Nora had been an only child for much of her life when her mom and dad were surprised with Michael. What had been a routine, healthy pregnancy, turned into a trade when Michael came home from the hospital and Nora's mom never did.

Gram, Dad, and the Harrises had rallied around Nora and baby Michael, even going so far as to make sure she had everything a girl could want, pooling what little money they had to buy her a car a few years later. Fate had struck again when her dad hadn't come home from duty—a traffic stop gone bad. Then, again, Tom stepped up double time, never replacing her dad, but always being there. Nora couldn't imagine life without him or Christine.

"Nora's here, and she's not in the sling," Tom called into the kitchen, as Nora bent down to give Gram a hug.

Tom's wife, a badass force to be reckoned with, came out of the kitchen in a huff. The former nurse gave Nora the steely eye. "Jesus, Nora, are you trying to push it? You were shot for chrissakes. Don't they have workman's comp anymore?"

Nora held up both hands in surrender. "They cleared me."

"Light duty?"

"Yes, ma'am."

"Desk duty?"

"Yes."

"Did you ask to go back?"

"No," Nora lied.

Christine narrowed her eyes with intense suspicion. "Good."

"Sit down, Nora, the potatoes are getting cold," Gram said, cutting through the air with a thin arm as if that settled everything.

They sat and ate, talking about nothing and everything, but mainly sports and people in the neighborhood. Nora let herself enjoy the pot roast and conversation, but all the while, her mind kept going back to Ethan—and Austin's pictures. This was big—maybe a career-making bust on whatever mob was running on Brightrock.

Her time with Ethan had been sweet and real. Everything Nora wanted. Then the brief interlude in the car had been enough to tease her desires and make a shiver pass over her even at the Harrises' dinner table.

"You alright over there? Don't need you going screwy on us after getting plugged." Tom raised an eyebrow in her direction, his fork hanging in midair as he watched her for visible signs of crazy.

"Tom, enough. We don't need to single her out," Christine said, but Tom still watched her like a hawk.

"I'm fine. Rock steady."

Tom didn't look convinced.

"Nora, I hate to be a bother," Gram said, leaning over and wiping her mouth with a napkin, "but I'd really like to try some pie. Do you think you could go cut some for us?"

Nora nodded, grateful for an excuse to escape Tom's perceptive glare. In the kitchen, she made quick work of the pie, slicing it onto paper plates and bringing it back out.

"Yeah, so I don't know," Michael said, pushing a clump of mashed potato around his plate with his fork. "I mean, you know. I don't need that kind of debt."

"Colleges?" Nora asked.

Tom cut off whatever Michael had been about to say. Her

heart went out to her brother. He could be a smart-ass, but he was smart as hell, and for some reason, the scholarships weren't coming.

"Notre Dame is a yes," Tom said, stabbing his pie with his fork and shoveling it in. "I told him all he has to say is when, and we'll load up the Buick and go take a look-see."

"Yeah, but I don't know. It's out of state."

"We'll figure out the money," Tom said. "You don't need to worry about that."

Gram nodded too. "I have some money set aside too. Been investing in Coca-Cola since your grandfather died."

"I'm in," Nora said. "I told you that from day one. I'll give what I can. It's just me and I can live pretty cheap."

"Don't count me out," Tom said. "I got my police retirement, and I can get more hours at the home center."

"Yeah, but that's for your insulin," Nora said, cutting him off.

Christine shook her head. "The cost keeps going up. Should be friggin' illegal."

"I'm fine. Doctors say I'm as strong as a horse. I have a little extra. We'll make it work."

Nora glanced at Michael, who stared at his plate with hard eyes.

"Where else did you apply?" Nora asked to get his attention.

He glanced up at her, the shame he was too young to carry clear. "Oh...you know, the usual places."

"Cornell, Duke, UMass, and Notre Dame, so far," Tom said, slapping an arm around Michael and giving him a shake. "And that's just the early applications. Smile, kid. You're smart, enjoy it. Half of the people on this Earth are dumber than the ground they walk on."

"But Tom, you've done so well for yourself," Nora jabbed.

Tom and Christine let out a howl of laughter while Gram chuckled, and Michael cracked a smile.

"Damn right," Tom said.

Nora left fifteen minutes later, with a bag of leftovers and strict orders to call everyone with updates on her arm daily, or else they all would be at her place. Walking back to her car, Nora slid out her phone, hoping to find a text from Ethan.

Her lips formed a thin line, and in a smooth move, Nora pulled a U-turn and headed back to the station.

CHAPTER 35

Ethan slid the phone back into his pocket, where he tapped it with his fingers through the wool of his pants. A gust of wind off the Boston Harbor tackled the constant humidity, letting fresh air rush into Ethan's lungs for the first time since he left his apartment building. He would have relaxed at the welcome respite, but his phone still sat motionless, like a deadweight in his pocket, its silence weighing on his mind.

Nora hadn't texted back when he'd said something glib and noncommittal. Lying by omission had been his go-to for years, satisfying the few people he needed to be close with. Nora wasn't buying that, though, and she never would. She was too smart and too persistent to be satisfied with mediocre answers that told her nothing.

The thought brought a smile to Ethan's lips as he surveyed the boats tethered to their docks in front of him. Gulls called to each other overhead, waving on the breeze in the fading sun. Ethan should've cut her out of his life and vanished like normal. Getting tangled up wasn't right for him or for his cause. Without him, Brightrock couldn't thrive financially, and he owed them so much.

A memory of his mom and dad fighting about what they could afford to serve for Ethan's seventh birthday dampened his smile. Born on Christmas the year the stock market crashed, Ethan had been used to thin stockings and hand-me-down clothes, but his seventh birthday had been the tipping point. While he never knew the details, the sounds of his parents' voices rising in the kitchen still haunted Ethan. He had clutched his old tattered bear and lay awake, wishing he'd never been born so the fighting about what to buy would stop.

Tears pricked at his eyes even now. Ethan sniffed and pushed them aside. He didn't remember what they had eaten, though he knew his parents would have come through. He and his family had it better than most of the country, but while the house they lived in was large, most of the money was gone. Ethan had often gone to bed cold, thinking of food.

The next memory came fast and still made him feel small. Ethan squeezed his eyes tight to try to keep it away, but all he saw was Austin in his navy whites waving goodbye to his teenaged younger brother. Standing by his parents, Ethan had felt scrawny, small, and worthless. The humiliation and pain burned his gut even now, and he gritted his teeth, opening his eyes to see his brother's beloved boat, which he'd named Bombshell, taxiing into the marina to pick him up.

Ethan waved his hand in greeting and made his way to board, slapping on a cheerful smile for his always energetic older brother.

"Looking sharp as usual," Austin said, reaching over to pull him into a hug. His accent came through loud, ignoring the letter r in the word sharp.

"You look like you almost shaved this week," Ethan said,

slapping his brother on the back. The gold dusting of what really was a pathetic excuse for a beard covered his jaw.

"Yeah, well, Caitlyn likes it."

"I like her, but there's no accounting for taste." Ethan ducked fast, so Austin's good-natured swipe sailed over him. "How's she doing? I'm surprised you didn't bring her with."

"She's great, and yeah, she wanted to come, but well, it's going to be a little crazy in a few months."

Ethan spun around so fast, he cracked his neck. "No shit?"

"Fucking A."

"Holy shit. Congrats."

"Thanks. Yeah, she wanted to come but has had a hard enough time keeping anything down. Didn't think the trip on the water would sit right."

"So you left her in that hovel of yours?"

"It's a cottage." Austin flopped into the captain's chair and tapped on his fancy GPS. Ethan loved boats, and he had to admit Austin's Bombshell was a beauty, but he never had the urge to own one for himself.

Austin fired up the throttle, backing them out of the marina. "Do you own all of Boston yet?"

"Not funny."

"Just Beacon Hill then?"

"Sadly, no."

"Just give it time." Austin glanced over at Ethan. "You look like hell."

"Thanks, bro. Nice to see you too."

"You need to take some personal time."

"Just got a new job, you know the drill. Probably a new name in a bit. Wait, who the hell are you now?"

Nora had mentioned Austin had died, but all that meant was a paperwork shuffle back on Brightrock. Austin would still be Austin to everyone on the island, but if he ever flew on a plane, he'd be whoever his passport said he was.

"I wanted Ignacio."

"Oh, I bet you did."

"Yeah, or like Horatio, Armistead, something cool."

"What did you get?"

Austin sighed. "Harold."

Ethan stared, slack-jawed before tossing his head back and roaring with laughter.

"Yeah, I know," Austin said, his mouth grim.

"I'm going to die if you tell me your last name is Potter."

"It's not."

"I'm going to call you Harry as long as you have that sorry excuse for facial hair."

"Yeah, whatever." Austin eased the throttle up again when they had cleared the marina. Boston looked beautiful in the fading sun behind them. Ethan could see the historic ships at the Boston Tea Party Museum on the water.

"We should make it in time for dinner before the renewal starts."

"Sounds good," Ethan said, not worried if they did or didn't. Timothy Chappell probably would find him and hold him verbally hostage about the portfolios for most of his decidedly short stay.

"Mom and Dad are thrilled you're staying for a few days. They talk about you all the time. Go on and on about the stocks and shit."

"Not me. Just the bull market," Ethan said, but his cheeks flushed with warmth.

"No, it's not. I shouldn't have that much money, and I have you to thank for that."

"Well, you should have enough to buy something other than that hovel you call a home."

"Dude, seriously. You're keeping everything going."

Austin kept talking, but Ethan wasn't listening. While his brother's words were meant as a compliment, their weight crashed onto Ethan's shoulders. He needed to provide and protect his family. As much as he wanted Nora, tangling with her made him feel like a traitor. If she ever found out the truth, it wasn't just him on the line, but everyone on Brightrock. His fingers traced the phone in his pocket, his only tie to Nora. With a grim frown, he stood, muttered something about a picture to Austin, and walked out of the forty-two-foot cabin cruiser's sumptuous cabin and out into the wind. He grabbed the railing and admired the view of Boston as it shrank with distance. Living a double life had never been easy, but he hadn't realized how hard it could get.

No, he could not allow himself to tangle with Nora. He needed to provide his family and community with a secure income. They relied on him. It was the only thing he could offer them, and if continuing to do so meant cutting ties, Ethan was more than prepared to do just that.

Though it pained him, Ethan slipped the phone out of his pocket, running his hands over the smooth surface. With a quick flick of the wrist, Ethan tossed his only connection to Nora St. Clair into Boston Harbor.

CHAPTER 36

"Are we there yet? I need to pee," Lizzy said, crossing and uncrossing her legs in Caleb's truck.

"Almost, I think this is the exit a few miles up," Caleb said shifting in his seat and taking off his sunglasses, tossing them on the dash. The fading sun had finally slid behind the mountains on either side of them in the Shenandoah Valley. The rolling green farmlands bathed in the sun's golden summer glow had been the perfect backdrop to their stories and songs as they had driven north.

They had been driving for the better part of two days and had finally crossed into Virginia on their way back to Brightrock, with a stopover to move out of her apartment and turn in the key.

An icy panic formed in the pit of her stomach at the thought of returning home. At least she had negotiated herself a week to return. Timothy Chappell was over a barrel and Lizzy knew it. She had called his bluff, at least for now. As long as she returned all would be forgiven in his eyes, until of course he realized what she was going to do.

Lizzy shifted in the seat again, her bladder testing physics, anatomy, and her patience all at once. Caleb looked over at her and smiled.

"I'm driving as fast as I can without speeding."

"Who's going to give you a ticket? The cows? C'mon, you can do better."

Caleb smiled again and just passed yet another of the countless eighteen wheelers on Interstate 81. Lizzy took a breath and watched him drive, soaking in the details around her. He looked so at ease, taking one day at a time behind the wheel of his truck. Before they had left, he had picked up an array of goodies from Maw Maw and Parrain, filled up the truck, checked the tires, and headed out.

They stopped once in Chattanooga but didn't have time to take in the sights other than the breakfast buffet at the hotel and the nearby gas station. They had been driving in Virginia for a while, but now were getting close to dinner about thirty minutes from their hotel and Lizzy's apartment.

"Finally, I thought we'd never get here," Lizzy said, wrenching open the door and making a beeline for the small, quaint country restaurant at the I-64 junction. Caleb must have hit the lock button twice, because she heard the truck's horn as she opened the door and made her way into the ladies' room.

A few minutes later she came out a new woman and found Caleb waiting for her while visiting with the hostess and admiring the pies on display.

"All better?" he asked with a grin, while they followed the hostess through a small, quaint dining room. The whole place reminded her of Maw Maw's house, had she lived in the country. The lace curtains, carved honey oak chairs, and the forest-green flowers everywhere felt rustic and homey.

"Much, but I'm still not used to this whole road trip thing," she said, pulling her hair around as Caleb held out her chair. She had tried to comb out her hair in the bathroom, but to her dismay still looked as though she had been sleeping in a car for two days. Just because she was on a road trip didn't mean she wanted to look like she'd been on a road trip.

"Y'all have a long drive ahead of you?" the waitress asked, setting two waters down.

"Two days down, at least one to go depending on traffic," Caleb said.

"You must be heading north," the waitress said with a knowing nod before she took their drink orders. "Fried chicken is our specialty, but everything's good and don't forget to save room for pie. Sounds like you need some home cooking to make the rest of the trip."

"What is home cooking exactly?" Lizzy said when she left.

Caleb drew his eyebrows together and let out a laugh. "What do you mean?"

"Like who decides that?"

"I guess it's regional," he said as the waitress came back with the two sweet teas and took their orders for fried chicken with all the sides as a sampler. "What would be home cooking for you? Chowder?"

Lizzy took a sip of her sweet tea and wondered what kind of diet she'd need to get on after her big adventure. "Yeah, lobster rolls, fried clams, what you'd expect, I guess. Parker House rolls are always a favorite on the table at my aunt and uncle's house for Thanksgiving. Missed them last year."

"You didn't go home?"

Lizzy shook her head and grabbed a piece of bread and butter the waitress had dropped off. If she was going to have to diet, she might as well enjoy herself now and with everything running through her mind, a few extra pounds was pretty low on the list of concerns.

"I had just left. Finally got some room to breathe."

"Did you like it better?" Caleb asked, taking a yeast roll for himself as well.

"I guess I thought I did but looking back all I did was order in food and hang around my apartment. Everyone else had somewhere to go. There were a few kids still around campus, but I mean, it's fine. Got what I wanted, went on a hike and toured around a couple orchards and whatnot."

Caleb considered her and then nodded before taking a sip of tea.

A few minutes later, the waitress dropped down two large plates heaped with steaming fried chicken and half a dozen small bowls filled with corn, mashed potatoes, and mac and cheese. They dug in together, each commenting on the food between bites.

"It's not like Maw Maw's but I'll take it. I haven't gotten the hang of frying. It's just not the same."

"I think it's so sexy that you cook."

"I'm glad. I love cooking. And I just like being at home. Feels natural." Caleb paused and watched her while he wiped his mouth.

"What?"

"I'm sorry you were alone for Thanksgiving. I was too last November, so I know what it's like."

Lizzy stopped and looked at him. He meant it honestly. "Like I said, I wanted some peace and quiet on my own."

He nodded, considering her. "Is that still what you want? To have your space?"

"I don't know."

"I'll understand. No pressure."

"No, no, it's not that. I guess I've just had a lot on my mind, but I hadn't really thought about it like that," she said. "I've wanted something for so long that when I finally had it, I just felt like I had to be happy. If I wasn't happy, I'd be letting everyone else down. I mean, this is what I had fought and wished for. I was a real pain when I didn't get what I wanted, so yeah, I guess I'm not sure. No? Maybe?"

Caleb nodded. "What do you think of when you think of being happy? Daydreams, that sort of thing."

"Ah Jesus, I have no idea. I'm all scrambled. What about you?"

Caleb blinked twice. "I think about my house, maybe putting in a new garden, cooking—just doing small, everyday things. Not just work, but more recently I think about you."

"Oh, come on."

"I meant what I said."

"You are persistent," she said, pointing her fork in his direction before diving into more mashed potatoes.

"Loyal, but unlike you I know exactly what I want."

"Yeah, I'm getting there, okay? It's just…complicated." She pulled her hands over her face. They finished the rest of the meal in silence, each with their own thoughts. Lizzy thanked the waitress when she came to clear the plates. They placed an order of apple pie à la mode to share and a couple of coffees.

"Let's talk about the apartment again. So what's the plan?"

"Came furnished down to the spoons. Just getting out my personal stuff should be easy. An hour, maybe two tops. It's only a one-bedroom. All I really have are more clothes and a few more toiletries. The big pain in my butt is the car."

"It's not at the airport?" Caleb said while fixing his cup of coffee.

"No, I left it at the apartment, hired a car, but driving isn't my favorite. I'd rather stay in the cab with you."

"That's high praise from someone who has complained about the state of the highway system since we left."

"Ha ha. Very funny. I don't even need it. I have my car back home. Caitlyn bought her own and stopped using mine, so it's sitting at Uncle Fred's now. I just picked this one off a lot when I got here."

"Whatever you decide to do is fine with me. Oh, hey now," Caleb said when the pie landed between them. "This looks great."

"Best seller, y'all enjoy. Here's the check, no rush, just take it up front when you're ready. I'll come back to check on you."

Caleb took a bite and motioned with his fork for her to do the same while he picked up the bill as if it was the most natural thing in the world. The sight of him in this little country restaurant on the side of a highway, smiling at her and grabbing the bill while reaching for his wallet, seemed like the most right thing in the world.

Caleb was wrong about one part though. She knew exactly what she wanted but was still working out how she could get it.

CHAPTER 37

Nora's dad had always said she'd been a tenacious child. Sitting on the ferry as it sped toward Brightrock, Nora watched Hyannis get smaller on the horizon as the warm sea breeze whipped by her. Part of her reason for the trip was her investigation, part was taking some personal time she was going to lose by the end of the year, and part was that she didn't like being ignored. All of it pissed her off.

Setting whatever feelings-crap she was dealing with aside, Nora's visit was long overdue. All the surface research she had done on Ethan checked out. Tax records, transcripts, and even his leases. What she couldn't find, though, was where he currently worked, and that bothered her. It was like Ethan Brooks had stopped existing.

With her shoulder the way it was, and the shrink report still ongoing, taking leave wasn't a problem. Whether she was at home on the couch or speeding toward Brightrock didn't change anything as far as she was concerned. What she did with her personal days was her own business. Not that she would know since she'd never had a reason to take personal days before.

The wind whipped through Nora's hair, tangling it into an angry frenzy of rebellious curls. She had elected to sit outside, hoping for some fresh air, but now regretted that decision in waves as the spray would hit her when the wind shifted. As if that wasn't bad enough, a father and son took pictures on the rail. The kid's happy expression while looking up at his dad made Nora look away.

Her own dad had been one of the greats. His sense of humor, wit, and no-bullshit attitude had taught Nora many of life's lessons before she could learn them the hard way, saving her a lot of grief. As she watched the dad in front of her crouch down by his son and point out where a dolphin had just jumped, Nora could hear her dad's old gravelly voice.

"If it smells fishy, but you don't see fish, guess what. There's fish there somewhere, whether you like it or not." Nora smiled to herself, pulling her lips in tight. She missed her old man like hell, the familiar feeling of pain setting up in her chest. All she had ever wanted to do was to make him proud.

A lot of people told her at the funeral about time healing all wounds, which was total horseshit. Grief crashed through someone's life, bringing devastation to everything. Over time, people rebuilt and daily life distracted from the pain more and more, but it still lingered behind everything like a dark shadow people couldn't see. All it took was a smell, sight, sound, or even something as simple as a can of soda or pack of cigarettes to pop the top of the pain, sending another wave of hurt crashing through everything again.

Tears pricked at her eyes as she watched the boy hop alongside his dad, holding his hand dutifully. She didn't know why she tried to hide the swipe under her eyes, but she did, pretending to scratch her nose. Nora puzzled over the evidence in her mind for the rest of the ride.

The call for Brightrock echoed through the loudspeaker above her, announcing their arrival. Nora stood tall and smiled to herself, grabbing her bag with her right arm and heading for the gangway. Whatever her personal feelings were, Ethan Brooks was hiding something, and she was about to figure that out for herself.

The ferry taxied into a picturesque harbor lined with giant granite boulders. Mansions on high looked out at the water while wearing their traditional cedar shingles. Yachts bobbed in the wake of the high-speed ferry as it slid toward the dock, which led to a row of shops and restaurants. Nora hadn't been here before, as another team had taken this part of the investigation. She had requested to go, but the department didn't see the need to spend money on a ticket when the case was pretty much a done deal. As they approached, Nora soaked up every detail, half expecting Ethan to leap out at her, and disappointed when he didn't.

A few other passengers disembarked with her, carrying large bags and hats for a day on the island now exposed by the media for what had happened last winter. The group of ladies with thick New York accents hauled overstuffed bags up to Kate's Diner, pausing to take a picture of the quaint waterfront buildings. Gulls called overhead in the late afternoon sun. The whole scene looked like a freaking postcard for New England tourism.

Nora soaked up the scenery as she walked the few blocks to the Cedar Inn, the only place on Brightrock that offered overnight stays. The large, covered front porch of the grey house faced the water with rocking chairs positioned for guests to take in the views. Red shutters matched the red door, but the real gem was the turret to one side. Nora hopped up the steps and let herself in the door, a faint bell announcing her presence.

The interior was painted yellow with bright white trim that reminded Nora of a lemon cake, except the inside smelled like banana bread. As she walked into the living room, the old oak floorboard creaked beneath the patterned rug. A breeze lifted the white sheers of the windows looking out to the porch. All of it looked elegant but relaxed in an easy way that invited anyone to just sit on the couch and chill.

Nora flopped down to do just that when a man with silver hair walked around the corner.

"You must be Ms. St. Clair."

Nora popped up off the sofa like a kid caught doing something wrong and clasped the outstretched hand with her good arm.

"Lieutenant actually, but you can call me Nora."

"Thank you for your service. I'm Alex. Ferry must have just come in. Sorry, we didn't hear you. Sal's in the garden."

Nora followed him over to a small alcove where she signed in and passed her credit card over to pay for the stay, hoping it wouldn't get declined.

She let out the breath she'd been holding in a rush when a small beep started signaling a successful transaction. The department wasn't paying for this, and the nightly rate had been way out of her budget, to say the least. She tried not to think of the money that could've gone to Michael's school and considered the rest of her lean savings account would have to do. She had to find Ethan and get to the bottom of whatever this was. Michael could have everything else.

The little printer started spitting out a curling receipt. Nora signed it in a scrawl just because and passed the pen back over to Alex, who started talking her through where everything was and what to expect for breakfast.

Nora nodded and smiled as he directed her over to a wine fridge where a cheese plate with some crackers had been laid out on the impressive island in the kitchen, then walked her over to a stunning back yard, manicured to a tee, where a jewel of a pool sat nestled in the lush paradise.

"Can I get you anything in the meantime?" Alex said as she followed him up a narrow staircase to her room.

"I'd love a map of the island if you have one?" Nora said.

"Sure thing."

Alex let her into a suite the size of her whole apartment that overlooked the bay outside. Warm yellows and light blues bathed in the light created the perfect space to curl up with a book and relax watching the seaside. The sheers covering a large window drifted a little in the breeze shrouding a window seat, plumped with pillows. Nora rounded the corner and looked in at a bathroom complete with a tub she wouldn't use and a large glass shower that had more showerheads than she knew what to do with.

"Here's the map," Alex said from the doorway. "We don't have many other guests right now, so just make yourself at home and text us if you need something and we've gotten lost in the house."

He smiled, crinkling his cheeks. Behind his artsy modern glasses, Alex's eyes sparkled with laughter and warmth. Nora liked him, and it didn't hurt that he and Sal clearly had a slice of heaven on Earth and were willing to share it.

It was too bad Nora wasn't here to relax. She was here to get answers.

Nora walked out of the Cedar Inn a few minutes later, map in hand, badge on belt. As she trudged along in her boots over the brick sidewalk, the hot August sun blazed down, melting everything in sight. Sandals probably would've been better, but Nora hadn't come to relax.

The gulls floated overhead on the picture-perfect New

England day in the quaint seaside shopping area. Boats sat like white pearls in the sparkling, dark-blue bay. As Nora walked, she noticed all of the manicured beds and polished signs. Everything about this place screamed Perfectville, which made her wonder what it was hiding.

She turned the corner and walked down to Kate's Diner, wondering if a few of the guys she worked with had been right. Maybe she had been on the job a little long, started to go too hard, lose perspective. In her defense, she did take time to have the occasional dinner with her crazy grandma and brother—at least, she had before she'd met Ethan. Once they'd started talking, Nora wasn't calling home as much.

Reaching the diner, Nora pushed through the door, ringing a bell above her. The inside looked like a typical tourist New England diner, down to the lobster traps on the wall. Nora could give points for the extra attention to detail, noticing the rich wood paneling that gave the interior a feeling of being in the hull of an old whaler. Some of the ropes even looked to be the real deal, no doubt picked up from an antique dealer somewhere on the island.

"Have a seat anywhere you like. I'll be right over with a menu," said a cheerful waitress, bustling by, holding two cups of coffee.

Nora slid into a small booth on the side and leaned back to observe the people around her. As the waitress hustled around the different tables, Nora could pick out the tourists from the locals. She pulled out her notebook and made a few notes when a menu slapped down on the table, followed by a glass of water.

"Hi there. Coffee, tea, soda?"

"Coffee. I don't need cream and sugar." With a quick nod, the waitress was gone in a flash. Nora appreciated a woman on a mission and flopped open the menu to look at the usual fare.

"In town for the weekend?" the waitress said, plunking a mug of coffee down with a little silver bowl filled with creamer.

"A bit. Following up on some investigations. I was hoping to meet Austin Brooks." Nora knew it was a shot in the dark and watched for any tell.

The waitress flipped open her folder and jotted down an order, not meeting Nora's eyes.

"You're a bit late. He's passed on."

Nora put her surprised face on, making sure to add in a sharp intake of breath for good measure. "No, that can't be. I talked to him a few weeks ago."

The waitress still didn't meet her eyes, now fussing with a pen in her apron.

"Yeah, it came as a bit of a shock to all of us."

"Do you know if he has any family or friends I could talk to? Maybe I could visit his grave?" Maybe she could trip up someone about the cremation.

"They scattered his ashes at sea, just like he would've wanted. You know Austin?"

"I had some questions for him about the terrorist attack a few months ago."

"Well, his parents live here, and I think his brother may have just gotten back into town."

"I'd love the chance to talk to them. Is their number listed?"

"No, but if you have a card, I can pass it along."

Nora thanked her and pulled out a nondescript card with just her name and number, no need to mention rank yet. The waitress studied it before slipping into her pocket and heading back to the kitchen. Sipping her coffee, Nora added to her notes.

The waitress knew more than she was letting on, but then again, there was no way this tight-knit community was going to give information to a random washashore being nosy. If Austin had died and been sprinkled into the bay, there was a dead end, but Nora's gut instinct told her it all was too perfect.

The waitress bustled by and set down her plate with what turned out to be a pretty delicious Reuben and fries. When the waitress came back, Nora was ready.

"Have you seen Austin's brother around recently?"

"He came in the other day, but I haven't seen him since."

Nora smiled to herself.

"You seem real interested in this. You a cop?"

"Depends. Is there a discount?"

The waitress let out a bark of laughter, laced with an accent only a lifetime in New England could earn.

"Sure. Why not? Love to support the men and women on the force. Had a ton in here after the bombing. Went through almost triple the amount of normal coffee. Paid my tax bill just from that month."

"Yeah, I'm just following up on a few loose ends. When did Austin pass?"

Now the waitress stopped and stared off into space. "Funeral was a maybe a month ago. I remember I bought a new dress. Couldn't get into my old one. Too much sampling the pie."

"Yeah, I get that. How'd he die?"

"No one really said. Heard a rumor it may have been an overdose. Never would've thought Austin would be that type, but then you just can't tell these days."

"Had he been addicted? Struggled in the past?"

"Nah, boy knew how to drink, though. I think he might've gotten on those pain meds for some old injury, but like I said, that's just a rumor. The family never said."

Nora asked a few more questions, but if the waitress

knew something else, she didn't budge. Thanking her and promising to return, Nora left to poke around elsewhere.

As she let the heavy wooden door close behind her, Nora hoped like hell she would run into Ethan. Of course, for investigative purposes only.

CHAPTER 38

"To your health." The chorus of voices echoed up to the rafters of the new town hall. Traditionally, the renewal ceremony had always been completed in the old, original meetinghouse, but as it had burned to the ground, the council had no choice but to relocate until enough funds could be raised to rebuild. Not that money would be an issue, but still, the council loved to overcomplicate everything, no matter how much Ethan managed in their portfolios.

Ethan swallowed the precious water, feeling the familiar warmth curl through his chest and stomach as it traveled down. Austin stood next to him. Caitlyn had stayed at the house. Being pregnant, she wouldn't partake of the water to maintain the average growth rate of the fetus. There was still so much they didn't understand about the water that kept them all alive, but what they did know, the people of Brightrock followed like gospel.

"Where's Lizzy?" Ethan whispered over to Austin.

"I texted her, and she said she couldn't make it," he answered.

"Didn't she miss the last one?"

"No, but the time before that, yes."

Ethan blew out a breath. "She's getting too comfortable with that."

"You know what it's like trying to talk to her about it. Stubborn as hell."

Mom glared at them both, shushing them into silence as the council droned on about the new building plans and a possible issue with securing the permits. Something about the board of health.

Ethan tried to stretch his shoulders while confined to the folding chair on the aisle. He hadn't heard from Nora but then again, why would he? His phone was at the bottom of Boston Harbor. His fingers itched to dive into his pocket and fire off a quick message to her. He had never had an issue with getting close to anyone before, but now he craved her like an addiction. Though he knew he needed a clean break, Ethan still intended to check up on her from afar once he was back on the mainland. Even if he couldn't be with her, he could still make sure she was taken care of. He had always been good at that sort of thing. It was easier for him to love people from afar.

The meeting adjourned, and the din of the crowd rose to fill the space. People shook hands, visited, and passed out trays of cookies, while the old-timers headed straight for their cars and bed.

A large, meaty hand clapped Ethan on the back. "Damn glad to see you, kid. I've been watching the market like a hawk. Nothing good, is there?"

Ethan smiled a broad grin at Alex, who he had known for his whole life. "Yeah, it's a little rocky, but we were due for a correction. Bull markets don't last."

"Never long enough. So how's Boston? Heard you moved from New York."

"It's going alright. How's the inn? Guests overrunning you since all the news?"

"Yeah, that's why I came to talk to you. We got one now. Kate at the diner said she was asking about Austin. A cop from the mainland."

Ethan's blood froze in his veins. A mix of excitement, rage, and shock flooded him. He thought if he ignored Nora long enough, she'd fizzle out, all pissed off at him for eternity. Apparently not.

His eyes narrowed, and he forced himself to keep his voice steady. "Do you think I might be able to speak with her alone?"

Alex sucked in his lips, so his mouth was a thin slash. He nodded slowly. "Yeah, I think you might want to do that. She seems ah, pretty determined. Tenacious really."

An hour later, Ethan stomped up the glowing steps to the old Victorian bed and breakfast he and his brother had helped restore. Sal and Alex really did do a beautiful job in managing the place, getting almost perfect reviews online. A feat in itself.

Ethan pushed through the door Sal had assured him would stay open despite it being well after midnight, hearing the little tinkle of a bell above him. The inside still smelled of banana bread and looked the part. The lights on the bookcases next to the fire cast a soft glow in the dark and cozy space. The floor squeaked beneath him, just as he wanted it to. He had no doubt Nora was up, waiting to see if he would show, searching for answers she wouldn't find.

Ethan circled slowly around the inside of the inn, admiring all of the elegant furnishings while playing with the numbers in his head, trying to calculate estimated expenses and profits, when he heard the soft creak on the stairs. He cocked a smile to himself, steeling himself for the fight that was to come. He could just imagine Nora now, no doubt with her gun either in her hand or holstered on her somewhere she could grab it in a flash.

He stopped moving and listened for any sound, the silence magnifying in the dim light. Minutes ticked by, and he almost gave up, when another creak gave her away.

"Out for a stroll?" Ethan asked, still facing the empty fireplace.

"Isn't it a little late for you?"

"I keep late working hours." Ethan spun slowly on his heel to meet her steely gaze.

Just as he figured, Nora walked down from the stairs, primed for a fight. To someone who hadn't studied her, Nora would look relaxed in her old police academy T-shirt and baggy sweatpants, but Ethan could pick out how she planted her bare feet on the rug, folding her arms in front of her. If he had been a burglar, he had no doubt she could've dropped him where he stood.

"Even on your days off?"

Ethan didn't bother to shrug. He was done playing the game.

"Why did you follow me?"

"Who said this had anything to do with you? I'm not entitled to a little time off?"

He cocked his head to one side. "Would that hold up in court?"

"I have a sterling record and haven't done anything wrong."

"Why are you snooping around?" Ethan took a step forward. "Asking questions about my brother? About me?"

"You know I have an investigation to run."

"It was my understanding that your role was finished."

"Funny thing for a guy to say who a few days ago couldn't wait to get his hands on me."

The anger pinched inside of him. "Nora, why did you come here?"

"You're part of my investigation. Still a person of interest—"

"No, Nora." Ethan took another step forward, closing the distance between them. "I don't think that's it."

"I'm just doing my job." She stared at him, narrowing her gaze until her eyes were like cold, judgmental slits.

"Is that so?"

"I'm a damn good cop."

"I can see that. You have me right where you want me. You're so smart, so tell me. Now what?"

"Excuse me?"

Ethan threw up his hands. "You followed me. You got me. You win. So now what? Am I under arrest?"

Nora frowned. "What in the hell are you talking about?"

"You had just gotten back to work—"

"Light duty."

Ethan nodded. "And now suddenly you're here to relax? On the exact same rock where I happen to be."

"Small world."

"I don't think so."

Nora glared at him. "What are you suggesting?"

CHAPTER 39

"Why did you come here?" He held up a hand when she started to speak. "And before you start, I want the truth." His hazel eyes met hers and tugged at something inside her.

"Funny use of words. I needed—"

Ethan took a step forward, closing the gap between them.

"What did you need?"

"I just wanted to know for sure what happened."

Ethan stopped just before Nora, his chest inches from her face. "I don't believe you."

"I'm a badass cop, remember?" Nora said, tilting her face up to meet his.

"So, you didn't come here to find me?"

Nora blew out a laugh. "That would be a desperate move."

Ethan's arms wrapped around her, and Nora didn't fight the touch, enjoying his warm hands on her back.

"Just interested in my dead brother, huh?"

"Yep," she said, closing her eyes now, so she wouldn't be

tempted to look at the perfect cupid's bow of his mouth in front of her.

"You wound me." Ethan sounded like he was smiling. He pulled her in close, so she could smell the faint tinge of his cologne.

"I didn't even try yet," Nora said, leaning her head against his chest.

"You know it's a shame you're just interested in a dead man when you have one right in front of you who has so much more to offer."

"Are you trying to change the subject?" Nora gave him a wry smile as he brought his mouth down to her. The second he made contact, she knew she was done.

His lips teased her own, soft and warm. He didn't pressure her, and she could feel his own amused smile melt away as the kiss deepened. Both of them shifted closer. Their bodies settled into each other, merging, so they were flush together. Ethan's hands moved along her lower back, guiding and pressing her into him and his strength. Nora reached up and pulled on the back of his neck, urging him forward and down into her. She wanted more, craved everything he could give her.

Ethan obliged, pulling her closer still. His tongue met her own, and together, they explored each other in a familiar dance that they both knew. Nora tilted her head to the side, pulling herself tighter against his hard body, feeling the heat inside her starting to tingle. She wanted him now and wasn't willing to wait.

Dropping her hands low, Nora slid them toward the hard length against her belly. Reaching him, she stroked his length through his pants, smiling against his mouth when he went still. She kept going, driving the pace in a steady rhythm, wanting him to beg through harsh panting. Her nipples tightened through her T-shirt, boring into his chest. Heat rose in her core as she continued to stroke while teasing him with her tongue.

As if he had heard her in an ancient way, Ethan's hands slid under her shirt and up her back, warming her skin with his own. One hand stayed behind to steady her as the other came around to her front, splaying his hand across her belly before traveling up. Nora felt herself turn to the side in his hands but stayed focused on her own rhythm. Ethan cupped her breast and kneaded in a gentle but firm way. It wasn't until he brushed a thumb over her nipple that her knees almost buckled. Ethan steadied her against him. His mouth took control, pushing in and exploring.

Her hands faltered when he started a pace of his own. Over her already blazing breast, Ethan sucked in a breath when he felt the change and pressed her to him again. His length strained into her belly, as he eased her down onto a sofa.

"My room," she said against his mouth.

Ethan gave her a grunt through panting breaths before pressing his lips hard against her as if branding her before pulling away.

"We're alone," Ethan said as he skimmed his mouth against her jaw, before moving to her neck below her ear. Nora felt his stubble scratch against her skin and arched her back to give him more access, urging him on. Ethan slipped his arm out from behind her and brought it around to her front as he teased both of her breasts under the old T-shirt, making her burn with need. Ethan shifted away from her hands and pulled her shirt up, revealing her breasts to his mouth. Sucking and lapping at her while working her with his hands, Ethan drove her to the edge, making her eyes close in bliss as he caressed and worshiped her as if she were divine.

His mouth moved to the other side, closing on the nipple,

making her squirm for his attention. Through her lashes, she could see the outline of his head and broad shoulders covering her in the generous living space. She split her legs to give him access on the now too-small couch, and he brought his hard length right against her burning core. She wanted more and squirmed with need against him. Answering the call, Ethan slipped a hand down her sweatpants and dragged a finger against her wet slit, making her jolt against the pillows.

In payback, he worked at a steady rhythm, giving her enough to pant with need but pulling back right when she wanted it most, working her into a frenzy. She gripped his head, trying to push or pull him to give her what she needed, and when he didn't budge, she moaned his name in a whispered rush, begging him.

Ethan's finger entered her, stroking and pressing with the heel of his hand while the other hand teased one breast and he lapped at her other nipple in agonizingly blissful torture. The heat between them burned. Nora clawed his shirt, wanting his skin against hers, but he didn't move other than slipping another finger inside her center where he pulsed against her, bringing her to the edge.

Her heart raced. Every muscle tensed against him. Nora watched him through lidded eyes as he covered her with his body, driving her to new heights, leaving her totally in his control so that every breath depended on him and his being as he fueled the fire within her body until it was raging against her skin. With a twist of his hand, he pressed his thumb right at her slit and shattered her. Nora flew apart. As the waves of passion rocked her, she clung to Ethan's shoulders, until the energy left her body limp in his arms.

Nora lay with her eyes closed as her breathing resumed its regular rate. Ethan tucked a piece of hair behind her ear, and when she opened her eyes, she could just make out the hard lines of his face in the dim light as he watched her. The emotion in his eyes struck her to her core. Her heart softened toward him, and she knew at that moment she would never find someone like him again.

Someone who could care for her with such passion and grace. There were no stained T-shirts or cheap fast-food dinners in a bag. Ethan believed in drinking a cup of coffee, sitting down and listening to refined music that was good for the soul. Everything about him that would have made her bristle, now made her long for his world and what made him different. He accepted her and everything she brought with her. He didn't ask, only gave. He cared for her, and if she was honest she was catching feelings hard, which would only make leaving so much harder. She could allow herself this night of passion, but in her heart, she knew this would be the end. They were too different, and he had too many secrets. One night to remember him by and then her life could get back to normal.

Nora brought her hand up and traced his jawline, bringing her fingers to trail along the length of his neck. Her fingers skimmed down his skin until she reached the collar of his shirt.

"I have two things to say. I'm on the pill and I want to see you," she said, her voice low and breathless.

"Bedroom. Now." He reached out and helped her off the couch before following her close up the stairs like a predator full of tense, male energy.

Nora smiled a cat-like grin, all her inhibitions gone. As they walked into the room, Ethan tapped the light switch, and brought the lamps on either side of the bed down low, to a dim glimmer.

"You're beautiful."

"I want to see you," she repeated, watching him.

Ethan's eyes burned into her own and made quick work of the dress shirt and pristine T-shirt underneath.

Nora drank in the sight of his chest in the low light. He had never mentioned working out, but it was clear he had spent some time in a gym from the taut muscles roping around his chest and stomach.

"All of you," Nora said, still looking at his waist.

"Your turn," Ethan said, his voice lower than usual.

Nora cracked a sly smile. "Nothing special." She pulled her shirt over her head and slipped out of her sweatpants and turned to face him. His eyes dropped from her own to take in the sight. His face melted, letting the hard mask he always wore drop away. He looked younger, giving Nora a glimpse of what he must have looked like as a boy, reverent with gratitude on Christmas morning. The innocence vanished when he studied her shoulder, the mark from the gunshot still an ugly blotch of healing skin.

"You're perfect," Ethan said, taking a step toward her.

She shrugged and nodded back toward him. "You're still covered."

Ethan stopped and with quick fingers, released his belt and popped his fly. The jeans fell to the ground.

God, the man could be on a calendar. In tight black shorts, he stood before her, a testament to the potential of the male figure.

"Still see clothes."

Ethan cracked a smile and slid them off, his full length popping free, pointing right at her. He moved toward her with that same predatory focus and gripped her hard around the small of her back, searing their mouths together in hot, impatient need. Their bodies tangled before collapsing on the bed.

He pulled her down onto his mouth, sliding his tongue to meet hers as they had in the car. He broke away from her mouth and melded kisses along her jawbone, down to the skin under her ear, before pulling her ear lobe in his teeth, giving it a gentle tug.

Nora moaned a little in response, her legs straddling him, her core rubbing against him. Her hands roamed over his body, kneading muscles as they went. Her fingernails dug into his skin, and she hoped like hell they left marks. She wanted her hands all over his body, something that could imprint this passion on him like a tattoo he could never lose.

Her hand clasped his length, making him go rigid before straining with need, tossing his head back away from her. She smiled to herself when she heard an audible sigh. She backed down the bed, trying to get off him, bring her mouth down to his waist.

Ethan grabbed her by the waist and hauled her up. For all her strength, he tossed her on the mattress and rolled over her.

"Didn't think you'd turn that down," she said breathlessly.

"I want to make you scream." He marveled at her.

Ethan brought his mouth down in a rush, tasting, licking, kissing, nipping every inch of her, paying particular attention to the tender, yellow bruised skin around her injury, while making sure to support his weight, so as not to crowd her. He kept the kisses going along her collarbone, before Nora arched her back, the invitation clear. Ethan let his mouth trail lower, planting kisses on her stomach, which tightened in anticipation again.

Ethan smiled when she squirmed to bring herself up to his mouth. He ran one hand along the skin of her drenched folds. Nora cried out for more, her pelvis leaving the bed, pushing into his hand. He slipped two fingers in her and caressed more breath from her, driving her until she panted his name in the form of a plea.

When she called out again, he circled around her core, seeing the waves of mounting pleasure in her face. Nora begged for more. Ethan lowered his mouth and shattered her, driving her into a frenzy that seemed to go on for an hour.

When the convulsions had stopped, Nora felt his hand languidly caress her body, and heard him murmur sweet words under his breath.

Ethan stared down at her with a look that could only be described as complete adoration. She let her lips form a slow smile, and when she raised one eyebrow, he returned the gesture.

Ethan rolled onto his back as she gripped his straining length. Nora worked him and showed no mercy, making him pant and strain just as he had done to her.

Nora bent her head low and covered all she could of Ethan in her mouth, reveling in his excited gasp and feeling his head fall back onto the mattress. She pushed him hard, her head and hand working him in a crazed rhythm until every muscle in his body was straining for release.

"Oh God, baby, I can't go much longer."

Popping free, Nora sat up and drank in the sight of him sprawled out across the bed in the moonlight, a magnificent prize for the taking. Ethan leaned up, his eyes blazing with a fiery passion, and flipped Nora over, taking control.

As Nora gasped for breath, Ethan released her just before she could cry out his name, denying her the pleasure she craved. With a quick thrust, Ethan shifted and crashed into her, expanding and stretching her core until Nora thought she might tear under his massive size. She held onto his arms and shoulders, her nails cutting into him as he drove her hard, riding her, and making every muscle quiver and tense. Nora gripped him, urging him on, stretching her legs to give him better access, giving in to his power and raw male control in a surrender she had never felt before.

She rose higher and higher, dragging in breath to fuel the blazing fire within her when with one final thrust, he sent them both over the edge into a dark blinding love.

CHAPTER 40

Minutes or hours later, Nora didn't know, her breathing resumed a reasonable pace. Ethan was lying on top but was carefully arranged so as not to crush or trap her. His breathing was steady and deep, and in the dim light of the dark night, she could make out his eyelashes resting on his cheeks. She watched him, combing her fingers through his hair, wondering what it would be like to have this, have him, forever. He looked so young and innocent asleep, the lines on his face the only clue to his age, no doubt carved by worry about business and his family.

Whatever had happened to his brother, and whatever he couldn't tell her, Nora could read in the thin lines carved into his forehead, that stuck out when he was resting and his guard was down.

Ethan sucked in a long breath and shifted his weight. His eyes opened slowly, once and then twice before he turned to see her. A wide smile lit his face full of love, reminding Nora of how her family had looked at her with pride and affection.

Tears pricked the corners of her eyes, and she sucked in her lips to try and hold them off. Not fast enough.

Ethan frowned, his eyebrows drawing together.

"Hey, what's wrong?" He smoothed her hair on the pillow while she tried to find the words to explain.

She sucked back in a breath, fast and hard. "Nothing, I'm good."

"I didn't hurt you, did I?" Ethan scrambled off, making her feel empty and cold.

"No, no. I just wondered what it'd be like if this were forever."

Ethan's look of concern was replaced by shock and then the innocent joy broke her heart.

"I'd love that, you know."

"Would you really?" Her voice hovered above a whisper. A fear swirled around the room that someone would hear them, and the jig would be up. She'd be caught and brought in for questioning regarding this inappropriate relationship but through the fog of fear, a glimmer of hope for a life she'd never dreamed possible shined through the grey clouds.

"I would. We could, you know."

Nora opened her mouth and closed it again, unable to find the words to describe how much that vision warmed her chest and made her ache for that reality. It had been so long since she had held the hope in her heart that she could find that love with someone else. Walking home after a day at work into Ethan's arms, where he'd be sprawled on the couch or working in his office in sweatpants while on the phone. The vision of them eating Chinese in front of a Red Sox game made her want to crack wide open under her rising emotions. She wouldn't have to be alone anymore.

"Ethan—"

"Just think about it," he said, shifting to his side and nuzzling her under her ear, just how she liked it. A strong arm snaked around her middle, pulling her to him. In the dark, their bodies tangled together in a languid dance of passion and unspoken emotions.

When they were finally sated, Nora propped herself up on her good arm and looked at Ethan. The moonlight streaming through the window of her bedroom hit Ethan's exposed chest, displaying an impressive set of muscles under flawless skin. Nora knew how perfect it was as she explored every part of his body, finding the closest thing to a scar on his back, near his ribs. A red blotch of skin the size of a quarter was visible on his back from his side, as if it was perpetually about to fall and slide away. Finding it now, Nora ran her hand over it, feeling Ethan stiffen as her finger touched it.

"Just like your brother," she said.

Ethan turned his head to look at her. His face looked so perfect, her heart could've broken on the spot. "What did you say?"

"Off the record."

Ethan frowned, a line forming between his eyebrows. "What?"

"Tell me off the record. I don't need to know where Austin is now and don't lie to me again because it'll just piss me off all over. I don't believe he's dead."

Ethan didn't move, just waited for her to continue. Not confirming, but not denying either. Nora took that as all she needed to continue.

"What did Mark Schmidt find out?"

"I don't know," Ethan said. "I was in the city when the attack happened. I never met the guy."

"I know that, but you have a feeling."

Again, Ethan said nothing. Alright, she could play this game.

"Had they met before?"

"Not that I'm aware of."

"Mark Schmidt had his dad's navy records in his house. With them, we found an old navy picture. Schmidt's dad is in it, and the guy next to him looks like he could be Austin's twin, I mean seventy years apart, but you know. Apparently, there was a guy on the ship with the same name as Austin."

"But as you said, seventy years apart," Ethan said with a note of caution in his voice.

"Right, but Mark Schmidt was reportedly an alcoholic with a traumatic past and some PTSD thrown in. He could have conflated the two. Did Austin ever mention him?"

"No. Never."

"Would anyone take a dislike to Austin?"

"He was a pain in the ass, but other than that, no."

"It was the same birthmark."

"What do you mean birthmark?" Ethan froze like a marble statue and stared at her.

"In another picture from the navy, the same sailor has a birthmark on his arm, which is eerily similar to Austin's. You can see it in a picture in the paper from a few years ago. He's at a wrestling match, screaming his head off. Want to see?" Nora asked.

Ethan drew his lips into a thin line and gave a curt nod. She slid out from under the covers, feeling the cool air hit her skin. She grabbed the file and darted back under the blanket again, feeling the warmth from Ethan and letting it ease her. A small voice reminded her that lying naked in bed with a person of interest while reviewing evidence after some hot sex was not a good idea. Nora pushed it out of her head and handed over the pictures. This was the most information she'd gotten out of Ethan, and she wasn't about to blow it, even if it was all off the record.

Ethan sat up and leaned over to turn on the light before studying them while he leaned against the headboard.

"I missed it at first, but there are two circles, which I believe are from Mark when he noticed it. Here, and here. They look identical. What I want to know is why he would go after Austin, thinking he was this other guy. I mean, obviously, these aren't the same person."

Ethan sat stone-faced in the bed.

"I can't let you do this anymore." His voice was low and filled with gravel, almost as if he were talking to himself. He pulled a hand over his face.

"You don't get a vote."

"Nora—"

"Don't start throwing up walls now. Off the record, remember?"

Ethan set both pictures down and turned to face her, his eyes sincere and honest. The emotion in them took her off guard.

"Did you research me?"

"Of course. It's standard. That's how I found where you worked."

"Did anything seem off?"

Nora opened her mouth and then shut it. She hadn't spent a lot of time poking around his file, mostly interested in getting the contact information. Once she had that, she paid him a visit, and then had been struck by how much—

Nora stopped cold and sucked in a breath.

"I expected someone a little older when I went in to interview you."

Ethan sat and didn't confirm or deny.

"You scrubbed your records?" Nora had heard of people with money doing similar things. Paying people off to have information removed, dates changed, and priors erased.

"Not yet."

Nora frowned. "Ethan, don't bullshit me."

"What if I told you we have good genes? Or that I could

live for hundreds of years." Ethan handed her the pictures back while watching her with an unnerving, laser-like focus.

"Oh for chrissakes, you can't possibly expect me to believe that. You're telling me this guy is the same as this guy?" she said, holding up the two pictures taken at least seventy years apart.

"No, of course not," Ethan said with a sarcastic and sad smile that didn't make any sense. He stood and glanced behind him. "That'd be ridiculous."

Nora stood too. "You know that's your problem. Every time I get close to something, you give me some bullshit and try to throw me off with some glib nonsense."

Ethan's mask of calm slipped a split second before the shield dropped back down into place. "There must be some explanation."

Nora didn't buy even one syllable of it.

"Do you know the penalty for adjusting personal information, or faking someone's death?" Nora tilted her head to the side as if considering the conversation light and pleasant.

"Can't say I do," Ethan said, matching her posture. "Never been one to break the law."

"Well, why don't I bring you in for questioning and we can review all of it there? You can even call a lawyer."

Had she been playing baseball, it would've been a homer. Ethan all but leapt toward her.

"This is ridiculous, Nora. What in the hell is wrong with you that you would even think for a moment that I would be so callous as to fake or manipulate my own brother's death? You're the one who showed up here—"

"I'm doing my job, Ethan."

Ethan narrowed his eyes and leveled a stare at her. "But the case was closed, wasn't it?"

"Cut the crap and tell me what I want to know."

"You don't get it, do you?" he said, taking a step toward her. Nora felt the need to step back but held firm.

"What do you mean?"

"There are some things you can't know, Nora." In the dim light of the bed and breakfast's bedroom, Ethan seemed larger than she remembered, swelling into every ounce of the football player she had read he was in college. The air around him seemed to crackle with dangerous energy that sent her hackles up as a warning.

"I just want to protect you. You know I care about you. I've already said I can't have you unprotected. The less you know, the better."

His voice rang true, and as much as she wanted to haul his ass in to interview, she had no probable cause to do so. A few old photographs wouldn't hold up as enough evidence to a judge. Standing there before her, he looked tired, the weight of her questioning weighing on him, dragging him down. A dark stubble coated his chin and cheeks, matching the bags under his eyes.

"How bad is it?" Nora asked. Her voice sounded far away, like a whisper to even her own ears.

"It's not bad. No one's being hurt."

"I've heard drug dealers say that."

Ethan let out a rueful laugh. "Only you would say that, and no, before you ask, I'm not a drug dealer."

"I never said—"

"No, you didn't, but you'd be lying if it hadn't entered your mind. I've done nothing wrong, and yet you continue to treat me like a criminal. I don't know why I like you."

"I don't know either, and I'm not..."

"Not what?"

"Treating you like a criminal. I'd be hauling you in already if I was."

Ethan's jaw tensed and any warmth they had just shared vanished.

"Do you think this is a game?"

"No, but apparently you do."

Ethan paced. From behind, all of his muscles tensed in his back, like a feral animal caged.

"This isn't a game for me. This is my fucking life. My family. Everything that matters to me, and everything I've sworn to protect."

"Oh, and you think I don't know what that's fucking like?"

"What would you do for your family? Do you know what it's like to sacrifice for someone?"

"Don't even start—"

Ethan rounded on her, his eyes crazed.

"But do you know?" His voice bounced around the room.

Nora's blood boiled. Grabbing a pillow, she slammed it against the floor to keep from hitting him. "I know my father's in his grave because he swore to protect. My brother can't afford to go to college, and the man who stepped up when my dad died is in debt up to his eyeballs with medical bills. I'm doing everything I can to help, and it's still not enough. Do you have any idea what that's like? Don't lord fucking words over me while you sit in your ivory tower with commas in your bank accounts. You don't have a fucking clue, and you never fucking will."

Ethan froze, standing like a stranger in front of her.

"You won't get anything else out of me."

Nora sucked in air, her breath coming in rapid pants. "I'll get a warrant."

"I'll be gone before morning."

"I'll find you."

Ethan bent down and pulled on his discarded pants from the floor. "No, you won't. You'll never see me again."

"You can't mean that."

Ethan stood and pulled the sleeves of his shirt over his arms. As he buttoned the front closed, he stared at her with unnerving calm. "I'm sorry, Nora. I really am."

"So I guess this meant nothing to you? Just more lies." Nora picked up the edge of the sheet and flung it in the air, exposing the bed where they had tangled in passion an hour earlier.

"Goodbye, Nora," Ethan said and shut the door.

Nora stood in disbelief and started rushing around to pull on clothes. She ran down the stairs right as a Land Rover sped off into the early morning light.

CHAPTER 41

Lizzy let herself into the little apartment, feeling the familiar weight of the keyring held together with a key fob shaped like an ice cream cone. Funny how the things she had picked out and carried with her for the better part of a century seemed so different after just a few months.

"I didn't realize you were so close to home when we met," Caleb said behind her.

She shut the door against the warm sea breeze. At Caleb's house the August weather had felt oppressive, but up in New England, it was just the right temperature to grill on decks.

"Yep, but I couldn't come up because of Caitlyn, remember?"

"Oh, I know. I've been in here before."

Lizzy stopped cold and looked at him while taking off her shoes and storing them in the closet. Having your current boyfriend talk with his ex in your house was new for her, and she didn't like the feeling.

Caleb held up both hands. "Nothing happened. She wasn't

happy to see me, but she hadn't picked up the damn phone or returned my texts so—"

"You're persistent."

"I told you it's loyal, and yeah, so I showed up and almost froze to death before we had a cup of coffee, during which time she made it abundantly clear where I stood, and off I went to Sal and Alex's Inn."

"Why did you stick around?"

Caleb shrugged and looked out the window that overlooked Easterly Bay. "I don't know. Nowhere else to go. Probably shouldn't have, to be honest."

"Um, excuse me?"

"Well, now I'm glad I hung around. I guess...I don't know. She just didn't look happy. After that kid died and her parents' funerals...I mean, she just took off with no notice and I was pretty concerned. Seeing her here didn't make me feel any better. She wasn't just sad, she was like...I don't know."

"Bitter?"

Caleb switched on a lamp Lizzy had ordered from Pottery Barn a while ago. "Yeah, I guess that's the best description. I just didn't feel good about leaving someone like that. Whether or not they wanted me here, I mean, it's not like I had to go back to work, so I figured I'd give it a month to see if she was okay and then head home."

"I still think it's weird another woman made you coffee with my coffee pot."

"It feels a lot different in here now," Caleb said, looking around.

"Well, I did take my stuff out of storage when she left. Convenient, huh?" Lizzy let out a bitter laugh. "Almost like I knew what was coming."

"You want me to move in your stuff from the truck?"

Lizzy shook her head. "Anything that was there isn't

particularly valuable. I brought all the good stuff with me." She raised an eyebrow in his direction.

Caleb shrugged and snatched her up, carrying her to the bedroom, before he stopped just inside the room.

"Don't worry. I bought new furniture. Gave my old set to Austin and Caitlyn as a wedding present. He has atrocious taste. Hadn't bought any, ever. I don't know how we're even related. His mom has excellent taste, so does Ethan. Austin must take after Uncle Fred. Wouldn't know the difference between wool and polyester if you tried to set it on fire."

"How old is he? Like really?" Caleb said when he plopped her down.

"Same age. Oh, that reminds me. Hang tight right there."

"Yes, ma'am."

"You southern boys are so cute."

"You know more than one?"

Lizzy stuck her head out of the closet with a sly grin and raised an eyebrow. "Maybe. I was in Virginia for almost a year."

Caleb made a noise of dissent in the back of his throat while she brought out a large box.

"I wanted to show you this, just so you know I'm not crazy." She pulled the lid and flipped it once, catching it with a hollow sound. "Time to break out the family photos."

"Well, it's only fair. Maw Maw's house is covered. There's no hiding the awkward teen years."

"An eye for an eye." Lizzy passed over an envelope and watched as Caleb pulled out a small, old and faded wallet photo of a toddler with a big smile in a dress.

They sifted through the box, watching her grow up.

"I was so much skinnier back then."

"I don't see it."

"How can you not? Look, there's my ribcage." She pointed to a picture of her in a swimsuit from the forties. She had always loved that high-waisted bikini and back then had always tied her hair up with a scarf. Her aunt had snapped the photo as Lizzy was hugging her knees on a beach blanket looking over the water.

"You don't have your angel wing."

"My what? Oh, that. We call it a firemark. Didn't know it looked like an angel wing."

"I thought it was a birthmark or a tattoo. What's a firemark?"

Lizzy tilted her hand backwards to rub her fingers over the smooth surface of her skin. "It's a red birthmark that shows up after we drink the water. Everyone here has one. They're kind of ugly. Not a great look with a bikini, so I usually cover mine up."

"No need. You're a knockout." Caleb shook his head and smiled, taking the picture between his fingers to look at it some more. "I'll bet every guy was after you."

Lizzy let out a bitter laugh. "Hardly. All of them looked at me like more of a sister, so there wasn't a whole lot of dates for me."

"They were just intimidated."

Lizzy leaned back into the pillows and looked at him. "You think so?"

"I know so. You said they're all so protective of you. Probably because you were the prettiest one on the whole island."

Lizzy felt a slow smile spread across her face. "You know, Caleb, I had meant to show these to you to prove to you that I'm older." She bit her lip. "You don't seem to be focusing on the weird part here. These pictures are before you were born. You understand what that means, right?"

Caleb looked up at her, not afraid, not suspicious. "You already told me."

"Now, I'm sure you're crazy. I have to say I expected a much bigger reaction."

Caleb shrugged. "I guess being raised Catholic, I know there's a lot of things I don't understand. One of my grandparents' houses is haunted. I've seen that myself."

"Really? How do you know?"

"The tenant committed suicide. House hasn't been right since. Weird stuff happens. Voices, things falling, messes, that sort of thing. Tenants come and go. Not saying you're a ghost."

Lizzy nodded once. "Thank you, I appreciate that."

"I guess what I'm trying to say is I believe you, and you're right. These pictures have erased any suspicion I had."

"You're taking this really well."

Caleb smiled. "It explains a lot."

Lizzy raised an eyebrow. "Oh yeah? Like what?"

"Why no one came to the bed and breakfast. Like why Sal and Alex always wanted to know where I was going, what I had found out. And the cemetery."

"The cemetery?"

"Yeah, not enough graves. Sorry, Parrain used to manage one, so I'm familiar, and you don't have enough plots. You have a few founders and one or two recent ones, but that's it. I had thought maybe you guys buried them at sea, but it was still odd."

"That's pretty observant of you."

"Didn't have anything else to do. Also, explains why when I asked Caitlyn when Austin had been in the navy, she didn't give me a straight answer. I could tell she was lying, but let it go. Didn't think it was my business."

"Parrain was right. You're smart."

Then Caleb did something she never would've expected.

He smiled and winked. "You deserve nothing less."

CHAPTER 42

Nora polished off a cup of black coffee and a slice of banana bread in the morning sun on her balcony. Drops of water from an early morning rain glinted on a hydrangea bush outside the big picture window. Had everything not gone to hell earlier this morning, it would've been a perfect day.

She mulled over what Ethan had told her early that morning and ran through the facts again, waiting for her phone to buzz with her answer from the chief.

Part of her mourned the loss of Ethan, as he had been the closest thing to a real relationship she'd known since she'd closed herself off after a nightmare breakup years ago, but she hadn't been assigned to this case for no reason, and even though it'd been closed, something wasn't right here. She had tried calling Ethan again, and just as he had promised, there was no trace.

When Ethan had accused her of suspecting him as a drug dealer, he'd hit it on the nose. Where else would he get that kind of money and enough pull to be able to change his credentials in the government systems? Bringing him down would be the highlight of her career, even if it shredded her inside. She needed her badge more. Defined herself by its weight and the years behind it. She couldn't let whatever had gone on between them cloud her judgment any longer. What she had done had been stupid and wrong, and it was only fitting she needed to pay the emotional price now.

Hearing the buzz, Nora yanked on a shirt and snatched her phone from the bedside table.

"Sir?"

The chief's voice rang through on the other end. "Lieutenant, I read your report and talked to the APA. This isn't enough to go on."

"Sir, with all due respect, I have evidence to suggest records have been tampered with by persons on Brightrock. Also, the large amount of income is suspicious."

"I understand that, but it's a no-go."

The news was a hit in the gut. Nora gritted her teeth, thinking fast for something to sway the chief while she had him on the line.

"Sir, if I could just get access to some—"

"Lieutenant, it's a no."

Nora collapsed on the edge of the bed she and Ethan had shared last night and braced a hand against her forehead. She had no doubt with his kind of money and influence, Ethan could vanish, go right up in smoke. Finding him in the first place had been hard enough. Now that he didn't want to be found, and with no warrant, Nora knew she'd never see him again. Her stomach clenched at the failure and the loss of something else.

"Sir, I've requested some time off—"

"Which I'm denying now."

Nora jerked her head up, mouth falling open.

"—another option. Department of Health needs assistance for routine checks on municipal utilities and recordkeeping. After the bombing and in the interest of public health and safety, I'm assigning you as support personnel as a follow-up from our homeland security unit."

Nora sat dumbfounded. "Sir, with all due respect, is this a glorified fire marshal position?"

The chief laughed on the other end, a short grunt of approval. "Yes and no. It'll get you access to records. Keep your eyes peeled, and if you find more, we might be able to get you that warrant."

"Yes, sir."

"I'll send you the contact information. This is the best I can do, Lieutenant. Gives you a week."

"Thank you, sir." Nora disconnected and set the phone down. Looking around the room, she expected to feel a swell of pride and anticipation at finding answers, but the drive that normally fueled her was gone and in its place was vacant air in her chest.

Brushing it off, Nora showered, dressed, and checked for the messages from the chief with her new orders and contact. Nora pulled out her computer to make some notes for her own records and put in a call to the Department of Health.

A series of voices directed her through menu after menu before placing her on hold for what seemed to be the better part of thirty minutes when a voice picked up.

"This is Evelyn Ross," a young, but confident voice said over the line.

"This is Lieutenant Nora St. Clair. I have orders to assist in your investigations on Brightrock Island following the attack by Mark Schmidt."

"Brightrock?" Evelyn seemed taken aback by the sudden offer to help, which led to more minutes on hold, so various bosses could call other bosses. All of it annoyed Nora.

Finally, Evelyn came back on the line.

"Alright, sorry about that. I'm new, and this is my first case. Just wanted to check."

"That's fine. When do you expect to be on the island?"

"Well, I wasn't planning on going soon, since they haven't been cooperating."

Nora frowned. That had been the first piece of interesting information anyone had said in the whole hour Nora had been on the phone.

"What do you mean?"

"Well, the town council has taken their time getting back to me, and they seem to be throwing up roadblocks. Asking for extra paperwork, then presenting paperwork that gives me everything I need, but I need to verify it personally, you know?"

"Sure."

"Yeah, well they don't seem too welcoming."

"I guess that's where I come in," Nora said, cutting off any more apologies. "So how soon can you get here?"

"Are you there now?"

"Yep, staying at the Cedar Inn."

"I'll book a trip out this afternoon."

Nora smiled to herself as she hung up. Evelyn might be new, but if she could get here by four o'clock, Nora would recommend her for immediate promotion. She checked the time and grabbed her map before heading out the door to get a look at the crime scene in person.

After half an hour, her shirt clung to her from the summer heat, but soon the mansions on manicured lawns gave way to a pine forest surrounded by chain-link. Caution tape still snaked through the wire diamonds, but someone had torn a section away from where the gate opened, and fresh tire tracks were in the muddy grass. She let herself in with her master key and followed what looked to be a driveway down a tunnel of pine trees for a quarter mile before the landscape opened up into a gravel parking lot and a pathway up to the ruins of what was left of the old meetinghouse.

Clouds swirled in the sky as she climbed up the hill, avoiding headstones and chunks of granite jutting out of the ground. Most of the grass was black around where the pressure cooker bombs had detonated, the burn an ugly stain on the landscape, like a violent bruise left over months after a fight. The muddy grass squelched underfoot while she circled around, eyeing the caution tape that fluttered in the wind.

Set atop a cliff overlooking the ocean, the old meetinghouse must have been something spectacular. One of the charred remains of the support structure stood proud against the sky. Most of the building was gone. The original cedar would've gone up like an old newspaper when exposed to the flame. Nora circled the heap of ash and blackened wood, putting an image to her notes about Mark's location. She liked to get her feet on the ground, hoping the perspective would shake something new from the evidence she hadn't seen before.

The sun was hot, but the breeze off the water on the cliff chased away the humidity she had felt further inland. She squinted and scanned the landscape, noting how few headstones there were, and noticed a much smaller building built into the hill. Made of stones and a slate roof, the squat little building would have held a push mower, a small car at most, but what made it unique was the seven locks bolting the thing shut. Nora marched forward through the grass and got a closer look.

It looked to be an old springhouse, with the door barely tall enough for an adult to squat through. Not that she could. The series of locks, which seemed to be of an older style, ran down one side of the iron gate, barricading anyone from entering. She pulled out her phone and hit the flashlight. Inside there was a small well that looked to be no more than a pit in the ground, the earthen walls absorbing her flashlight unlike the smooth shine of concrete. Several plastic five-gallon buckets sat upside down next to the hole in the ground as if they were drying. On a shelf, a dozen pitchers sat upside down, next to a package of Dixie cups. Nora studied the locks. All of them were free of rust. She picked up one in her hand and felt it slide in her fingers, leaving a dark stain of new oil.

She snapped a few pictures and headed back. If Evelyn had any interest in water, she was going to have a field day with this.

CHAPTER 43

"These records are the most organized I've ever seen," Evelyn said the next morning as she rifled through yet another filing cabinet in Brightrock's town hall.

Over a shared dinner at Kate's Diner last night, Nora had shown Evelyn the pictures she had snapped on her phone of the suspicious well and the fresh tire tracks. Nora was no scientist, but apparently her hunch had been right, as Evelyn had almost spit out her pasta when she realized what she was looking at and the repercussions the unfiltered groundwater could have.

The next morning, Nora had sent messages requesting access to the water on behalf of the Department of Health, copying her captain and chief on the email for backup. Evelyn's jurisdiction meant there was no need for a warrant as the old springhouse was on protected land, but the seven locks were old, and as much as Nora wanted to go nuts with some bolt cutters, the brass had requested she play nice and let Evelyn's bosses forward the request to the town council.

Much to her dismay, the town council was giving new

meaning to the phrase dragging their feet. Evelyn and Nora had been using the time to go through the records at town hall to make sure all of the building permits, and God knew what else, had been filed correctly. Nora would've stabbed her eye with a pencil at the mind-numbing amounts of boredom had she not had her own motive for rifling through the endless files.

With the smell of dark roast coffee wafting throughout the small conference room, Nora sat across from Evelyn as she looked through old building permits filed with the state, skimming for anything that mentioned Austin or Ethan Brooks.

Everything she and Evelyn had found had been in immaculate condition. Every code had been met, and every permit was up to date with not a single error to be seen, which of course meant there was a deeper lie. There wasn't a local government in the world this error-free. Even's Austin's death certificate, which, while vague, matched all the information Nora already had back in her office.

As for Ethan Brooks, there were two. One was listed as born on Brightrock in 1929, but the records were vague. Nora had kept looking, refusing to believe Ethan was almost ninety. There must have been a mix-up. What he had told her couldn't be right. In a nearby file, Nora also found a different Ethan Brooks had also been born in 1970, to the first Ethan Brooks, mother deceased. That sounded more like it, but still was wrong and again the record was vague and lacked any real information. His joke about having good genes haunted her. He looked thirty not fifty, so where was the record for the thirty-year-old Ethan? The possibilities made her temples ache. It was clear there were lies, but where was the truth?

"Excuse me, ladies?" An almost ancient, but surprisingly

spry man with horn-rimmed glasses and a British accent strode forward with a cane.

"Lieutenant St. Clair," Nora said, holding up her badge.

"My apologies, Lieutenant," the man said, looking at her with alarm and disdain from his three-piece suit. "I wanted to introduce myself as a member of the town council. I am Dr. Timothy Chappell, and I am responsible for all record-keeping here. I believe you requested to meet with me. I trust you're finding everything in order?"

Evelyn stood and introduced herself. "All of the records seem to be in order."

Dr. Chappell broke into a smile that Nora didn't believe. "That's wonderful news. I'll have my secretary show you out."

"That won't be necessary," Nora said, cutting him off. "We haven't finished all of the files and still have work to do."

Dr. Chappell looked like someone had given him a wedgie. "Of course, Lieutenant. Might there be something in particular you are looking for so I can point you in the right direction? We want to give the Department of Health and the police our full support."

His face was so straight, Nora almost believed the lie. Evelyn opened her mouth, but Nora beat her to it.

"Health records for everyone on the island. We can have the names removed."

It was his right eye. Nora wouldn't have caught it if she hadn't been searching for the tell.

"I hardly see how that is pertinent to this investigation into a drunk man's attempt on the lives of our citizens. Under HIPAA, their privacy—"

"Is our utmost concern, and will be kept anonymous and not be made public. This is merely for investigative purposes to track the overall health trends of the people on this island to allow the Department of Health to alert you to any public safety issues," said Nora. Evelyn bobbed her head once in agreement.

"I'm going to be reporting this to your superiors. I cannot risk the privacy of our citizens based on the opinion of two—"

Nora cut him off before he could insult her further. "Also we have requested access to the well or springhouse within the preserve. The one next to the site of the terrorist attack. We've been waiting for the town to return our emails."

His face froze in a mask of horror and rage. "I beg your pardon?" He recovered quickly—Nora would have to give him that.

"The one with seven locks."

Evelyn jumped in. "Given the images I've seen already, I'm going to need to complete a full panel on the water. It appears people have been drinking from it, despite the fact that it lacks basic filtration—"

"And it's a hole in the ground," Nora finished. "Ms. Ross here has strong concerns about the safety of the residents."

"The locks are there to keep people out. That well is on a nature preserve and is in no way—"

"Dr. Chappell, are you willing to obstruct the Department of Health's investigation and risk the health and safety of the people on Brightrock?"

The old man sputtered, trying to work his mouth to come up with some legal jargon.

"Last time I checked," Nora continued, folding her arms over her chest, "the good people at the Health Department outrank all of us. Putting up barriers is illegal. Ms. Ross, did I get anything wrong?"

"No, that pretty much covers it."

Dr. Chappell's face was contorted with rage that only spurred Nora on. Something was in the well that he didn't want them anywhere near.

"So if someone were to get in Ms. Ross's way with her investigations as part of a routine follow-up to a domestic terrorist attack, I would be forced to get involved." Nora tilted her head to the side, wondering if the arrogant bastard was going to have a heart attack right in front of her.

"Are we clear, Dr. Chappell? We all have the same goal here. To protect and serve, am I right?"

CHAPTER 44

Ethan sat in his new office behind a desk that held business cards with a new name. He had still managed to find a job in Boston, but while the familiar anonymity of the city welcomed him home, there was little comfort except for the now frayed business card he kept with him at all times with Lieutenant Nora St. Clair's number fading in ink. He couldn't part with his last link to her and hoped that once he waited enough time, he could see her again from afar.

Timothy Chappell and the elders had done a remarkable job with his new credentials and résumé, so that he needn't have started at the bottom again, blending into the upper middle of a decent investment bank. Coming into the fold, Ethan, now David, hadn't even bothered to unpack or settle in. He wouldn't be in this small office for long, despite Timothy Chappell's strategic insistence that lying low for a while would be better.

Ethan reached in his pocket and flipped the card over in his hand, running his fingers over the worn edges, letting the charts roll by on the screen, calculating expenditure growth as a matter of habit when the phone rang.

"This is David." The name didn't roll off the tongue, not that he cared. He'd get used to it, just like everything else. If this is what it took to provide for his community, then they could call him whatever they wanted.

A British accent clipped into his ear, the diction holding firm to the old style. "Hi David, this is Timothy Chappell calling to speak about my investment accounts." Whenever on a public line, Chappell always insisted on talking by the book.

"Yes, sir. I'll pull them up right now." Ethan reached into his own bag to pull out his personal computer, where he kept the confidential files.

"Great. I'll need to talk quickly. The Department of Health is coming and insisting on investigating the record-keeping personally."

Ethan froze. The weight of the words seeped through to him. "Well, sir. I'm sure everything will be in order."

"Yes, I agree, but I'm worried. They are personally coming to inspect the oldest water supply, and a police escort has now been assigned."

A wave of chills rushed over his skin. He struggled to find words, while his brain raced through the possibilities, options, and of course, Nora's involvement.

"I had heard from another person that you may have some contacts in this field. I am at a loss for what—"

"Sir, can I call you back?"

"Yes, of course."

Ethan dug out his private cell, which was already buzzing with Timothy's number on the screen.

"How soon are they coming?" Ethan whispered while eyeing the shut door in front of him. As a precaution, he had checked all of the corners for possible bugs and found none.

Finance lent itself to private rooms, which was a blessing, but Chappell still insisted.

"They're here already."

Ethan gripped the phone so hard, the case dug into his skin. "Warrant?"

"No, blocked. I didn't need to call the APA. There wasn't enough to bring against us, but—"

"The Department of Health doesn't need a warrant," Ethan finished for him.

"No, though the presence of a police lieutenant—"

"St. Clair?"

"Yes, Alex said you had been introduced." Chappell let that sentence hang in the air. The silence that followed crackled with condemnation, though the conservative town elder didn't say a word on the matter. He had allowed Ethan personal privacy as long as he was discreet and the rate of return on investments met expectations.

"We have, but are not on speaking terms."

"Perhaps you have sway with her?"

Ethan balled a fist and held it against his forehead. "I don't believe so, sir."

"I need you to try. Convince her not to take samples of the water. Legally, the Department of Health trumps everything, and there's nothing I can do without causing further attention."

"Perhaps they won't find anything in the analysis?"

Chappell hissed on the other end of the line. "I would rather not take that chance. Call her. Convince her. Do whatever is necessary to block this testing. I'm stalling as long as I can."

"What about the desalination and town water?" Ethan asked, referring to the water plant installed to provide regular drinking water after the wells had run low years ago.

"That's how I'm stalling, but they've called for a full

report as the cause for further analysis. They're including all private wells. For whatever reason, that cop wants the spring tested."

Ethan swore under his breath. Chappell didn't correct him, which told Ethan how scared the elder was. This was unprecedented.

"I'll do what I can."

Ethan listened to Chappell's cautions, requests, and praise before hanging up and staring hard at the wall across from him. He let his hand run along the edge of the card in his pocket.

On his last night with Nora, Ethan had been transformed but vowed never to speak to her again. She had the power over him to violate everything he was and stood for. Ethan had never broken his vow of secrecy, but with her, he had told her all only to have it rejected as another lie and spat at his feet with a venom that burned every cell in his body.

He couldn't take her rejection of him and everything he stood for. He had failed by telling her, hoping to gain her trust like his brother had with his wife, betting that Nora could love him or at least care for him enough to listen and consider the possibility of what Ethan was.

Now he had to call her and beg for her to set aside her own oath in order to protect him. Ethan already knew what the answer was going to be when he picked up the phone. Though it made him more of a hopeless failure and traitor to his island, Ethan craved hearing her voice again and prayed she would answer as the phone rang in his ear.

CHAPTER 45

Nora finished another slice of Sal and Alex's banana bread in the warm breakfast room. Both the room and the food really were exceptional over the past week she had spent on Brightrock. Outside, the sunny August morning looked inviting but the heat of the day would smother anyone caught outside after noon. Inside, the Cedar Inn was bright and cheery, not to mention filled with fans and sweet, sweet air conditioning. It would have made for a perfect getaway from the city, but that's not why she was there.

She tried not to look at the couch in the other room. Housekeeping had fluffed the pillows, so they stood plumped and perfect, leaving no trace of the activities that were seared into Nora's memory.

Ethan was always going to stay there, locked deep inside her mind. She wouldn't see him again, but at least privately, she could revisit her memories. It was clear now he'd never intended to tell her anything. Nora had been a fool to go along with all of his games. The best she could do was find out what he was hiding and deliver justice, as was her job.

She might be alone, but she had her badge, a job to do, and that was that. She owed that to her dad and to herself. Pining after some guy wasn't going to help her make captain but catching him in a lie and uncovering whatever was going on here on Brightrock Island might.

Her cell buzzed on the table. Nora didn't recognize the number and tapped the button to silence. If it was important, they could leave a message. She needed coffee first. She had tossed and turned all night, trying not to think about Ethan.

Nora's lips formed a thin line as she stirred her coffee, counting the bubbles as they popped while thinking of the times they had shared together, including the time he had ordered a latte with that ridiculous heart. Only once before had she allowed herself to get so close to someone, let her guard down, put someone above, or at least close to, her job, and it had ended in heartbreak. Because of that she had shut everything out. No one other than her immediate family and Tom and Christine had crossed that line in her heart for years, but somehow Ethan had charmed his way in before driving right out. Nora couldn't decide if she felt hungover or grief-stricken, but either way, it pissed her off, and she tried again to shove the unwelcome thoughts into the corner of her mind.

The twinkling of a bell followed by a door slamming signaled Evelyn's arrival. "Morning! Got any more of that bread?"

Nora passed over the basket. "Any news?"

Evelyn swept down in cut-off shorts, a tank top, and yellow cap. Her short hair showed off big purple earrings that would be a prime target for an attacker, Nora thought. Instead of saying so, she popped another bite of banana bread into her mouth and watched Evelyn do the same, as she sat down.

"Holy shit, this is good. God, I already ate like half a loaf before I went out." Nora watched as Evelyn took another bite and slumped down into the chair opposite her. "This is why I can't be trusted on vacation. I mean, I try and be good, but then banana bread just pops up, and I mean, what am I supposed to do? Not eat it? Yeah, right."

"Did you go to the lab?"

Evelyn jumped up and grabbed another cup of coffee from the coffee bar in the kitchen and plopped back down before cutting another slice of bread. "Lab? Here? Pfft. No way. I just went on a walk. How cute is this little town?"

"Adorable. Have you gotten results back from the water?"

Evelyn devoured another slice and chewed. "Yep. You were totally right."

Nora leaned forward and put her cup down. "What did you find?"

"It's unreal, actually. There's no way anyone should be drinking that."

"Someone took water from there. Recently," Nora said, thinking of the buckets and tire tracks.

"Well, if they're drinking it, shit's gonna get weird."

"How do you mean? What did you find?"

"Uranium and arsenic like...woah. I mean, bad. Massachusetts has always had high levels in wells, hence, you know, my job." Evelyn reached into an oversized bag and slapped down a stack of papers before swiping a few crumbs of banana bread off it.

Nora leaned forward and read it over, coming up empty. "What the hell does all of this mean? All I see are numbers and PPB."

"Parts per billion. The higher it is, the worse it gets."

"Isn't arsenic a poison?"

"Yes, but there's more to it than that. Inorganic compounds cause a ton of problems, everything from skin and stomach problems, lesions, to cardiovascular shit, cancer, impaired nerve function." Evelyn took a sip of coffee. "The uranium causes cancer, but you probably knew that. See that number right there? No, that one. Yeah, that one. That's enough for me to call the feds. Highest level I've ever seen."

Nora stared down at the numbers. "Why would the town go to this water? We saw the buckets. Someone is using this well. Recently."

"With those levels, they're lucky to be alive." She popped more bread in her mouth. "And if they are, they won't be for long."

"So, now what?"

"Cancer...oh, you mean the well? Yeah, it'll have to be sealed."

"Like a cap?"

She shook her head, making the earrings swing. "We have to stop the water supply. Gotta stop the source, so it can't bubble up somewhere else. Have to excavate and pour concrete down at the source of the spring to seal it off. We don't want anyone getting near this water again."

"Why hasn't it been done before?"

"From what I can tell, the town council has reported their own research for years. Numbers were never sent in for analysis for this particular well. The rest of the water on the island is good. According to our records, they installed town water a while back. Something about the local water supply dwindling. Anyway, all of that is treated and desalinated. The Cape is working on installing that now. People are pretty happy about it. Especially the fire departments."

"But they never talked about this well?"

"Nope. It's probably a natural spring they found by their old meetinghouse when they arrived, but whatever, there's no way anyone can drink that."

Nora nodded once, thinking of Timothy Chappell's reluctance for them to visit the well. She'd bet her badge he knew about this. Why would he try to protect it? "Alright. Then let's shut it down."

CHAPTER 46

Ethan hopped down from the plane and marched off the steaming tarmac that glistened with the remains of a late afternoon thunderstorm. The charter pilot he had hired last night waved him off while Ethan walked toward where Austin's Ford was waiting with the keys in the ignition. He and Caitlyn had dropped it off as a favor. They just thought he had arrived back for the surprise meeting Chappell and the council had called yesterday.

The meeting that he was going to was everything he could do to prevent the end of time for all of them.

A humid blast of wind pummeled into him but did nothing to warm the cold void in his chest.

He had tried so hard to make sure his family and friends would never need to worry, but now it was his doing that ultimately would bring everything crashing down. Four hundred years of secrecy and protection down the drain because he had gotten too close and couldn't handle Nora.

Lieutenant St. Clair, he corrected himself, as he shut the

door and cranked the engine. He didn't usually drive himself, but then he wasn't used to begging someone to abandon a search on the fountain of youth. He doubted the latter was as easy as driving.

He navigated the roads of his childhood back to the Cedar Inn, where he knew Nora was still staying according to Sal and Alex. He pulled the truck right in front of the Victorian facade, dark with the fading sun behind it.

Ethan crunched over the wet gravel and up the steps. He pushed through the front door, hearing the twinkle above him from the little bell. Ethan stopped and stared at the couch in front of the dark fireplace. His memories of being with Nora on that couch felt like a lifetime ago.

A creak up the stairs made him turn around.

Nora's golden eyes glowed in the light. The hard cop edge only softened slightly when she recognized him. She relaxed her stance and descended down the stairs, her body tense like when they had first met. Predator and prey all over again. Ethan would've bet money her gun was on her.

"Coming for another nightcap?" Nora folded her arms across her chest and propped herself up on the doorjamb.

"I need to talk to you."

"Last time we did that, you took off. Tried to ping your phone, but the last time it made contact was over the water. Hasn't resurfaced since. That's frowned upon in the eyes of the law."

"Nora, I need you to call off the sealing of the well."

Her golden eyes narrowed. "Why?"

"There's something you don't know about that well. Something special."

"What?"

Ethan swallowed. He stared at the floor and rubbed his hand over his chin, feeling the stubble.

"Still won't tell me. Figures."

"You won't believe me."

"I'd say try me, but you won't, and I've lost patience dealing with you. Besides, there is nothing I can do. Done deal."

Ethan's heart dropped into his stomach. He closed the distance between them and took her by the shoulders. Nora didn't stop him, but her stare didn't warm either.

"Nora, please. That well—"

"Is dangerous."

Ethan frowned. "What?"

"The lab results came back. It's being sealed as soon as the state people can get here. It's full of uranium, arsenic, and a bunch of other shit too. Totally deadly. We're looking into who has been accessing it as they're at serious risk for all sorts of problems."

"Nora, that water keeps us alive. Remember how I told you about my genes? I wasn't joking. I was born on Christmas Eve in 1929." Her eyes widened in shock. He sounded desperate to his own ears but didn't care. "It's true. That water is what does it. We drink it every season after we turn eighteen. It slows the aging process. You need to understand. You need to help me stop them."

"I couldn't find your birth certificate. There was one from Christmas Eve in the twenties and then another from the seventies. It didn't make sense." Her eyes darted back and forth, while she frowned a little, searching his eyes.

He gave her shoulders a little shake. "Don't you see? The later one is a fake for my employer. Please, Nora. I'm begging you. If you want to arrest someone, make a big splash, take me. You said you thought I was a drug dealer, so arrest me. I'm going with you, but I need you to stop this. Please."

"Ethan—"

"Nora, I will do anything."

"Ethan, I can't."

"But you can—"

"Ethan, stop." Nora shook her shoulders and stepped back. "You're talking crazy. I don't know what's going on here, but I know enough about you to know you're not a dealer and that water's not safe. It's out of my hands. Job's done. Done deal. That's it."

"Nora—"

"Don't you get it? I live to protect and serve. That's who I am. That water is dangerous. Timothy Chappell was trying to hide it. I don't know why, but I'm close—I can feel it."

Ethan felt the blood drain out of his face. His hands fell to his sides. "Nora—"

"Ethan. I'm sorry. I can't help you."

"You said your family is struggling—"

"Don't even suggest it. I will arrest—"

"I can make all of that go away. All of their worries, bills. Everything will be taken care of. Discreet. Your brother's college, the medical bills. You need a safer apartment. I can make all of that happen, and no one will know."

"I'm going to pretend you didn't just try to bribe a cop."

"Please consider this. I can make everything easier. Not just for you, but for everyone you love. Donations to the department. Everything."

Ethan watched her eyes, pleading with her to reconsider, to let him take care of her and everything she loved. Even if he couldn't have her himself, caring for her from afar and protecting Brightrock would give him more than enough pleasure. He watched as her golden eyes looked at him, in the now dark foyer.

Nora closed her eyes and drew in a breath. When she opened them to look at him again, the pain was evident. He knew the answer before she spoke, and as she opened her perfect mouth, Ethan felt his heart break like it never had before, slicing through his soul with complete and utter defeat.

"I'm sorry, Ethan. The answer is no."

CHAPTER 47

Lizzy drove the little Ford Escape up and down the winding road, bumping along behind a line of cars. At least one adult from every family had been summoned to the meeting at the ruins of the old meetinghouse.

Caleb gripped the I'm-going-to-die handle as she turned and bounced off-road to head into what was marked as a reserve, surrounded by a chain-link fence around the perimeter. Through the lush trees, the sun speckled down onto the ground covered with a soft bed of shaded leaves. It was a perfect New England summer day, but Lizzy couldn't relax her shoulders or release her grip on the steering wheel as she drove this road for what would be the last time.

"Are you sure about this?" Caleb asked her for what must have been the thirtieth time.

"Yes." Lizzy's stomach knotted with the single syllable as if her body knew she was agreeing to a slow suicide. Giving up the chance to live longer flew in the face of the will to live. She would miss her family but hoped exceptions could be made. Perhaps if handled correctly, she could still have some contact with her cousins, aunt, and uncle.

They had discussed the plan last night when the emergency town hall meeting alert came through on her phone. Lizzy would renounce her membership and withdraw from the town charter. As was tradition, though it hadn't happened in years, the town council would offer her a last drink of the water. Lizzy planned to save it in case Parrain needed some, as Caleb had shared with her stories of the old man's declining health.

Caleb drummed his fingers on his knee next to her. He had urged her to reconsider, worried not having the life-sustaining water would make her vanish. She had assured him that no such thing would happen. She hoped she was right.

"What's this meeting about anyway?" Caleb asked, now tense and stiff as a board. He had insisted he come in case something happened. He wanted to stay in the car, not wanting to get her in trouble, but Lizzy had convinced him to walk in with her after the meeting had started. Lord knew she was going to need a hand to hold.

Lizzy drove into the clearing and parked the car. The burned ruins of the old meetinghouse had been cleaned up and now were draped with blue tarps and scaffolding. Her heart broke when she realized she'd never get to see the old meetinghouse restored if she went through with her plan today. She would never see it again.

"Who knows. They call random meetings enough for it not to be totally weird. Could be a comma in the fourteenth clause of our NDA."

"Jesus. That bad, huh?"

Too nervous to answer, Lizzy shrugged and watched as family and friends walked on the rocky hill toward the ruins of the old meetinghouse. The entrance remained, with the addition of scaffolding as an exoskeleton supporting the remaining portion of the roof. Underneath the beginnings of construction, the front looked the same. A jagged pile of rubble sat in place of the northwest corner. Seeing the hole in person pierced her heart all over again.

Lizzy's lips parted as she stopped, taking in the damage for the first time since the day of the explosion. Caleb's hand touched her shoulder as his arm came around her.

"I had no idea what to expect."

"You hadn't seen pictures since the explosion."

"I didn't want to look. I was here for the fire and heard of the repairs. Austin and Ethan assured me it was fine enough to rebuild." She swallowed the rest of her words, hearing voices from the other side of the old meetinghouse.

"Come on." She led him toward the voices, accepting his hand in her own.

They walked in the fading sun, over the torn caution tape, the kind law enforcement used, past the small springhouse that contained the well and water Lizzy could thank for her century on this planet and would be leaving behind today. The locks were off, even though it wasn't renewal day.

Her stomach knotted at the thought of never partaking in the ritual again, but she trudged forward, squeezing Caleb's hand tighter. He squeezed back and gave her a tight-lipped smile with a quick nod.

Having him there with his loyal, loving, quiet confidence scared away any doubts in the back of her mind. Her heart swelled with love as they crested the hill.

In the golden sunset, everyone she had ever known and loved sat before the town council in a tableau of her life, her past before her and Caleb beside her, hand in hand. She stood on a precipice between her old life and her future. Her heart in her throat, everything from her old life came back to her in a series of images and memories. Her mom's smile and her dad bouncing her on his knee, her aunt and uncle taking her in next to her cousins Ethan and Austin.

From there, she had images of running through the gardens of her aunt's house trying to keep up, then excelling in school, sitting at the old meetinghouse hearing the secret about Brightrock Island. She remembered toasting the water in her new pewter cup, a gift from the town, coughing the water down in disbelief.

From then, her time at college had always been dampened by the feeling of being different, an outsider with a secret, longing to get close to the other students. Her Aunt Mary kept her focused through weekly letters and visits over the breaks.

Lizzy searched for her aunts in the council and found Aunt Mary and Aunt Tee seated behind Timothy on what looked to be sturdy chairs pulled out for the occasion, whatever it was.

Lizzy frowned at the worried look on both women's faces. Tee looked anxious, her hands twisted in her lap with her lips drawn into a thin line. Aunt Mary, who had always carved a fierce path in front of her, sat stoic, the lines in her wise face deeper than normal. Lizzy had never seen them both look so unsettled, and after almost four centuries on the island, there hadn't been much they hadn't faced.

She stepped forward, but Caleb stopped her. Taking her hand in his own, he placed it in the crook of his arm and covered it protectively with a smile.

"A lady like my Elizabeth always needs a gentleman."

His warm green eyes shone with love and pride.

"I love you."

"I've loved you for a long time."

She blinked back tears through a smile and let him escort her down to where the group stood outdoors, facing the town council with the sparkling Atlantic behind them. As they approached, faces turned and smiled with delighted surprise before fading to shock as she walked forward like a bride with an outsider, her head held high, facing the most spectacular sunset she had seen in years.

The hell with what they thought. If she was going to break every rule in the book, she was going to do it her way. Caleb had been right. Their bodies told everyone why she had come without any words.

Austin sat next to Caitlyn, his arm tossed around her shoulders. Ethan sat next to them, seemingly struggling to appear relaxed, instead looking like a caged animal with his hands on his knees, his fingers drumming. One by one, the three of them shifted to look at her, their smiles running away when they saw who was on her arm. Ethan didn't seem surprised or confused. He smiled a sad sort of smile and gave her a brief nod. He looked almost jealous, but for the life of her, Lizzy couldn't understand why.

As they walked arm in arm down the aisle of chairs, Lizzy smiled. Whether this was like a wedding or her funeral, it didn't matter. She had what she needed, and this was good-bye. The warmth of the sun on her face and the sea breeze tangling her hair was like a blessing from the universe, the perfect backdrop for closing this chapter and starting her final life with the one she loved.

There was no procedure for leaving. No official renouncement of the island, the water, and the people, but as they walked forward, Lizzy felt they were doing the right thing. The elders saw her coming, with an outsider. Lizzy frowned a little when there was no outrage at Caleb's presence, no screaming over bringing an outsider to the most sacred of sacred places. She stopped about ten feet in front of them, meeting her aunts and Timothy Chappell square in the eye, ready for whatever fight she needed to make. It didn't matter anymore; she had made her decision.

Caleb adjusted his arm under hers, bringing her closer. He had no idea what was about to happen, and she admired the hell out of him for standing strong next to her in what must have been a bizarre transgression against the laws of nature to which he was accustomed.

A silence fell over the crowd as people held their breath behind her, all watching with keen interest at what was sure to be a dramatic event that would go down in the long history of the island.

Timothy stood from his folding chair, an old man weighed down by the centuries of guarding the secret of their island. The bags under his eyes were darker than normal. His thin hand gripped the top of a walking stick, which shook like a tiny branch in the wind. "Elizabeth, I believe I know why you have come." His shrewd eyes assessed Caleb with open distrust.

Lizzy took in a steadying breath and opened her mouth to speak when he continued.

"But you needn't worry. Times have changed, and I have an announcement to make on behalf of the council." He gestured with his right hand toward the empty front row. "Please take your seat."

Lizzy opened her mouth to argue, but the old man simply waited for her and Caleb to move. There was no yelling, no outrage at bringing an outsider here, instead only polite patience, as Chappell waited for her to sit. Caleb led her along and sat, taking her hand in preparation for whatever was about to happen.

Lizzy planted her butt down on the metal folding chair in shock and disbelief. She turned around to gauge the reaction of others and found the same look of bewilderment.

Timothy looked out at the crowd with a tight-lipped smile that quivered with emotion.

"Thank you all for coming on such short notice. I've no

doubt kept you waiting long enough." Any remaining cold arrogance flew away with the wind, as he seemed to be blinking back tears. "I believe, my friends, our time has come to a close." A ripple of shock went through the audience with an audible gasp and swirling questions demanding more information. He held up a gnarled hand to stop them.

"The council and I have tried to protect our ways from the outside world for almost four hundred years. For those of you who do not know, the Department of Health has ordered the well be drained and sealed off." He paused while the weight of his words sunk in for everyone. "This, of course, so they tell me, is for our protection."

An abrupt outcry filled the silence that followed his words, people demanding answers, calling out suggestions. Timothy shook his head. "The Department of Health opened an inquiry into our town and found our compliance lacking. The water tests have come back, and as I'm sure is no surprise to anyone, the results were outside the normal range. We are out of options. I'm afraid I have failed you." Timothy coughed to cover a sob and looked down to sniff away his emotions.

The audience sat in stunned disbelief until someone said, "Surely, there must be a way."

Timothy shook his head. "I'm sorry. The well and spring will be filled in and sealed tomorrow. We thought it would be fitting to have one last toast to your health before then. Please gather your cups."

CHAPTER 48

Lizzy sat at the table of her aunt and uncle's grand dining room in shock. Austin and Caitlyn sat across from her, neither drinking the coffee in front of them. Ethan hadn't joined them. He had headed off toward Kate's Diner, looking as though he might be ill. Caleb shifted in his seat, admiring the armor on the wall, having exhausted the introduction pleasantries. None of them were in the mood to chitchat.

Uncle Fred and Aunt Katie sat holding hands at the end of the table, each looking unsure of what to do next.

"I knew I was getting older, but I didn't expect to have just twenty years left," Fred said with a laugh. "Suddenly, I feel like an old man."

"Fred, stop," Katie said, looking like she was on the verge of tears and trying very hard not to show it. She had taken two pills for a headache when they all got back to the house but still rubbed at her temples.

Austin banged his hand on the table, making them all jump. "This can't just be it. We can't stop trying. They said they were going to seal it—"

"You heard Chappell—" Fred started to say.

"I know, but can't we seal it? If we make them think we've cut it off, how often are they going to check? Really?"

Fred shook his head. "I asked Aunt Tee about it after the renewal. She and Mary looked it up along with the rest of the council. It involves pouring something like concrete down there, so none of the water can seep out. It's a permanent installation. They both said the council's looked at it from every way possible."

"What about bottling the water?" Caitlyn asked. Not having had the water more than twice, she looked concerned, but not nearly as much as the others.

Fred shook his head. "No time, and besides, we don't know how it holds up. They tried that a while ago. Didn't seem to work."

The six of them sat in silence watching their coffees grow cold as the reality of the time passing set in around them. Before, Lizzy had felt like she had more time than she could handle, spending away years like nothing. Now, she felt the sting of regret when faced with a mere fifty more years to go. The selfishness of her thoughts and actions up until now hit her with alarming clarity. She squeezed Caleb's hand and wished like hell there was some way to change everything. After all, Katie and Fred had enjoyed a lifetime together, but Lizzy had just found her life partner, and even though they had fifty years ahead of them, that felt like nowhere near enough time together.

Caleb squeezed back and cleared his throat. "How did y'all avoid detection for so long?"

Fred spun his coffee cup in thought. "The springhouse is in a nature preserve. We found some rare bird species and filed all the paperwork to protect the land."

"So they—I mean the state—left you alone?"

Austin drummed his fingers on the table. "Yeah, pretty much. Not much they could do with a bunch of trees and birds."

"So why now?" Caleb looked from one to the other.

Fred shrugged. "Something with the Department of Health."

Austin leaned back and folded his arms, his jaw jutting out in thought. "Probably because of the giant bombing in a building that should never have been in a preserve."

Caleb nodded and cracked his knuckles.

"Did you have an idea?" Lizzy asked, studying him.

"I don't know. I was just thinking about when this happens with oil. What prevents the government from staking claim to something."

"We're all ears," Fred said, watching Caleb with a curious look.

"Tell me a little more about the history here," Caleb said, leaning forward on his elbows.

"Like how much history?" Austin asked. "I mean, not to put too fine a point on it, but we've got a lot of that around here."

"The beginning. How did this all start?" Caleb looked around at all of them.

"Showed up on a boat, drank water, didn't die," Austin said, getting up to head to the sideboard where he poured himself some amber liquid that looked like whiskey. "No, no. Sit," he said when his mom started to get up to help. "I got it. I know my way around the kitchen. Anyone else want anything? Mom?"

"Sure, honey," Katie said, resuming rubbing her temples like she was in a painful dream.

"Dad? Lizzy? Caleb?" Austin asked, uncorking another bottle.

"Who owned the land before you—or the first people—got here?" Caleb asked, accepting his glass from Austin.

"I don't think anyone was here. What do you think, Dad?" Austin said, taking a sip of his drink while standing behind Caitlyn.

He shook his head. "Maybe the local American Indian tribe, but I had thought they were on another island. Chappell would know more."

"Tribe?"

Katie looked up and nodded. "I don't know if they were part of the Wampanoag, but American Indians were in the area. Came a few times in the beginning, according to Aunt Tee and Aunt Mary."

"Do they have a reservation or anything like that here on Brightrock? Any members still alive?"

Austin shrugged. "Jane, Chappell's wife, but I haven't seen her in years. She's still alive, right, Mom?"

"She hardly ever comes to any social function. I think Timothy brings her water home from the Renewals," Katie said, looking up and squinting her eyes against the pain in her head.

"What were you thinking, Caleb?" Fred asked, ignoring their questions.

"Well, it may not work, but I have an idea."

Caleb explained what he knew in a few short sentences. Before he had finished, Lizzy pulled out her phone and dialed Ethan, who knew more about the laws and council. He answered, sounding at least three drinks in, but sobered up as he listened, asking sharp questions to clarify what Caleb was saying.

"You think that helps?" Caleb asked when he was done. Lizzy held her breath. Everyone else did the same.

Ethan thought it through on the other end of the line,

now on speaker. "I'm not sure, but it sounds like it might to me. I'm calling Chappell now."

Austin slapped Caleb on the back and shook his shoulders. "Lizzy, I'm glad you brought him back. He might've just saved the day."

CHAPTER 49

Timothy rushed outside, clutching his leather folio. In the August heat, his tweed coat felt heavy, but he needn't have bothered with shedding it when time was of such essence. He had been in his office at the new town hall when the phone call had come through. Ethan had told him in a series of short words what he had failed to consider during all of this time, and now with the Department of Health planning to seal the well in the morning, he wasn't sure he had enough time, but there was no choice. He would have to make do.

The sound of his shoes, clipping on the brick pavers beneath him, gave an unsteady and quick rhythm, hampered by age. Sweat formed on his brow as he walked toward the house in the fading light, thanking God it was close to the town center. As he had been one of the first founders, his home still remained the closest to the original hub. Back then, there had been only seven houses and no need to walk very far.

Rounding the last corner, his chest began to ache with exertion. Fearing a heart attack, Timothy slowed his pace but continued toward the brick house on the spot where he had lived for almost four hundred years. The original had been made of wood, with small windows, but over the years, Timothy had renovated and replaced the structure when building techniques improved and times had changed. Their current home had been built around the turn of the last century but had been modernized for comfort while leaving sufficient evidence of the historical influences to feel like home.

Jane's garden swayed in the evening breeze, while Timothy walked up the slate walkway toward the old oak door. Climbing the steps was an exercise in agony and determination. Timothy clung to the iron railing for support and haste, while his breath came in quick rasps.

The door opened, and Jane stood, her smile vanishing when she saw him.

"What's happened?" She rushed forward, grabbing his folio and taking his arm, never mind the fact she was almost as old as he.

"There's no time. We have to move fast." Each word came out with a separate pant, as his body halted him in protest.

"Come sit down in your chair. I'll get you some water. This isn't good for your heart."

Timothy allowed her to steer him toward an old wingback sitting in the front room surrounded by shelves filled with books he had amassed over the years. While they had a TV, Timothy found the screen vulgar and still preferred to read the newspaper on a matter of principle.

Jane moved back into the room, carrying a glass of water with a small white pill.

"Aspirin, just in case." Her dark eyes narrowed in focus as she watched him swallow the medicine without protest. Her dark hair had turned white a long time ago, and Jane chose to keep it long, wearing it up in a bun almost every day.

Tonight she had already let it down for bed, combing it with her fingers out of nerves. She eased down in her own matching chair, pulling her flowered housecoat around her.

"You have a solution." It wasn't a question. Timothy had always appreciated and relied on Jane's quick wit to match his own. Her intelligence had been the first thing he had noticed about her back when they had first met after he had arrived on the island. Her beauty and kindness still struck him, but her mind was still as sharp as when he had first seen her with a few others on a bleak winter's day.

Timothy took another drink of water and nodded. "I don't know why I didn't think of it. We need to draw up a charter." He looked at her, meeting her dark almond eyes. "In the old style."

"How will that help?"

"Native land is under a different jurisdiction, and as such, the government and the Department of Health do not have the authority to manage internal affairs."

"How did we not know about this before?"

"That man, Caleb, works in oil and as such knows the land laws better than myself, apparently. There's a new initiative to help tribes reclaim land rights, a law passed by the previous administration and quietly handed over to the Department of the Interior's Bureau of Indian Affairs. I just checked the code myself after learning about it. It's true and if we do this right, it should work."

Jane sucked in a breath and let it out slowly, the sound telling Timothy more than words ever could. After well over three hundred years of marriage and life, he and Jane spoke without sound.

"I presume that's where I come in." A small smile grew on her face. Being the only remaining native person on Brightrock, Timothy had always encouraged Jane to come out and be social with the others, but no matter his best efforts, Jane always felt more comfortable with him alone in the home.

"Do you still remember the old way?"

Jane looked away, her white hair lying to the side of her shoulder. Her tan face showed signs of a life well-lived, filled with joy and laughter, but even those lines were thin. Her beauty radiated outward like a sun. "It's been a long time."

"You must remember, Poppy."

Jane smiled at his nickname for her. Timothy reached out, taking her hand in his own, just as he had when she'd arrived at the water's edge carrying a basket of food up to the hill as a token of peace from their tribe on Cape Cod. Her people had been a distant relative to the Wampanoag and as such had communicated legal matters not in written text, but in the form of wampum belts on swaths of fabric. One included with an English charter would be a sign of agreement to the terms within, reserving a portion of Brightrock Island as native lands to be held by the tribe and descendants.

Jane met his eyes, raw determination in them. With a curt nod, she closed them once. A vow and promise to succeed.

"I'll start now. Do you have parchment or whatever is appropriate?"

Timothy stood. "In my desk."

Jane gave him a sly smile, the same one he had loved for over three hundred years. "Still have the quills?"

Timothy let out a short laugh. The sound caught him off guard, and he wondered in the back of his mind how long it had been since he'd last relaxed. All of the worries, fears, and legal matters of the secrecy of Brightrock weighed on him day and night. While other people felt constrained by the rules and regulations the council of elders imposed, Timothy knew of no other way to ensure the secrecy and security of the island and the sacred water. He knew he was unpopular, but someone had to be the conservative voice. If someone didn't get to laugh, it probably would be best if it was him.

"Do we need to get some goose feathers and a penknife?" Her eyes sparkled with laughter, and her shoulders fell from her ears, her relief evident.

"I do still remember how to cut them, as a matter of fact."

"I have no doubt you do." Jane stood, releasing his hand, and glided over to a shelf with an old woven basket. The beads she needed were inside. With a small prayer of thanks to God for Caleb Broussard's quick thinking, Timothy leaned forward out of his chair, and feeling older than he had in a long time, shuffled over to his desk. He smiled to himself as he pulled out the paper.

He had always known the old ways would come in handy.

CHAPTER 50

Boston
December

Nora pushed through the crush of bodies on the frigid December evening. It almost made her want to commit murder on the spot. Then at least she would have something to do with her hands. She always felt lost without pockets, but she didn't want to show up at her brother's winter awards night looking like a bum. Some of the high school seniors would be signing with colleges, some had gotten scholarships, and that Michael had been invited surprised no one since he had been on honor roll forever. That was the only reason she was even wearing this dress to begin with. She hadn't touched it after the date with Ethan and had forgotten to go shopping to get something new. She was glad she had ignored her original idea of throwing it out. At least she had something presentable to wear.

"Nora!" Tom waved her over from a row down toward

the front of the gymnasium, acting as part ceremony space, part sardine can.

Nora clambered over a dozen other people in the high school auditorium before reaching Tom, Christine, and Gram, muttering excuses as she went, feeling awkward never knowing whether to put her ass or her boobs toward them. Both felt wrong.

"Hey, you made it. Can you believe this place? Thank God we came with your grandma. Parking is outrageous."

"It's a good thing I brought the handicap tag," Gram said as Nora leaned over to give her a hug. She had to duck around Gram's signature bright red hat which matched her pantsuit and scarf.

"Damn lucky," Christine said, looking up and studying Nora's arm over her glasses while fanning herself with the program. "We'd still be in east Egypt."

"Sit down, sit down," Tom said, unbuttoning his suit jacket as he eased into the stadium seating chair. "We're going out tonight after. Got reservations and everything."

"Don't you even think about treating," Nora said, cracking open the program.

"Sure am. You can screw off if you think about stopping me."

"Bull," Nora said, not even looking up. She was faster with a credit card, and a lot sneakier. "That reminds me, I have a little something for you. Want to help with the payments, since you've done so much for us."

"Ah, keep your money. Family is family."

"I'll be pissed if you don't take it." Nora looked over at him.

"We're all good. Friggin' blessed."

"Oh, come on with that."

Christine leaned over. "You didn't tell her?"

"Tell me what?" She glanced between the two of them, trying to figure out what the hell they were up to.

Tom straightened up and patted his chest twice with a meaty fist. "Debt-free, baby."

Nora felt her stomach lurch in her gut. "What?"

"Insurance companies must've figured out their shit...sorry, stuff," Tom said when Christine slapped him in the chest.

"Yeah, and they even called collections and cleared everything up, including bills that had nothing to do with the insulin."

"What? I mean, that's great, but how?" Nora's brain worked overtime as she tried to come up with alternatives to the solution plaguing her.

Christine shook her head. "Beats me."

"I was telling Christine that eventually we'd get a break, and we did."

"I put some money in the poor box." Christine looked up and made the sign of the cross.

"She was feeling guilty, but we've earned this."

Christine made a sound of dissent with a single grunt.

"Don't be like that. It's great."

"Yeah, that's—"

"Incredible," Gram added from a few seats over. "And about time."

"Sure is," Christine said, cracking a smile. She beamed at Tom for the first time in a long time, giving Nora a glimpse into her softer side.

Tom gave her a tight smile and patted her leg twice. "I can't get choked up yet, we haven't even started." His accent dropped the r, in true Boston style, tugging at Nora's heart even more.

Tom swiped at the corner of his eye and sniffed. "Yeah, so

I'll be damned—yes, I said damned, Christine—I'll be damned if anyone else is paying for Michael's award dinner."

"That's very kind, Tom," Gram said, leaning over. "But I wanted to treat. Would you believe that my social security checks have doubled? My investment returns too. Almost tripled what I was getting before, and I haven't changed a thing! Marge at the senior center was jealous. It's a Christmas miracle!" Gram waved her arms out with the program. "I feel like Tiny Tim, you know, at the end of The Christmas Carol?"

"I'm treating, and that's final. I owe it to your father," Tom said.

Nora had to blink away tears and shifted in her seat as the music swelled around them, cutting off the debate.

"Where's Michael?" Nora said, leaning over as the opening procession started, and students walked out, wearing big smiles and dress clothes.

"That's the best part," Tom said.

"There's more?" Nora asked, her stomach dropping again.

"He's on the stage," Gram said, leaning over.

"Full ride."

"WHAT?" Nora's mouth dropped open. The women behind her hissed at her outburst.

"Hell, yeah. I knew he had it in him."

"Oh, my God. That's great. Jesus...where to?"

"Anywhere he damn well pleases," Christine said, fanning herself again, almost giddy with joy.

Gram leaned around with a broad smile. "We got the call last night. An anonymous donor at the last minute. Didn't even apply for it. Called the school and mentioned Michael by name."

The air left Nora's lungs in a rush before coming back too

hard, in short bursts. The floor started to move underneath her feet, and the hot, stale air made her head swim.

Ethan.

Nora had no proof. She hadn't seen him since that fateful last moment when he had begged her to call off the search, put up a block, obstruct justice as she had called it. She had denied him. She said no, and with a single word had put her job above the best man to walk into her life since Tom and her dad. With those two letters, Nora had cast him back out, and though she was a damn good investigator, she knew in her gut she could search for years and she would never see Ethan again. His phone had been cut off, and all records had dried up. Ethan didn't want to be found, and Nora certainly wasn't going to get any favors from anyone on Brightrock Island. Her heart wrenched in her chest, and tears flowed freely down her cheeks, streaming to her chin where they dropped off like rain to land in her lap as the house lights dimmed and students walked on stage.

"Look! There he is! MICHAEL!" Tom stood and waved like an idiot until Michael saw them in the sea of faceless family, offering a sheepish smile and wave. Tom flashed a thumbs-up, and Michael returned the gesture with a laugh that split Nora's heart in half with joy and gratitude for the man she loved and would never see again.

For the first time in her life, she regretted following the law. She had threatened his family, and in return, he loved and supported hers from afar. It was game over.

In the dark auditorium, as the names of students rolled through the packed hall while snow fell silently outside, Nora wept.

CHAPTER 51

New Orleans
December

"So, you're really going to live here?" Uncle Fred asked Lizzy. Quiet music played in the cathedral while the guests took their seats. Caleb and the groomsmen had already walked down. Lizzy, Uncle Fred, Maw Maw, Parrain, and the bridal party waited in a small room off to the side of the vestibule.

She smoothed the white silk over the skirt of her wedding dress. The soft fabric felt cool against her manicured hands. The emerald-cut diamond on her hand glinted in the candlelight of the cathedral around them. She loved the weight of it, feeling protected and cherished at the same time by the small band of gold.

"That's the plan. Think you and Aunt Katie can visit?" she asked, looking up at her uncle. He had always reminded her of an absent-minded professor. With his wispy hair,

Fred looked like a grad student in need of a brush and haircut.

"Oh, I'm looking forward to it! We've haven't traveled much. Can't wait to soak up some of the local culture."

"We have a guest bedroom. Now that Caleb's been transferred back stateside, our schedule's open. I'd love you to come anytime." Lizzy smiled and realized just how much she meant it.

A few years ago, she couldn't wait to get away from the same people she had known her whole life. Now, the thought of her life without her uncle's gentle smile or her aunt's kind-hearted fussiness made her stomach drop. Austin's confident grin and Ethan's confident smirk had been a part of her life for longer than she could remember. Aunt Tee and Aunt Mary had always been there for every step, yin and yang of unconditional love. And even though he found comfort in stoic apathy, and could be a real pain in the ass, Timothy Chappell had been the first person she saw after her parents had died.

Lizzy remembered that night almost a century ago like it had been yesterday. Standing in a nightgown at the top of the stairs, Lizzy had clutched her tattered bunny rabbit and watched as the doctor pulled a hand over his face and shook his head slowly. She had known then she wouldn't hear her dad's laugh or see her mom's smile again. Timothy Chappell had come into the dark house and picked her up, taking care to wrap her in a warm coat before carrying her to his brick home in the cold winter air.

He had brought her inside his warm house and sat her down in front of the fire in his library, which smelled like pine and was filled with books. A beautiful woman with long dark hair with streaks of white glided into the room wearing a long floral robe that swirled around her legs. Jane, who Lizzy had never seen before, tried to feed her, bringing a spoonful of hot soup to her lips. When that didn't work, she'd offered her a cup of warm milk, then a piece of chocolate. Lizzy didn't remember if she ate it or not but could still feel the warmth of Jane's arms around her, pulling her onto her lap, rocking her back and forth while singing a soft song in a language she didn't understand.

With some distance and her newfound freedom, Lizzy now had the grace to see all of their strengths instead of their flaws. Funny how after a few months away, Lizzy appreciated everything and everyone so much more than she ever did before. To think Timothy had been the bane of her existence a few months ago. Now, he had been instrumental in rewriting the code to be able to send water in flasks for members living away from the island.

Having the option was nice, but Lizzy was looking forward to aging like normal with the man she loved in a new state with a new extended family. They would still visit Brightrock like any other couple, and Lizzy looked forward to it. If they happened to be present for renewal, then so be it, but it wasn't going to run her life anymore.

The music swelled around them and she looked at the people in the line up around her.

Lizzy slid her hand into the crook of her Uncle Fred's arm and took a steadying breath.

"Ready?" he asked with a grin. He looked so dashing in his black silk tuxedo.

"More than ever."

Lizzy smiled and heard the organ of the cathedral strike up "Canon in D."

"Oh cher, I think that's our cue," Maw Maw said before turning and enveloping Lizzy in a firm hug. "Welcome to the family, Elizabeth. We're so happy for you and Caleb."

"Caleb's a lucky man," Parrain said with a smile that pulled the lines in his face tight.

Lizzy thanked them both and watched as they took each other's arm and walked down the aisle radiating love as they had no doubt done for fifty years.

Lizzy had to blink fast as the tears tried to come back and realized she wasn't the only one. Next to her, Caitlyn dabbed at her eyes.

She leaned over and whispered, "You know, I have you to thank. If you hadn't come to Brightrock, I wouldn't have met Caleb."

Caitlyn laughed and waved her off. "I think we both got something out of me moving. You two really are perfect together." She handed over Lizzy's bouquet of flowers, ever-green with white roses and holly dipped in gold. Caitlyn stood like a Roman goddess in dark-green silk, her own smaller bouquet covering her belly. She would've been glowing even without the flickering candles around them in the cathedral.

Austin nodded in agreement while staying close like an overpaid bodyguard with something to prove. "The church lady is waving us down, babe. We gotta go."

"I guess that's our cue. Congratulations," Caitlyn said, taking Austin's arm. He held her like she was made of glass, placing his hand over hers.

"Welcome to the club, cuz," Austin said with a wink. Caitlyn beamed at him as he slowly led her down the aisle. Love poured out from between the two of them as they walked, carrying their unborn child into the golden grandeur of the cathedral dressed for Christmas.

Lizzy watched from the shadows, picking out Caleb way at the end, waiting with a patient smile and waving to the multitudes of Cajuns filling the pews. Her side had made an appearance too.

Aunt Tee and Aunt Mary sat side-by-side behind Timothy and Jane Chappell, all of whom had traveled together to New Orleans, defying doctor's orders. Seeing them all in the pew—Timothy who hadn't left the island in over a century, and Jane, who rarely left her own home—brought tears of gratitude to Lizzy's eyes. She dabbed at them with her handkerchief, trying not to smear her makeup. Aunt Katie sat beaming in a champagne dress next to Ethan, who looked smart in a tux that probably cost more than the limo outside. Lizzy and Austin had talked about getting him a date, but he declined every girl they'd mentioned.

"Don't look so sad," Uncle Fred said, giving her a little shake. "It's your wedding day. You look beautiful."

"I was just thinking about Ethan."

"Ethan?"

"He looks so...I don't know—lonely."

"Don't worry about him. He'll be alright. Besides, you're the bride. It's your day." Uncle Fred leaned in close and lowered his voice. "Listen, I don't want to make you self-conscious, but you're the best-looking one here."

That got a laugh out of her and Lizzy had to blink back a few more tears. "Thank you, Uncle Fred."

"Anytime, Lizzy bear." He gave her shoulders a little squeeze when he said her childhood nickname.

Lizzy blinked away happy tears. Before she could reply, the church lady appeared out of the dark vestibule and fluffed Lizzy's long lace veil and train. It was go-time.

"Canon in D" finished, and trumpets swelled filling the magnificent arches with a rich, booming sound. Everyone stood and beamed as Lizzy walked down the aisle through the people she had known her whole life, and the people she would grow to know.

Caleb stood at the altar in a tuxedo that made him look like a New York model as opposed to the quiet, loyal man she loved. His hands were clasped in front of him, relaxed. The corners of his mouth tilted up in a smile filled with awe.

"Wow," he mouthed to her.

Lizzy grinned.

Uncle Fred stopped when they reached the front and turned to give her a hug and a kiss on the cheek.

"I wish you two all the best," he said in her ear. "Love ya."

Lizzy sniffed back the tears and watched as Fred faced Caleb, pausing and rolling onto the balls of his feet much to the amusement of the congregation. He reached out and shook Caleb's hand twice and leaned over to whisper something in his ear before clasping him hard on the shoulder. He turned around and gave her a wink before retreating to his seat next to Aunt Katie.

The priest began the service with a deep voice, magnified to every corner by the small mic on his collar. "Dearly beloved, we are gathered here today—"

"You're breathtaking," Caleb said as everyone turned to the hymnals and the organ boomed behind them for the first song.

Lizzy lowered her lashes and grinned. "I knew I looked good in white."

Caleb nudged her while everyone started to sing, his green eyes looking down from his smiling face with love beaming out from within him. "You are always breathtaking. I love you."

Lizzy mouthed the words back and sang along, feeling happier than she could ever remember.

CHAPTER 52

Boston
March, fifteen months later

Even though it had been the biggest drug bust taken down in recent memory, Nora could've done without the media. Standing on the stage for the second time in less than two years, receiving another award, made her choke back a smile and more, only because her grandma and brother were in the front row, each beaming with pride. Tom sat behind them and was making a point of clapping his thick, meaty hands so that his applause was louder than God himself, while Christine grinned and clapped at a frantic pace.

When all of the brass had finished their speeches in front of the cameras, about how much safer the town would be, Nora's family practically rushed her in an array of hugs. Gram got to her first.

The small arms gently enveloped her while she whispered in Nora's ear, "Good job. Knew you'd get 'em."

Nora didn't have a chance to reply when Christine slid over and gave her a squeeze. When she leaned back to look at Nora, her grin was even wider. "Justice was friggin' served."

Michael stepped up in his shy sort of way. He had been at school for seven months, choosing to put his scholarship to good use at Columbia. The change in him was telling. He stood a little straighter but still gave her a little shake around the shoulders like he always did, just like their dad had.

Not to be outdone, Tom barreled forward in a dress shirt and striped tie and threw both arms around her in a bear hug to end all bear hugs. As Nora rocked back and forth, Tom thumped her on the back several times. He sniffed a few times and said, "So proud...so, so damn proud." Words failed him for a few moments until he pulled himself together. "Glad you had that fancy armor. Lousy criminal would've hit you for sure. Thank God you weren't wearing the cheap stuff."

Nora felt the tears flood into her eyes and shut them hard to stem the flow of utter bawling that would come forth if she let it. It was no good. A thin trickle slid down each cheek while Tom's hand thumped away on her back, rocking her back and forth. After that, the floodgates opened, sending tears pouring down. Nora choked back a sob when Tom pulled away and looked at her through tears of his own on his big teddy bear face.

With her heart in her throat, Nora navigated the rest of the room with her family following her as she got pats on the back and compliments from a sea of beaming faces in uniform. Her heart swelled with pride, but a hole remained. She caught herself spinning around to scan the room, looking for a familiar square jaw and warm eyes like she had seen before.

In the past, Nora would have looked for the first exit from such an overblown media parade, ducking around people to leave first, but now she kept circling, coming back, and looking around the room. Each time, her heart sank a little more, which was shit. She'd been searching for Ethan for months. His payments to Tom and Michael had continued. Nora knew it must be him because honestly, what were the odds of someone showing up out of thin air to magically take care of her family? Zilch.

Ethan haunted her like a ghost she craved to touch. His presence was evident in the smiles of relief on the faces of the ones she loved the most. It didn't stop there.

The 5th Division had received a considerable endowment, the security on her apartment building had been upgraded along with a new kitchen ordered for units like hers. Her heart ached for him. She wanted him. Needed him. And as she scanned the thinning crowd again, her heart broke once more when she didn't see any hint of him. Nora knew in her heart from the moment she'd met him, she would never love anyone in the way she loved Ethan. No one could replace him, and her heart seared in her chest every night at the close of another day. Immortal—or whatever was close to it—or not, she had lost her heart to him totally.

Nora filed out the door following her family and answering the chorus of attagirls flung her way from the last of the uniformed crowd. Tom had reserved dinner at Natale's, adamant she deserved nothing but the best for her big bust, something he claimed had made her career. Stepping out into the freezing cold, Nora hunched her shoulders against the wind. Thanksgiving had passed, and Christmas trees had gone up, come down, and long been shoved back into the attic or left on the curb. For the first time in years, everyone had gotten more than one present, courtesy of continued good fortune with her investments, which of course made Nora wonder even more. New Year's Eve and Valentine's Day had passed while she was at work, picking up a shift so the guys in the department could take off and spend time with their significant others. Now, everyone was gearing up for St. Patrick's next week. Tom and Christine had even mentioned they'd like to get everyone together at a pub for a couple of rounds, their treat.

She walked alongside them all before turning off to head to her cruiser, while the rest headed to Tom's Buick. Nora still felt the sting and wondered if the emptiness would haunt her forever. Walking in the cold night alone, Nora cried silent tears, letting them slide down without shame. When she had last seen him, she hadn't fully believed she would never see him again. She had been so convinced she could find him, or that he wouldn't be able to resist.

Alone in the parking deck, she knew she'd lost. Taking down that drug ring had been an effort not only in duty but as a personal challenge. Nora laughed to herself. It came out more like a sob. She had believed if she won another award, received another honor, that he would come like he had before. All of this had been for him. When she had dressed in her uniform, she had taken extra care with her hair to make sure it looked perfect for their reunion that she had been so sure about.

Now, for the first time, she realized her mistake. She'd been wrong. The reason she had been so obsessed with whatever happened on Brightrock wasn't Mark Schmidt, the bombing, or the water. It was him. She loved Ethan and never would see him again. The pain struck her in her chest, and upon reaching her car, she took a moment inside to rest her head on the steering wheel and let it all go. With her forehead on the fake leather, she wept for everything she had thrown away. All of the confidence in her bluff, risking her heart, betting Ethan would blink first and come back to her.

Without him, even at the top of her game, Nora was incomplete and heartbroken.

A tap at the window jolted her upright. Standing outside in the dark of the parking garage, in the most beautiful wool coat she'd ever seen, Ethan smiled at her.

Nora flung the door open and threw herself at him. Through the tears, the words were muffled against his broad chest as she hugged him tight against her.

"I'm so sorry. I'm so sorry." She repeated herself again and again through the sobs, not giving a damn if anyone saw them.

Ethan squeezed her close, pulling away only to kiss her hard on the mouth.

"God, I've missed you," he said, his voice a reverent prayer.

"I've missed you like hell. Bastard." Nora leaned back and wiped her face with a swipe of her gloved hands. "You didn't have to do all of that either."

Ethan grinned at her. "I have no idea what you're talking about."

Nora laughed and sniffed again. "You shouldn't lie to a cop."

He grinned wider and hugged her to him again. "I would never. God, you look so beautiful in that uniform. I couldn't resist." Ethan leaned down and crushed her to him with a desperation that she felt.

"So it's true then?" she asked after another heart-melting kiss. Even with the time apart, the second her body had touched Ethan, the fire had come raging back. "You're really, truly old?"

Ethan leaned back and barked out a laugh. "You have such a way with words."

"Well?"

His face grew grave, and a familiar pain and sadness came

rushing back into his features. "Yes. I was born well before your Gram."

Nora wrinkled her nose. "That's not the best way to sell me on us being together."

"Do you want to be together?"

"Are you asking?" Nora said, grinning through the tears still streaming down her face.

"Oh, God, yes."

Nora laughed as he pulled her to him, letting the strong arms encircle her with tenderness.

She jerked back and stared at him from arm's length, gripping the sleeves of his coat in case he vanished right in front of her. "I never take out the trash."

Ethan stopped and looked at her. He blinked twice. "What?"

"I said I never take out the trash. I just smush it down until I test the laws of physics. Also, my family is good, but we're loud, crass, and flawed people. The flaws come out during holidays and sports games."

Ethan chuckled and planted a kiss on the top of her head.

"Deeply flawed. We're deeply flawed people who mainly communicate in movie quotes. Just want to let you know what you're up against. I'm supposed to be at Natale's now for dinner. We're late."

"We?"

"Yeah, if you're going to be with me, you gotta take my family. Then, it seems like you already have. But they're easier to love from a distance. You'll see that for yourself in about thirty minutes."

"I'm sure I'll love them," Ethan said with his lips against her forehead.

"I love you."

"I love you more, Lieutenant."

Nora looked up at him and felt the wave of emotion slam through her chest. "Promise you'll never leave again."

"I never did. You know that."

"Um, I beg to differ."

Ethan shook with laughter against her. The smell of his subtle, expensive cologne reached her and made her melt into him more.

"I promise. Shall we take my car?" A black Escalade was parked about a dozen spaces away.

"But I need my cruiser," Nora said, the words more out of habit than protest as Ethan had already started walking with his arm around her toward the luxury car.

"We'll get it later. Besides, this way we can make up for lost time."

"I'm armed."

"You know how that excites me." Ethan smiled at her with a face full of laughter.

Nora stopped and turned to him. "How will this work? I can't leave my family."

"I'll never ask you to."

"When the time comes can...I mean, will I even be welcome on Brightrock? Like forever? I don't even know if I want that. I mean, I do, but there's like a lot to sort through. I don't even understand everything you were telling me, like about the mystery water? I heard it wasn't sealed before I got reassigned. Eventually, though, I mean, I want as much time with you as possible."

"Oh, we have time. If you want it, we have all the time in the world."

Nora walked in step with him now, her head reeling with the what-ifs of what she was saying. "What would I do there? I'm a pretty terrible cook, and I clean only when non-relatives visit."

Ethan swooped a lock of hair back over her ear, love

shining out of his face. "Funny you mention that. We need experienced law enforcement."

"Really?"

Ethan nodded.

"I mean, the chief was talking captain a bit ago; I don't know if now's the right time."

"Nora."

She stopped and looked at him. "Yes?"

Ethan turned and cupped her face in his hands. "I promise you. We'll make it work. I love you."

"I love you too." The words tumbled out as an honest statement of fact. Nora had never been surer of anything in her life.

Ethan kissed her and then continued. "I need you in my life. I want you to be happy. We'll take everything a day at a time. We don't need to figure it out tonight. Will you marry me?"

Nora's mouth fell open. "You just said we don't need to do all of this tonight."

Ethan closed his eyes and shook his head. "I know. I'm sorry." He muffled a curse. "You don't deserve to be asked in a parking garage. I should take you to paradise, a tropical island, maybe Paris and woo you there. I'm—"

Nora planted her mouth against his. "I'd love to. I have no idea how anything will work, but yes."

Ethan clung to her like a man seeking a life raft, crushing her to his body as they giggled like teens. Nora's phone buzzed at her hip, then vibrated again and again.

"Shit, sorry." She grabbed her phone. "I know, I know. I'm sorry. I'm coming, Gram."

Ethan smiled again at her and held the door open to the back of his hired Escalade.

"Yes, I figured you'd park in the handicap spot. Yeah, I know the bread's warm. Save me some. Go ahead. I'm on my way. No, really, I am. It's fine. Actually, can you get another seat?"

While Gram peppered her with questions, Nora turned to Ethan, letting her eyes devour his broad, powerful profile. He sat relaxed in an exquisite suit staring at her with a mix of pride, adoration, and a hunger that sent a thrum through her body. Feeling her heart burst with love, Nora said into the phone, "I'm bringing someone I think you're all really going to love."

ACKNOWLEDGMENTS

There are so many people in my life that have made this book possible.

None of this would've happened without my dear friend, Jenn, who's own writing inspired me to revisit a cherished childhood hobby almost a decade after I had written anything. Without her acting as my cheerleader through emails and editing, this book would've come out years later.

My husband, Kevin, has supported and invested in me since the beginning. He has done everything in his power to give me the time and space needed to create this book. I can never appreciate him or my son enough.

I owe a tremendous amount of gratitude to Kate Studer, who took this complex story in her expert hands. This book had so many moving parts, and her comments were invaluable in helping me shape each character and their unique timeline. Everything she suggested elevated the work and helped me tell the story I wanted to tell.

Once again, Caroline Teagle Johnson created a stunning cover, that captured the spirit of the Firemark series and my vision for Lizzy and Caleb. I am so grateful for the opportunity to work with her, and for her patience as we revisited so many pictures of the sky.

I am thankful to have met Ann Suhz and Ann Riza in New York. Their attention to detail and careful eye polished this story to perfection, not once, but twice. All of their comments and research has made me a better writer, and for that, I am deeply grateful.

I wanted this book to act as my love letter to the places where my family is from, but while backgrounds are helpful, stories are about people. I'm very appreciative of my family and friends for helping inspire me. There is a lifetime of people to thank, and I hope I have captured the ways I have been blessed with love in my life. Unlike on Brightrock Island, people and places change over time, but through the real magic of stories, we can keep what we love alive forever.

ABOUT THE AUTHOR

Kathryn K. Murphy writes action-packed, small-town romance novels bursting with emotion.

If you want to know when Kathryn's next book will come out, please visit her website at www.kathrynkmurphy.com, where you can sign up to receive email updates.

www.ingramcontent.com/pod-product-compliance
Lightning Source LLC
Chambersburg PA
CBHW021101110726
47900CB00007B/1980